AN UNEXPECTED CATCH

ADVENTUROUS HEARTS

BOOK TWO

ABBEY DOWNEY

WILD HEART BOOKS

ISBN: 978-1-963212-09-9

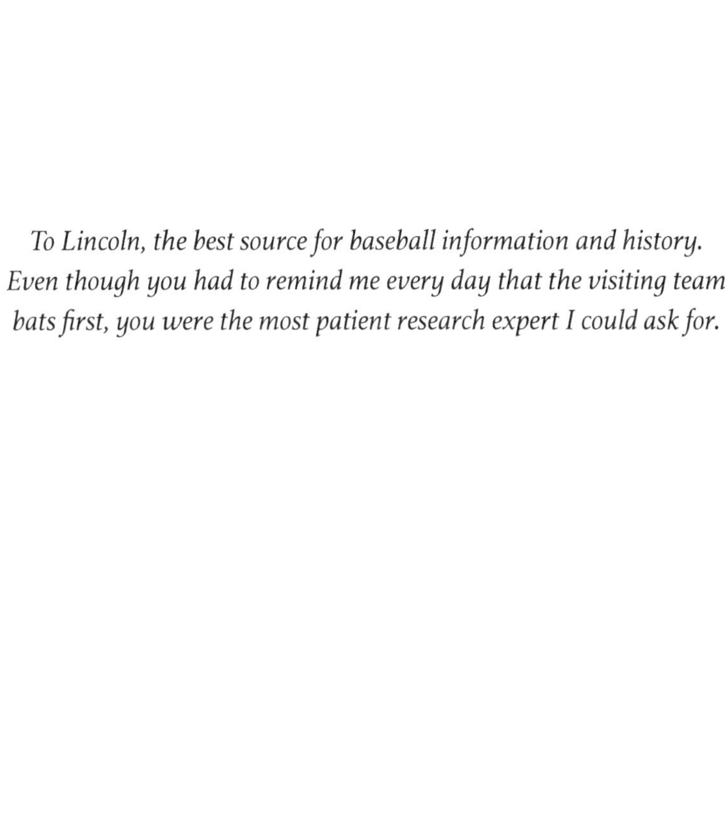

To Lincoln, the best source for baseball information and history. Even though you had to remind me every day that the visiting team bats first, you were the most patient research expert I could ask for.

CHAPTER 1

MAY 25, 1907
CHICAGO, ILLINOIS

"Miss Curran, say you'll be my wife. I'd let you attend the games to watch me play."

Beatrice Curran tugged her hand against the sweaty grip of a young man in a dust-covered pinstriped uniform kneeling in front of her until he finally released it. Wiping her palm on her skirt with no effort to hide the motion, she arched an eyebrow while glaring down at him. "Bernie Hall, I'll do no such thing. Now go clean up. You're a mess."

Stepping around him, Bea marched down the hall she'd been traversing before the rookie third baseman stopped her, guffaws echoing through the passageway as the other players teased Bernie. The nerve of that boy thinking not only that she would find him a good prospect for marriage, but that *allowing* her the opportunity to attend his games would make it a more tempting offer. She was the only female umpire in baseball, respected and sought after by teams in several leagues. No player was going to tell her whether or not she could attend a baseball game.

She rapped her knuckles on the door at the end of the hall, and after a deep voice welcomed her in, it was a relief to slip inside the office. She far preferred the silence and stillness of the room to the chaos in the player-filled hallway. Bea lowered herself into a padded leather chair and reached up to rub a tight spot on her neck.

Behind the desk, Chicago City League President Charles Rosen grinned knowingly. "A tough game?"

"The game went fine. But constantly spinning around to see what's going on behind me takes a toll. I know it's not easy on the budget, but you ought to think about having two umpires at games. The major leagues do."

Charles continued to watch her. "Or you could think about moving to stand behind home plate like most umps are doing now. Bea, I know you. You didn't come in here to complain about a sore neck. What do you need?"

He had no idea how hard that question was for her to answer. She needed a bigger purpose in life than calling baseball plays. She needed unlimited funds and the support of men who usually thought themselves above her in order to make her dreams happen. She needed to meet a man who wasn't a baseball player and could see past the aloof show she had to put on all the time and still care about the woman she was inside.

But right now, she'd settle for Charles's understanding when she revealed the decision she'd recently made. "I need to tell you this is my last season working as an umpire."

For once, she'd surprised him. Charles had supported her career from the beginning. He'd been the one to give her a chance when her dear friend, Marjorie King, had volunteered Bea to fill in for an umpire who hadn't shown up at a game they were attending. Many of the players had argued against allowing a woman on the field, but Charles had simply smiled and told them to let her show what she could do. She'd proven her ability, and Charles had continued to hire her for more and more games every season.

Now, though, he clearly didn't know what to think about her announcement. "You didn't actually agree to marry one of those fools, did you?"

Bea couldn't help the laugh that escaped her lips, despite the pang of regret that hit her at the same moment. She wasn't against marriage in general. If pressed, she would have to admit she liked to imagine what it would be like to fall in love. But she *was* against marrying a conceited athlete or any man who felt he had a right to control her. "You know better than that. Baseball players are all the same. Cocky. Arrogant. Respectful enough when they have to be but not the type to accept that a woman could be just as or more intelligent than they are. No, I'm simply ready to move forward with a plan that's been in my mind for several years."

Charles leaned back in his chair, lacing his fingers in front of his chest. "Tell me about it."

Faced with the opportunity to share her dream out loud, Bea licked her dry lips and drew a fortifying breath. "You know I've been working with the women's baseball team at Western College. I've met so many young men and women there who have an interest in physical education."

That was the easy part to explain. The part that remained a dream and an uncertainty was more difficult. Bea pushed her chin up, feigning a confidence she didn't feel, encouraged by Charles's thoughtful interest. "While the college has a physical training department, it only exists to integrate exercise into the students' curriculum. The woman who hired me to manage the women's baseball team, Miss King, runs the women's gymnasium program now. She's retiring at the end of the summer, and I'd like to take over and see the department expanded to include a professional course that would train teachers. Imagine if all the nation's schools embraced instruction in the importance of movement and sports, teaching children how to care for their bodies and how they work."

She paused to let Charles absorb her vision. And he seemed to, as his thoughtful expression turned into an agreeable nod. "I see your passion for this. But do you have to quit? I don't have many umpires I can rely on as much as I do you."

A comfortable warmth spread through Bea at his words of appreciation. "It's time for me to move on. But as I said, I'm committed to this season. Even if I'm hired at the college, I won't take over until late fall, when the new term starts. I don't intend to leave you shorthanded, and I want to say a proper goodbye to all the teams. They may be a bunch of arrogant fools, but I'll miss them."

Charles stuck out his hand, and Bea shook it with a hitch in her heart as he held her gaze. "Bea, I'm thankful for having had the chance to work with you, and I'll wish you the best when the season ends."

A knock at the door interrupted them. Charles called for the visitor to enter, and his assistant, Frank Arthur, stepped into the room. Bea nodded a greeting as she settled back into the chair again, able to relax now that she'd said what she needed to.

Frank handed Charles a stack of papers with rows of neat typing filling them. "The records from today's games and the lineups for tomorrow, sir."

Charles shuffled through the pages, stopping to pull one out and hand it to Bea. "You haven't seen the new lineup for the Lincoln Parks, have you?"

She shook her head, taking the paper from him and perusing it with interest. The Lincoln Parks had rearranged much of their team during the off-season, and she hadn't been at any of their games in the three weeks of play so far. Frank leaned over her shoulder to point out one name in particular. "Emmett Worland is expected to be their new star. He's a standout pitcher."

Unfortunately, Bea already knew that name. "And quite the womanizer, from what I've heard."

Frank's cheeks turned pink at the blunt assessment, but Charles let out a snort. "Quite right, Bea. I've heard the same. You'll have your hands full with that one. If I was a betting man, I'd wager he'll propose to you before the game is done."

Bea raised both hands in a careless gesture. "Just like all the others. And he'll get no different treatment. He might think he's the most irresistible man ever to walk the earth, and many women might agree. But I certainly won't."

Charles's delighted laughter accompanied Bea as she rose and stepped past Frank on her way to the door. Turning back, she smiled. "Thank you both for your support over the years. It hasn't always been easy to work in this sport, but knowing you two believe in me and will defend me has helped."

Then she slipped from the office before she became emotional. There were still months of games left to referee. Becoming a weak mess of feminine emotions—even if it was only Charles and Frank who saw it—would lessen her authority on the field. She'd fought hard for that authority, and she refused to let it be taken away before she was ready.

As for whether she was ready to change the course of her life and move into academics instead of being on the ballfield, well, that remained to be seen. All she knew for certain was that while baseball had defined her for the last few years, she was tired of being an oddity, the female umpire who drew spectators to games and constantly turned down proposals from players.

As much as she prayed for it, it was too much to hope for a man to come into her life who would respect her while also supporting her dreams and her desire to work for herself. But that didn't mean refereeing baseball games was all she could hope to achieve. God had placed a bigger dream in her mind, and she was going to step out toward it in faith that He would make the way.

~

Cheers roared from every side of the baseball field, boosting Emmett Worland's spirits enough to ignore the pain that always burned in his shoulder after pitching a full nine innings. Another win. They were only a few weeks into the season, but the Lincoln Parks were undefeated so far, confirming that Emmett's choice to join the team was a solid one.

As he jogged toward the dugout, Emmett paused by a group of spectators who leaned over the low fence separating the seats from the field. He focused on one young boy, ignoring the clamoring ladies gathered around the child. "You play ball, young man?"

The boy only nodded, his eyes widening. Emmett grinned and lowered himself so he could look straight into the boy's face. "You wouldn't happen to be a crackerjack pitcher like me, would you?"

That little face lit up, and the pain in Emmett's body completely faded from his awareness. People responding to him with pleasure and excitement rather than the cold dismissal he grew up with was the whole reason he'd pursued baseball in the first place.

Reaching out to ruffle the boy's hair, Emmett held his awestruck gaze. "You keep playing, then, you hear me? I want to see you on one of these big fields someday."

The boy beamed, but Emmett was momentarily distracted —against his will—by the simpering ladies who leaned out over the fence trying to catch his eye. One reached far enough that she started to slip over onto the field, leaving Emmett no choice but to grab her arm and help her right herself. The woman batted her eyelashes at him. "Oh, thank you ever so much." She added a blushing giggle. "You're such a hero."

The rest of his team was gathering their gear and leaving the dugout, so Emmett took the opportunity to escape the tittering woman and her friends before the encounter got out of hand. He didn't need any more rumors about his supposed romantic endeavors.

His teammates would expect him in the locker room for a post-game meeting, but Emmett stole a few more minutes to greet fans and encourage young players on the way off the field. It was the best part of the game for him, so he wasn't going to rush himself. Unless more damsels put themselves in distress to get his attention.

Eventually, his teammate, Boot Kearney, called his name from the open doorway that led to the offices and locker rooms. "Come on, Worland. We're waiting on you."

With a final wave that brought another round of cheers from the loitering onlookers, Emmett ducked into the dugout, grabbed his glove and a few extra bats that remained, and joined Boot for the walk to the home team locker room.

Given his tall, thin frame, Boot's uniforms always appeared to be swallowing him up. But he was a favorite with his team-mates, the first to welcome newcomers with a warm smile. While they walked toward the locker rooms, Boot clapped Emmett on the shoulder, the impact causing a sharp pain to radiate up his neck and through his skull. Emmett did his best to hide it, forcing a smile to cover the ache.

The Lincoln Parks had hired Emmett because he was the best pitcher in the independent league, where he'd spent the last three years. Now was not the time to let a little pain get in his way. The headaches that still plagued him after he'd been struck by a hard-hit baseball back in the fall would go away soon enough, so he hadn't told anyone on his new team. There was no reason to worry them about his health.

The locker room was a chaotic mass of men, clothing, and gear going every which way. Players shouted across the room to each other, offering more criticism than encouragement, but usually not mean-spirited. This was his second-favorite part of a game—the aftermath when the adrenaline started draining out of his body and the camaraderie of the team bolstered him, win or lose.

Emmett soaked it all in as he changed out of his previously white uniform, noticing a smear of mud across the words *Lincoln Parks* embroidered on the chest. With a pang of remorse for the effort his grandmother's laundress would have to put into cleaning it later, he shoved the uniform unceremoniously into the large leather bag he liked to carry.

Before he'd finished cleaning up, Emmett heard his name and turned to see the team's bat boy. The ten-year-old had been blessed with the moniker Alphonso, but the team called him Kid. "Hey, Kid. What do you need?"

Without explanation, Kid handed him a slip of paper before turning and bolting from the room, scurrying between players and bags as if he couldn't escape the madness fast enough. Emmett's heart dropped as he turned the note over and saw his grandmother's wax seal. His gut told him he wouldn't be happy about the message it contained.

Behind him, Boot leaned close to peek at the handwriting. "You getting love notes from pretty fans now, Emmett? Share with the rest of us for once, would ya?"

Emmett waved the paper in front of Boot's face. "If you'd like to rendezvous with my grandmother this evening, I'd be more than happy to give up my place. Unfortunately, when she summons me, the expectation is that I show up immediately."

Boot dropped onto the wooden bench behind them and rubbed a pomade-covered hand through his hair. "You never sound happy when you talk about her. Is she really that bad? My gram is the sweetest little lady you ever could meet."

A rough laugh was the only response Emmett could muster for a moment. "No one would ever call Aileen Montrose Buchanan sweet. They call her a force in Chicago society. They call her one of the richest widows alive. They call her the back-bone of the Chicago Women's Athletic Club. But sweet? Never."

Several of the other men had started listening in and now felt entitled to share their opinions. Hank Forman leaned forward with his elbows on his knees, his unkempt brown hair flopping into his eyes. The long legs that made him a good first baseman bent at an extreme angle to accommodate the low bench. "Why do you go, then? Ignore the woman."

If only it could be that simple. His grandmother had provided for him despite her immense grief after his mother's death. She'd given him the best education possible, all the opportunities her sizeable wealth could buy. She'd expected him to follow in his grandfather's footsteps and run the family stockyards, expand their fortune, take his proper place at her side in Chicago society.

Emmett hadn't done any of that, and she refused to forgive him.

But she was still the only family he had.

Shrugging, Emmett picked up his bag and waved to the other men. There was no way to explain his complicated rela-tionship with his grandmother to his teammates. "I'll see you at practice on Monday. Good game, fellas."

He left amidst a chorus of congratulations and made his way to the nearest electric streetcar stop. The homes along the streets grew ever larger and more imposing until the last stop before the Gold Coast, Chicago's most elegant neighborhood. Of course, nothing as common as a streetcar could be found amongst such wealth, so Emmett walked the remaining few blocks until he passed the massive, castle-like Palmer mansion and his grandmother's estate came into view.

Funny how he'd spent twenty-two of his thirty-two years of life there, but he still couldn't think of it as home.

Trudging up the stone walkway to the familiar but still impressive front entrance, Emmett reflected on what others must see. His grandmother had never been one to do things in half measures, and when Mr. Palmer's house had been touted as the grandest ever built in Chicago, she'd refused to come in second and insisted on having a home built next door that would be just as magnificent. No one in their right mind would argue whether she'd succeeded or not. Both houses were awe-inspiring in their own ways.

For Emmett, though, his grandmother's house elicited a wide range of emotions, none of them amazement.

Forcing his mind away from thoughts of the past, Emmett pushed the button to ring the doorbell, one of the latest improvements Grandmother had installed in the house to impress her friends. It was only moments before the butler, Hugh, opened the door wide and welcomed Emmett with his typical greeting. "Mr. Worland, welcome home."

"Good evening, Hugh. I'll see myself to Grandmother's study." Emmett passed the aging man with a pat on the shoulder and a smile. Then he drew a deep breath to fortify himself for the task ahead. Facing Aileen Montrose Buchanan when she wanted something he wasn't willing to provide was intimidating at best. *Terrifying* might be a better word.

The door to the orderly, sparse room was wide open, so Emmett stepped in and cleared his throat to let Grandmother know he was there. Her gray head remained down, intent on reading what looked like correspondence from a friend, but she lifted one finger in acknowledgment of his presence. How very like her not to be at all enthused by the obedience of her only grandchild.

Finally, she dropped the letter onto her desk and gracefully raised her head to examine him. He should have gone upstairs to change into a nicer suit and clean up a bit after the game, but it was too late now.

Grandmother released a deep sigh as if his appearance burdened her, then she gestured for him to enter. "Come. Sit down."

Emmett lowered himself into one of the fine upholstered chairs, trying to keep dirt off as much of the seat as he could manage. But he couldn't keep the tinge of sarcasm from his words. "It's nice to see you, too, Grandmother. Yes, we won our game today."

Her lips thinned into a tight line. "Emmett, you needn't be rude. Of course, it's good to see you. And congratulations on your victory."

From anyone else, those words would have been nice to hear. But from her, they fell flat, like meaningless small talk rather than genuine sentiments. He'd better get this over with before it turned into one of their many arguments. "Thank you, Grandmother. What did you call me here for?"

She entwined her slim, wrinkled fingers together as she paused before speaking. "We have a family problem, and you are the only one who can solve it."

That didn't sound promising. "And what might that problem be?"

"Your reputation."

Of course. It always came down to image. And Emmett's inability to conform to what she thought his image should be. "I'm not what the papers make me out to be, Grandmother. I don't go around leading ladies on, flirting and seducing them. They just flock to me. They're always there, hanging on to my every word with no encouragement from me. How can I fix my reputation when I didn't do anything to earn it in the first place?"

She leaned forward, her icy blue eyes burning into him. "Didn't do anything? Is that the story you're telling? My dear, I wouldn't know how you should go about it, as my character in Chicago society has always been pristine. But rumors about you are once again threatening to stain that spotless reputation, and I won't have it. I cannot continue supporting your lifestyle if it's going to disgrace our family."

Her veiled reference reminded him harshly that if he'd shown more discretion in the past, they wouldn't be having this conversation. If only he'd never met Charlotte Ford. While he might claim not to have done anything wrong to cause a stir in the papers, the reality was that his very public mistakes when it came to the presence of women in his life wouldn't be easily forgotten. He would always live under their weight.

Emmett took a deep breath to keep the frustration from showing on his face. That would only give Grandmother cause to turn smug. She was all too aware that baseball wasn't exactly a high-paying career, though some of the major league teams were starting to pay quite well. In fact, she often reminded him that if he'd attended Western College as she'd wanted him to instead of abandoning any higher education in favor of baseball, he could be wealthy in his own right. As it was, though, Emmett couldn't keep playing without either her money or taking a second job, which would limit his practice time and conflict with games.

She left him no option.

He had no idea how, but he'd have to find a way to put a stop to the rumors that he enjoyed trifling with the hearts of Chicago's unmarried ladies.

CHAPTER 2

*B*ea tugged the shortened blue skirt she wore for games into place, then straightened her white shirtwaist and navy tie. She checked that her hair was securely pinned back in a low chignon that accommodated her baseball cap while keeping the tendrils from distracting her during the game. With one last glance in the small mirror, she nodded at her reflection. Ready to work.

Walking out onto the field before a game was always an interesting event, especially this early in the season when she hadn't refereed for all the teams yet. New players liked to test her, thinking a lady umpire was a joke. Until they realized she was all business—and likely more capable than most of the male umpires.

Today's matchup between two Chicago City League teams, the Lincoln Parks and the West Ends, was sure to be a good one. Both teams had started the season strong, and she would have to be alert and focused so she didn't make any mistakes that might affect the outcome of the game.

The teams were warming up, the Lincoln Parks players on

the right side of the outfield, throwing balls back and forth. The West End players got into their positions on the field, the manager throwing fly balls and grounders to help them warm up.

Bea watched from the fence while the visiting team returned to the dugout, several players stopping on the field to talk with their manager. With him standing only a few feet in front of her, Bea couldn't help but watch the Lincoln Parks' new pitcher. He had the broadest shoulders she'd ever seen and was one of the taller players on the field. Only the slightest bit of dark-blond hair stuck out from under the back of his cap, meaning he must keep it short.

To Bea's surprise, she found herself wondering what color his eyes were. That is, until he turned, caught her looking, and shot her a crooked, confident smile. Blue. His eyes were a piercing, distracting blue. But he also wore the look of a man who knew the women in the stadium were all staring at him. Bea dropped her gaze as if there was nothing worth seeing and refused to meet his eyes again while the other players returned to their dugout.

But the pitcher wasn't going to allow her to ignore him. His voice reached her ears despite her best efforts. "I'm Emmett Worland. This is my first year in the City League."

Bea considered ignoring him or pretending she hadn't heard. But he'd given her no cause to be rude, and she worked hard to keep personal prejudice out of her work. "I'm Bea Curran. I hope this will be a good game for you, Mr. Worland."

A stray ball flew their way. Without hesitation, Mr. Worland wheeled back a few steps and reached up to pluck it from the air with his glove before it hit Bea. Then he threw the ball across the field to the opposing pitcher as easily as tossing a crumpled-up paper into a fireplace. "I've heard of the lady umpire but didn't think I'd get the pleasure of meeting her this early in the season."

He didn't sound patronizing, as many of the men did when they met her. But a man who went through female companions as often as he was said to must be well practiced at smooth talking. "Well, now you have. Let's make this a clean game, Mr. Worland."

An actual smirk settled on his face as he ran forward to intercept a ball an outfielder was returning so the game could start. With his arm outstretched, his entire body reaching while balanced precariously on one foot, she could see why ladies flocked to see him play. He exuded absolute confidence and comfort on the field. And his lively blue eyes, wide grin, and athletic build didn't hurt either.

She managed to drag her attention away from him as the first batter came out of the dugout, and she took her spot behind the West Ends' pitcher to start the game. The crowd wasn't as large on Tuesday afternoon as it was on the weekends, but there were plenty of spectators to fill the air with cheers and taunts. Closing her eyes for a moment, Bea let the atmosphere wash over her, the smell of dirt and grass a balm to her soul. She did love being on a baseball field.

She opened her eyes ready to work. The first half of the game progressed without incident. The calls were easy to make. No one got upset with her. Both teams put on a good show for their fans.

By the sixth inning, the Lincoln Parks had earned a two-run lead and shifted into a more relaxed style of play.

And then Mr. Worland started speaking to her again. "You really are as qualified as they say."

She couldn't help responding, thanks to his rather astonished tone. "I wouldn't be here if I wasn't."

When his catcher tossed the ball back after Mr. Worland struck out the first batter of the inning, he caught it with an easy reach. Another batter approached the plate, and Mr. Worland got in his stance, glanced around the field, then pulled back and threw the ball with a force that always seemed impossible from Bea's vantage point. The batter didn't swing at the perfect pitch, so she called the first strike.

Without turning, Mr. Worland spoke again. "I didn't mean that as an insult. I'm pleased to have such good officiating for our games. The lower league games can be a mess due to bad calls."

Was he trying to flatter her? And if so, was it because he thought he could sway her to preferential treatment for his team? Or was it an attempt at flirting?

Bea chose to ignore him this time and focus on the game. He struck out the next two batters without hesitation, and the West Ends' pitcher took the mound in his place. Bea was horrified to realize she rather wished the inning would end so Mr. Worland would return.

Shaking off such an unacceptable thought, she watched the game with more care. The later innings were often more intense and contested than the early ones as teams got lax or desperate, so she needed to keep her wits about her.

Wishing a handsome pitcher was back in her line of sight would not help in maintaining her record of excellent calls.

But then he did walk into her vision again, this time at the plate with bat in hand. So far in the game, he'd proven to be an accomplished hitter, on top of being a skilled pitcher. Bea could see why hiring him had been a significant news item for the Lincoln Park team.

She found herself almost holding her breath as the West Ends' pitcher wound up and released the ball. She was actually hoping Mr. Worland would hit it. If she didn't get herself together, this game could be a failure for her.

The crack of the bat striking the ball with intense force snapped her back into the moment. The ball sailed over her and the pitcher, landing in a roll between the left and center fielders, causing them to scramble for it while Mr. Worland reached first base without even needing to hurry. Her chest expanded with completely unwarranted pride.

The next batter took his spot at home plate, and Bea returned her attention to the matter at hand. The bat once again connected, and the ball flew, not as far this time, heading straight to the shortstop waiting next to her. Bea twirled around to watch the man sweep the ball up in his glove and toss it toward the waiting second baseman as Mr. Worland ran for all he was worth. He slid through the dirt, his foot touching the base a mere breath before the ball nestled into the baseman's glove.

Bea spread both arms out, sweeping them parallel to the ground. "Safe!"

An uproar arose from the stands and the field. The dust from Mr. Worland's slide had made it difficult for anyone else to see the play. But Bea knew he had touched the bag before the baseman caught the ball.

She stood firm as the West Enders reacted with varying degrees of anger and frustration. It happened often enough that she'd learned to simply walk back to her place and be alert, watching for anyone who grew upset enough that they needed to be ejected from the game.

Usually, that worked fine.

But this time, as she returned to her spot, a presence loomed behind her. Before she could turn, a whoosh of air indicated something intense happening. Whirling around again, she found the second baseman storming toward her with Mr. Worland rushing to force his arm against the man's chest to stop his advance.

Bea took an involuntary step back. The second baseman towered over her, a hulking, burly man. But Mr. Worland was a match for him, putting his large frame between the other player and her and using a deliberate, calm tone. "Remember, laying a single finger on the ump gets you thrown out. And it won't change the outcome of the game except that your team will be without a good second baseman. It's not worth it."

The two stared each other down for a long moment while Bea's breathing refused to return to its normal rhythm. Finally, the second baseman turned and stomped back to his position. "Get your foot on this bag, Worland, or I'll have my pitcher throw that ball and tag you out."

Mr. Worland met Bea's eyes, tossing her the most ridiculous wink. "I apologize for that scene. Are you hurt?"

Bea shook her head, unable to form words to respond. Mr. Worland nodded and kept his gaze trained on her as he backed toward the base. She whipped around to focus on the pitcher and upcoming batter again. Being proposed to by players was one thing. Having her physical safety defended by one of them was quite another. It felt much more intimate and visceral than any of the players getting down on one knee.

So why did her mind insist on reliving it over and over?

~

*E*mmett splashed his face with lukewarm water from a basin in the locker room before rubbing a ragged cloth over his head, thinking back over the game. It had taken all their skill after the incident in the sixth inning, but the Lincoln Parks had pulled out a win.

Staring at his own reflection in the mirror next to Emmett, Boot grinned. "I liked your dashing hero routine out there, Worland, saving the umpire in distress. Clever way to get her attention."

Emmett shook his head while pulling his shirt over his arms and into place. "I wasn't trying to get her attention. I saw a situation that needed handling, that's all."

Boot's eyebrows remained raised. "That's not how it looked to anyone else. Fellows have been chasing the lady ump for years. You're the first one who's tried rescuing her."

Emmett didn't respond, instead returning to his spot on a bench and leaning down to tug his shoes on. If his grandmother heard about this from the same angle Boot suggested, she'd be livid. He had to be more careful. It had been his protective instincts that started the rumors that he was a womanizer in the first place. He'd have to guard his reactions better if he was going to get away from that reputation.

Which might not be too difficult if only she wasn't so fascinating.

The others weren't ready to quit talking about her yet either. Comments flew around the room.

"Did you know she plays baseball along with being an ump?"

"She manages a ladies' college team. Can you believe that? A whole team of girls playing baseball."

"I heard she's a humdinger of a basketball player too."

But, as often happened in the locker room, the men eventually took the talk too far. The stout right fielder, Tom Barden, released a gruff laugh. "I'd let her tell me what to do any day. Think I could convince her to give me a private lesson on the rules?"

Emmett sprang from his seat. "That's enough, Barden."

Tom just continued to laugh. "Oh, right. Worland's made a claim on her already."

The others joined in the amusement. Knowing nothing he said would change their minds—and would instead make the insinuations worse—Emmett grabbed his things and left the room. Word of a fistfight with his teammates wouldn't do him any favors in his grandmother's eyes either.

One thing Emmett liked about being on a city league team was that most of their games happened in Chicago, so he didn't have to leave his hometown for weeks at a time. He walked out of the field into a perfect—albeit hot—spring evening. The city was alive with sounds and people, some ending their workdays, some just starting. Chicago made him feel vibrant in a way other towns hadn't. It was one reason he'd chosen to take the Lincoln Parks' offer.

The other reason for staying close to home didn't bear thinking about.

Baseball had been his world for too long to let anything take it from him. It had been his comfort when Grandmother was absent. His purpose when the rest of his world was cold and harsh. He wouldn't give it up until someone pried it from his hands.

Before he made it farther than the field entrance, the sound of a lady's heels clicking on the bricks by the gate caught his attention. He looked over his shoulder to find Miss Curran glancing away as if trying to keep him from noticing her.

Which would be impossible, no matter the setting.

She'd looked beautiful in her element on the field, but she was still charming now after changing into a sensible, light-blue dress and tucking her brown hair up under an equally sensible hat. He smiled, undeterred by the way she turned up her pert little nose at him.

"Miss Curran, I hope that incident on the field wasn't too unpleasant for you."

Her shoulders drew back, and she straightened her spine to face him at her full height, although she missed matching his by at least eight inches. "I've been in the midst of worse and managed fine. Emotions run high on the field, and not all men have mastered the self-control an umpire must possess."

He found his smile spreading into a grin. It was no wonder she'd hardly been bothered by the intense moment. This woman was stronger than any ladies he'd met before. And he liked that quality far more than he'd ever imagined.

Silence fell between them, and she started to step away, but Emmett was reluctant to bid her goodbye. He'd never been good at small talk, so he had to search for something to say that might keep her there longer. "What made you start refereeing baseball at this level?"

He hoped the pang of dismay didn't show on his face. How such a personal question had slipped out, he had no idea. It was the kind of thing he tried not to ask women, as they tended to take any interest from him as a sign that he wanted their undying affection.

But instead of simpering or refusing to answer, her head tilted to one side as if she was considering it seriously. "I'm rarely asked such questions. Most players propose to me without so much as a passing interest in who I am. My brother-in-law, Sam, played for a company team in Iowa for several years. My sister and I attended many of his games, but at one in particular, the umpire never arrived. They were almost ready to forfeit the game when Sam asked if I would do it. I had plenty of knowledge of baseball from practicing with him and even stepping in to play now and then, so I agreed."

"And I can see why they kept requesting you if you worked from the start like I saw today."

Unexpected laughter filled the air, the light sound warming his heart and making him wish he could hear it every day. Her brown eyes danced with merriment, crinkling at the corners. "I didn't. At only sixteen, I was terrified of those men. But I held my ground when I knew I was right, and I taught them some rules they didn't know that made the games run much smoother. When I moved to Chicago, Charles Rosen very much appreciated that quality. He's the one who started requesting me for the City League."

Emmett could envision a slightly younger Miss Curran, but less confident wasn't something he could imagine. To his dismay, the moment of distraction gave her a chance to nod in his direction while starting down the sidewalk toward the train station. "Goodbye, Mr. Worland. I'm sure I'll see you at another game soon enough."

His heart thumped, his intuition telling him he ought to come up with some way to continue the conversation, but his mind was unable to conjure a sensible word. "Can I escort you home?"

The question blurted from his mouth before he could consider it. He flinched. He sounded like a love-struck school-boy, not a thirty-two-year-old man. Miss Curran must have had the same thought because one brow arched as a sardonic smile turned up her lips. "No, thank you. I'm quite capable of handling the trip home by myself, as I do every day."

The chance he shouldn't be trying to take was slipping away. He had a feeling their next meeting would be all busi-ness. "You can tell me more about the questions no one asks you," he cajoled.

She turned serious this time, no amusement lingering in her soft brown eyes. "Mr. Worland, I have to maintain a neutral relationship with players at all times. If we were to be seen together socially, it could cast doubt on my integrity. And I've worked far too hard for my reputation to let that happen. I'm sorry, but I won't see you again until the next game."

The mention of her reputation brought Emmett's reality crashing down upon him. She was the sort of upstanding lady of quality that his grandmother might approve of as his wife. But Emmett had no intention of marrying when he was unable to support his own family. And right now, he couldn't even support himself. Until he broke into the big leagues, he couldn't pursue any woman. Doing so without plans to marry in good time would only confirm his grandmother's belief in his false reputation.

Stepping back, he gestured for Miss Curran to proceed. She

sent a half smile his way that he liked to think held a bit of regret. But then he forced himself to put her out of his mind. Maybe someday he would be in a situation to experience the love of a good woman. But until then, he had one purpose in life—baseball.

CHAPTER 3

Sitting in Marjorie King's office at Western College, Bea allowed herself to slump in the hard wooden chair, watching a cobweb float in the corner of the high ceiling. Sun streamed through the small window, highlighting Marjorie's piles of papers and books and turning the ever-increasing streaks of gray in her blond hair to silver. "The girls can't play worth anything. What am I going to do with them?"

While some administrators might have taken offense over an employee complaining to them about students, Marjorie chuckled at Bea's assessment of the women's baseball team and didn't argue with it. "Don't lose hope, dear. They have heart. They want to play, and they try hard. That's half the battle."

Bea twisted a string that stuck out from the sleeve cuff of the old shirtwaist she wore for practice with the college's women's baseball team. The weight of being tasked with helping the women improve—and knowing the board of regents was watching to see if she could do so—sat heavily on Bea's mind. "Yes, but the other half is concerning. How do I help them? They might be willing, but I'm good at strategy and planning, not coaching. They're a chaotic mess. The outfielders

24

bump into each other more often than not, and our batting is terrible. They need more than I know how to give."

Raising one eyebrow, Marjorie voiced the opinion Bea had already rejected several times since beginning practice with the team two months ago. "You could always seek help. Some teams have started bringing in assistants who coach the players while the manager focuses on coordinating strategy and schedules. You know plenty of excellent baseball players with wisdom to impart to the ladies."

A snort escaped Bea's lips, which would have embarrassed her in front of anyone else. But Marjorie wasn't a stickler for propriety. In fact, a delighted glint appeared in her eyes at Bea's response, making her appear much younger than her fifty years. So Bea explained without apology. "Those players would be more likely to propose to the girls and whisk them out of college than to help turn them into a winning baseball team. Women's teams must become more than a curiosity if we're going to prove to society that we have as much right to athletic pursuits as men. Those girls need to be taken seriously. And I need the team to succeed if I'm going to convince the board I'm qualified to take over your position when you retire."

With a tilt of her head, Marjorie rooted out the deeper meaning behind Bea's words. "You're speaking out of your own past experience, it seems. You had to fight hard to prove your ability as an umpire. But asking a man for help isn't going to diminish what you've accomplished or the girls' right to play. Not every player is seeking a wife. Find a married one. Or one who doesn't want to settle down."

For some reason, Mr. Worland's face flashed in Bea's mind. But she pushed that thought deep into the back of her mind. He not only asked to escort her home the night before— proving he would pursue her just like so many other players— but he was said to have formed relationships with ladies in every town his previous team visited. The women in Chicago flocked to him, vying for attention that he didn't hesitate to give them. He was wholly unsuitable.

Standing, Marjorie walked the two steps to a bookshelf and pulled out an attendance ledger, speaking absently while thumbing through it. "You know I have many connections in Chicago society, Bea. I recently heard an interesting tidbit from my long-time acquaintance Mrs. Aileen Montrose Buchanan. I have no doubt you've heard of her."

It wasn't a question. Everyone in the Windy City knew who Mrs. Buchanan was. She was *the* pillar of society. She was included in every important function. She ran a multitude of charities. She'd funded half the college building projects in honor of her late husband, an esteemed alumnus. "Of course. But I wasn't aware you were close."

Marjorie shrugged. "No one is close with Mrs. Buchanan, exactly. But we've been in the same social circles long enough that I have some part in her life. And she does open up on occasion. The other day, she mentioned that she threatened to cut off financial support for her grandson if he doesn't stop his flirtatious ways."

"And?" What did a rich, spoiled boy losing access to his lavish lifestyle have to do with her baseball team?

"And he happens to be Emmett Worland, pitcher for the Lincoln Parks and the man you mentioned more than once since stepping foot in my office today."

Heat worked its way up Bea's neck despite her best efforts not to be embarrassed. Had she mentioned him that much while telling Marjorie about how the City League games were going?

Focusing on the problem at hand, she let her mind work through all Marjorie was implying. Mr. Worland was the rich, spoiled boy who was being forced to clean up his behavior. Bea knew the salaries of players at the semi-pro level. He likely depended upon his grandmother's wealth to allow him to pursue his baseball career. He wouldn't be able to corrupt any of her players without putting that at risk. And she couldn't deny he was an excellent baseball player.

Still, Bea shook her head. "Not him. I need someone serious and committed, and I'm confident he's not either of those. He's the same as the rest of them. Selfish. Cocky. Thinks no one can tell him no. He won't be a good influence on the girls. Their parents trust us to protect them and their reputations. His presence would endanger that, no matter what his grandmother threatens."

Marjorie tilted her head with a slight shrug. "It's your team. I was offering an option, but I'll leave the decision up to you. Please, consider the idea, though. You might find him to be a better fit than you think right now."

Realizing how late it was, Bea thanked her friend and rose. "I need to get to practice. Do you want to walk with me?"

Marjorie grinned. "I certainly do. I can't stand sitting here inside on a day as beautiful as this one."

Bea and Marjorie left the athletic building and walked across the picturesque campus in silence, enjoying the sound of Lake Michigan's waves hitting the shore that bordered the east side of the college. They arrived at the baseball diamond before any of the girls, while the men's team was still practicing. Standing at the plank fence that separated the spectator benches from the field, they watched the young men practicing plays. Would any of their three managers fit her qualifications for helping the women's team?

But she didn't have to contemplate it for long. She knew how they would respond if she asked. The college leadership and the men's team, in particular, had been not only unaccepting but often downright in the way of the women's baseball program. She'd been told they would receive no funds from the athletic department, and they could only use the field when the men's team allowed it. They could be asked to leave it at any moment if the men needed the field, whether they had a good reason or not.

No, no one associated with the college would be of help to her. Not until she proved the women's team was as valuable as the men's.

Marjorie spoke up again as the men finally started gathering their equipment and leaving the field. "Bea, I wanted to mention the music department's senior recital again." Marjorie held up both hands, preemptively stopping the protest Bea had given several times before. "I know, you don't see any reason to go. But making the right connections will be part of your job if you take over for me. Donors are vital to the college. And Mrs. Buchanan's interest in college programs determines where many of the alumni are willing to put their money. She'll be in attendance, and that means you should be, as well."

"Marjorie, what business do I have attempting to get in the good graces of a woman like that? I'm a female umpire from a small town in Iowa. She'll take one look at me and know right away that I have no business handling her donations."

Bea's team began to arrive, all in their shortened skirts with hair pulled back in a variety of simple fashions. Several of them sported billed ball caps like the men wore to keep the sun out of their eyes. Her heart filled with emotion. These women were every bit the players the men were, but they needed better direction than she could give. She was a good coordinator, not a good teacher.

Turning to face Bea, Marjorie commanded Bea's attention again. "You have every right to take over my position, Bea Curran. Don't you dare talk about yourself that way. You'll come to the concert and delight Mrs. Buchanan like you do me, and she'll be ready to pour money into the women's teams."

The chances of that happening were nearly nonexistent, but Bea never could argue with Marjorie when she got her heart set on something. At least she enjoyed music, so attending the senior recital wouldn't be a complete waste of her time. And who knew? Maybe Mrs. Buchanan was more open and accepting in reality than her reputation made her out to be.

Plus, it wouldn't hurt to dig up more information about her grandson. Only to decide if he might be helpful to her team, of course.

❧

A week after the first game Emmett played with Miss Curran as the umpire, they met on the pitcher's mound again. This time, however, Emmett was determined not to make a fool of himself.

Ever since their conversation at the gate of West End Park the previous week, he'd felt ridiculous for the way he'd acted. Of course she would refuse to spend time with him outside of games. Not only did she have her professional reputation to consider, but his own was hardly sterling enough to make a lady like her feel comfortable in his company. Grandmother had made that more than clear.

So he'd committed to keeping his comments on the mound when she was officiating completely baseball-related.

Which would be much easier if she didn't look so pretty in dark blue.

Emmett attempted to focus on the game ahead as he warmed up with his team. They were playing the Cleveland Spiders, a team that had a reputation for being scrappy and playing aggressive baseball, the kind of group that tended to be volatile in competition. He had his work cut out for him if he was going to get the Lincoln Parks through with a win while staving off any fights between the men.

But keeping his mind on the game was more difficult than usual that day. It started with the Spiders, who flocked to Miss Curran when she appeared at the edge of their home field while the Lincoln Parks were warming up. They'd never played a game with her officiating, and while he understood the novelty, the way those men stood around her and captured her attention was too much.

It wasn't at all like what he'd done at their first meeting last week, of course.

And the way her lips turned up in a smile as she accepted their compliments with knowing, aloof grace certainly wasn't causing the sudden burning in his chest.

Then there was the crowd. The Spiders' fans filled most of the seats in Lincoln Square Park. But they were as unfamiliar with the lady umpire as the players. More than once, Emmett overheard the men who trekked from their seats to the fence to call for the attention of the Spiders' manager, Bucky Mack.

"Mack! Hey, Mack! What kind of joke is it that there's a woman on the field?"

"You're not letting her tell our boys what to do, are you?"

With gritted teeth, Emmett managed to contain himself while Mack calmed the fans, but it left him in a strange mood. He walked two players in the first inning, something he hadn't done since his youth playing with friends on the field their fathers' company teams used. In the second inning, he allowed two runs, putting the Spiders ahead.

All the while, he was aware of Miss Curran's watchful eye behind him.

Returning to the dugout after the Spiders' first baseman caught a pop fly to get the third out, Emmett dropped onto the bench and rubbed a hand through his hair before replacing his ball cap. Down the bench, Hank crossed his arms over his burly chest and glowered at Emmett. "Get it together, Worland. You're losing this for us."

"Maybe you should help by getting a run, then," Emmett snapped.

Boot sat himself between them, breaking the tension. "What's going on, Emmett? You look like a mess out there."

He debated playing dumb, not revealing what was going on in his mind. But connecting with his teammates could make all the difference in the way they worked together on the field. So he took a fortifying breath and let the words out. "I'm distracted. My grandmother demanded that I redeem my reputation, or else she'll stop supporting me so I can play instead of running the family business. How am I supposed to do that when I didn't do anything to earn that notoriety in the first place?"

The two men watched in silence as another teammate lined himself up at the plate and hit the first pitch squarely to right field. He made it to first base while fans cheered, and their teammates clapped. Boot finally responded as Hank started his at-bat with a strike. "What if you make an effort to show what you *are* instead of trying to prove what you're *not*?"

It took a minute to decode that, during which Hank struck out and the next man in the lineup walked out with his bat. "I see what you mean. But how would I do that?"

Boot shrugged as he grabbed his bat and started for the deck to get in a few warmup swings before his turn. "Do the nice, honorable things you always do, but in public."

The idea made sense, but Emmett still had no idea how to prove he was a better man than the papers said without it seeming contrived. He hadn't been aware he did nice, honorable things that no one saw.

When his turn to pitch in the third inning came up, he could feel the game falling apart. The Lincoln Parks had only scored one run, and they all seemed frustrated and desperate, which was never a good way to play the game. When the first opposing batter walked up, Emmett narrowed his focus to the ball in his hand and the catcher's glove. He made it all he could see, hear, or feel. The ball leaving his hand and flying straight into the glove.

It worked for the first two batters. Three quick strikes on each. But then he became aware of Miss Curran behind him again. Her sweet voice calling the strikes grew distracting. He knew when he released the first pitch that it was a perfect hit. Sure enough, the Spiders' batter slammed the ball hard, and it flew past Emmett and the shortstop. The outfielders scurried to reach it but were a moment too late, and the batter was safe on first.

The Spiders called a time out, and Emmett couldn't help a glance behind him at the lovely umpire. Despite his determination to focus, he found himself asking her the question burning in his mind in a low voice. "Miss Curran, how would you suggest a man like me might prove he isn't what people say?"

Her brown eyes flew to meet his gaze in surprise. "If you think you can redeem yourself in my opinion, Mr. Worland, I'm sorry to tell you it won't work. I've known far too many baseball players just like you. I've even seen some try to settle down and commit to a woman. It never lasts, and there's a lifetime of pain she has to pay for it."

The words hit Emmett like a stray ball to the head. "Haven't you ever met a player you respect more than that?"

Without responding, she turned to call the end of the time out and restart the game. Emmett found that the rapid pulsing in his veins caused by her words was a better motivation than anything he'd tried to that point. He struck out the next batter with his usual ease.

Back in the dugout after the inning, her comments settled in his mind and became a challenge. If he could find the thing that would change her opinion about him, everyone else would see who he truly was too. He just had to prove himself to Miss Beatrice Curran.

That couldn't be as difficult as she made it out to be.

CHAPTER 4

As hard as she tried to remain impartial, Bea's heart dropped every time she had to let one of the Spiders walk. So she was already conflicted and frustrated when the shortstop reached second base behind her.

"Ump! Hey, ump!"

She glanced over her shoulder, saw nothing was happening related to the game, and returned her attention to Mr. Worland's pitching.

But the Spiders player didn't stop. "Ump, keep making those calls for us. Walk Henderson."

Without giving him the satisfaction of looking again, she responded, "Only if they're pitched that way."

The man hooted with laughter.

The inning didn't improve for the Lincoln Parks when the Spiders scored twice before the teams switched places.

Then the shortstop took his position on the field to her right and started up his annoying calls again. "Ump! Did they put you out here to distract us? 'Cause it might just work. Imagine, a lady calling baseball games. Can't be real."

Bea gritted her teeth, but he continued.

"Where's the real ump? They hiding him in the dugout, going to bring him out halfway through as a gag?"

That was enough. Bea held up her hands to stop the game, asking the batter to step away from the plate for a moment. Then she turned toward the shortstop. "If you don't find some respect, I'll be forced to eject you from this game. I've heard about your team. None of the others are any good at shortstop, so your removal might be an automatic loss if the Lincoln Parks start hitting to center. Do you want to risk it?"

His jaw went slack, and he blinked at her for a long moment. Then a grin stretched across his face. "No, ma'am. Keep up the good work."

The respect in his eyes sent a wave of warmth through Bea. It was always a gratifying moment, although she wished she didn't have to work so hard to earn it in the first place.

But it was the way Mr. Worland's eyebrows rose in approval of how she'd handled the player that turned the warm feeling into a flush creeping up her neck.

The rest of the game wasn't easy for the Lincoln Parks. The Spiders played great baseball, and she could see Mr. Worland wasn't pitching anywhere near as well as he had the previous week. His question for her in the middle of the game had been unexpected, and Bea couldn't help thinking back on Marjorie's revelation about him. Did he feel his portrayal as a rake was unfair? He seemed genuinely frustrated and curious about her opinion. Was it possible that Marjorie was right and he wouldn't be as bad for the women's team as Bea assumed?

She tried to shake off that idea, but it kept plaguing her as she watched Mr. Worland return to the pitching style she'd admired last week, giving his team a chance. The rest of the game was hard fought, with many close calls she had to make, but the Lincoln Parks came up one run short in the end.

And still, the thought that Emmett Worland might be good for her girls wouldn't leave Bea alone.

While she cleaned up and changed, Bea forced her thoughts to turn toward the music department recital. As usual, Marjorie wasn't wrong. Making connections with those higher in society was one of the very few options available to further Bea's cause. If she wanted to expand the athletic department, she'd have to show an unwilling board of regents how it was going to be funded. There was no hope of finding anyone willing to part with money from the athletic department's already tight budget, so donations or fundraising were the only options. For either method to be successful, she'd need to know the right people.

So she found herself walking into the Franklin Music Hall that Friday evening, wearing the only gown she owned that was appropriate for such an occasion. Usually she didn't mind wearing the pink silk with puffed sleeves and lovely silver embroidery running down the front of it. But knowing the social standing of those who would be in attendance at the event made her more aware than ever that the frock was several years old and likely hopelessly out of fashion.

Still, Bea would go to great lengths to secure funding for her team. So she reached up to make certain the ribbon circling her hair was secure and squared her shoulders. The Franklin Music Hall was one of the college's most touted buildings. It sat tucked against the lake shore, as picturesque as the rest of the campus. Large windows let the sounds of the musicians tuning their instruments out into the night. Huge columns flanked the steps that led to several sets of ornate double doors where fashionable guests entered.

As she passed through those doors and entered the hall, Bea immediately caught sight of one of her players, Sarah Blaine, who was performing in the concert. Sarah lit up when she saw Bea and excused herself from the older couple she'd been speaking to, making her way straight to Bea. "Miss Curran, I'm so glad you're here. Miss King said you might be."

The pleasure in her voice was almost enough to make up for how out of place Bea felt. "I can't wait to hear you perform, Sarah. I'm sure all the guests will be impressed with your skill."

Sarah beamed but then glanced around the room, one hand rising to adjust the lace along her neckline. "I'm not so sure. These people are used to going to the opera and professional concerts. We're just a few aspiring musicians."

Marjorie joined them as Bea reached out to loop her arm through Sarah's and responded in a low voice. "You act as if this is a professional concert, and they'll believe it. Go with confidence."

Sarah's slumped shoulders straightened, and a determined glint appeared in her eyes. Bea released her to go prepare for her performance and turned toward Marjorie, who skipped any greeting. "You have a way of inspiring confidence in those girls. I'm so pleased you plan to give more of your time to them."

The words were kind, but they sparked a tremor of concern in Bea. "I hope it's the right decision. I'm afraid I'm not the most fitting person to attempt to expand the department. Look how difficult a time I've had finding support and funding for the baseball team, much less to create a new certificate program."

Directing Bea's attention toward an elegant older woman across the room, Marjorie smiled. "We're taking care of that right now."

And before she was quite ready, Bea was face to face with Aileen Montrose Buchanan, queen of the socialites and easily the most intimidating woman Bea had ever met. She was taller than Bea had expected—or maybe her perfect, rigid posture made it seem so. The older woman's gown was impeccable, and her hair, laying in a perfect twist against her head, seemed to recognize that she would not withstand any nonsense from it. Her thin lips didn't so much as twitch upward as she listened to Marjorie's introduction. "Mrs. Aileen Buchanan, this is Miss Beatrice Curran. Bea, Mrs. Buchanan. Oh, and I believe you already know her grandson, Mr. Emmett Worland."

Without warning, Mr. Worland himself stepped out from behind his grandmother, whose imposing presence had kept Bea from noticing him. Bea swallowed, fighting unexpected dryness in her throat. As attractive as he was in a pinstriped uniform, standing before her in a black formal suit, she could see how so many women fell prey to his advances. His shoulders were impossibly broad, and the fitted coat he wore showed off every inch of his muscular, athletic frame. She prayed her voice wouldn't betray those ridiculous thoughts when she spoke. "It's a pleasure, Mrs. Buchanan. And yes, Mr. Worland and I are acquainted."

~

*E*mmett tried to keep his glance at Miss Curran brief, but her beauty in that pink dress was impossible to ignore. He was keenly aware of Grandmother watching his every move, though. He'd only agreed to attend the concert as a way to prove he was willing to participate in her idea of a respectable life. He'd never imagined he would be graced with Miss Curran's company there.

And while he wasn't sad to see her—could never be—the presence of such a beautiful woman who was also strictly off-limits did make the evening more complicated.

Grandmother's life-long friend, Miss King, grinned at them all, looking downright delighted. "I offered to help keep the students organized behind the scenes during the concert, so I need to get backstage. I'll join you during the refreshments afterward. Bea, you should sit with Mrs. Buchanan and Mr. Worland. You're all my guests, so please, get to know each other a bit."

Then, as if completely unaware of what she'd done, Miss

King fluttered away in a cloud of purple skirts. Now he faced the task of proving to his grandmother that Miss Curran was a baseball acquaintance, not one of his supposed flings.

Instead of pressing the matter, however, his grandmother scanned the room, finally nodding toward a group of empty seats toward the front. "Well, Emmett, you might as well escort us to our seats."

The last thing he wanted was to offer his arm to a lady with Grandmother's intense stare trained on them, but he had little choice. She'd spent plenty of money over the years ensuring he had impeccable manners, and he was expected to prove it when they were in public. So he held out his arm to their lovely companion. "Of course. Miss Curran, may I?"

She hesitated. He approved of the move, even if it did sting a bit that she didn't seem to want to be in his presence. But if she remained unaffected by him—uninterested, even—it would help him show he wasn't the rake he was accused of being.

Finally, she slid her hand through the crook of his arm, holding her body away to touch him as little as possible. He steered them toward the seats Grandmother had indicated, and they were soon settled, Miss Curran between him and Grandmother. He didn't mind the seating arrangement one bit until Grandmother began the line of inquiry he'd been dreading. "Miss Curran, please enlighten me as to the nature of your acquaintance with my grandson."

He couldn't help wondering if Grandmother's intimidating stare made Miss Curran as nauseous as it had often made him over the years. If it did, she showed no signs of such, responding with a level of confidence he admired. "I'm an umpire in the Chicago City Baseball League. Your grandson has pitched in several games I was officiating so far this season. He's quite talented."

She offered it as a compliment to his grandmother, that was

clear. But the words still sent an unexpected thrill through Emmett. When was the last time someone had given him a genuine compliment like that, not at all couched in subtle criticism? His teammates congratulated each other on a game well played, but rarely commented on specific talents. The newspapers didn't compliment players without using it as a tool to spring into critique. And his grandmother hated that he played baseball. While she participated in many athletic pursuits, she'd never had a single kind thing to say about his entire sport.

So it was nothing short of a shock when Grandmother leaned toward Miss Curran, curiosity lighting her faded blue eyes. "You mean to tell me you, a young woman, *work* as an *umpire*?"

Clearly not aware of his grandmother's distaste for the sport, Miss Curran nodded with more enthusiasm than he'd seen from her in any other setting besides the field. "I am. And I'm quite good if the papers can be believed."

A laugh, an actual humor-filled laugh, burst from his grandmother. Emmett was speechless. She was the most cheerless woman on earth. How was Miss Curran charming her so quickly and completely?

The older woman relaxed back into her seat and patted Miss Curran's hand as two students walked onto the stage, one moving to stand in front, preparing to sing, and the other taking a seat at the piano in the corner. "I do hope to hear how that came to be while we enjoy refreshments after the concert."

Miss Curran agreed, then turned her attention to the stage. Emmett watched her profile long after the music started, trying to discern how she'd brought out such good humor in his grandmother. Without looking his way, she finally leaned toward him, her voice low. "Is there a problem, Mr. Worland?"

Embarrassed at having been caught staring, he turned his gaze to the students. "No, no problem. I apologize."

"Then perhaps you should pay more attention to the

concert." He couldn't help one more glance in her direction, though, when he heard amusement in her tone. He was rewarded with the knowledge that a slight smile was tipping up her soft lips. So she did have some levity in her, something more than the serious, focused umpire he saw on the field.

He did as she instructed from then on and kept his attention trained on the concert. The student musicians were quite talented, making it an enjoyable hour. But even if he appeared focused on the performances, a significant part of his mind refused to ignore the beauty sitting at his right side.

Once the final student performed and the program was closed by an emotional music instructor, the attendees began rising from their seats to find the refreshment tables in the lobby. Emmett escorted Miss Curran again, the two of them trailing behind Grandmother as she made her grand exit with many eyes following her progress through the room. It was a relief to be behind her rather than holding her arm as he usually was, giving all those people the opportunity to assess him as well as the illustrious Aileen Montrose Buchanan.

In the high-ceilinged lobby, tables held a variety of foods for the concert-goers interspersed with arrangements of pastel flowers. Small sandwiches, tiny squares of cake encased in solid frosting, bits of fruit—everything was designed to be held in one hand. Emmett took two sandwiches and tried to eat with small bites as he'd been taught, but he was hungry. There had been no time for a meal between the game that afternoon and the time his grandmother had declared he needed to be ready to join her.

Unfortunately, Miss King approached their group right as he shoved an entire little cake into his mouth. It was a good thing his grandmother greeted her first, giving him time to chew and swallow. "Marjorie, that was a charming concert. Please give the music director my compliments."

Miss King accepted the praise with a graceful nod. "Thank you. I will, of course."

Taking a sip from her glass of punch, Miss King then turned to Emmett. "I hear you've been having a very good season with your new team."

Emmett nodded, taken aback by the sudden turn in the conversation, although he should have expected people to ask about his career. People other than his grandmother, of course. "It's going fine. We've had a few losses, but overall, we play well together."

Arching an eyebrow at Miss Curran, Miss King seemed to be waiting for something. When Miss Curran's eyes widened and she gave an almost imperceptible shake of her head, Emmett couldn't resist the curiosity that rose. "Was there something you wanted to say, Miss Curran?"

All three of them watched Miss Curran for a long moment while she swallowed hard and visibly fought for words.

Finally, Miss King turned back to him. "Are you aware Miss Curran manages our women's baseball team here at the college?"

"I've heard that, although I don't know Miss Curran well enough to have firsthand knowledge of how she spends her free time," Emmett replied in the most neutral tone he could manage. The truth was, he was desperate to learn just that.

Miss King seemed to pick up steam, growing more animated as she explained. "She does. But to be honest, they're a mess that not even her skill can tame."

Emmett glanced in Miss Curran's direction as she uttered a strangled groan, but Miss King didn't even bat an eye as she continued. "We've been considering the idea of bringing in an assistant manager to help her. Someone with a different perspective who can coach the ladies in ways Miss Curran has found challenging. Someone like you."

At least she got right to the point, because Emmett never

would have guessed they were planning to ask for his help with a women's baseball team. Immediately, he looked at his grandmother, certain he knew what she would think of him spending hours working closely with an entire team of impressionable college women. While the idea of helping them might have appealed to him under normal conditions, he couldn't agree while fulfilling her demands. "Me? I'm hardly qualified to advise a team of students. And working with a women's team isn't something that interests me."

He'd chosen the words deliberately to shut down any arguments in favor of him considering the request, but Miss Curran's tight-lipped expression made him wish he could take them back.

"We have our answer, Marjorie. I told you he wasn't a good choice." Her tone was frosty enough to freeze him in his tracks.

Emmett's heart pinched. Why he hated to upset Miss Curran that way, he wasn't sure, but he'd almost rather face Grandmother's censure than hers. If only he could show Miss Curran that he was doing it to protect the ladies on her team and himself, not because he had any disdain for women in sports. Why couldn't anyone see he was trying to do the right thing?

CHAPTER 5

*B*ea let the ball sail from her fingers, watching it fly straight toward Bethany Sims's glove. Bethany readied herself, her glove held high to pluck the ball from the air—until it hit the ground five feet behind her. Bea sighed as Bethany scrambled to get it, grabbing the grass several times before finally getting the ball in her glove and spinning around. She threw it in the general direction of Sarah Blaine, who occupied second base. Sarah ran a few steps and caught it, but with a loose hold that allowed it to slide from her grip and drop into the dirt next to the base.

It had been the same story for the last hour as Bea had fought to get the girls to tighten up their fielding. Dropped balls, missed pop flys, lopsided throws that went wild. They couldn't get it together.

And Bea was all too aware that it was because she wasn't the best manager.

Yes, it was undeniable that she had the necessary knowledge and plenty of skill with a ball. But that didn't translate into being good at instructing or guiding others. She was a better coordinator than a teacher.

She needed help.

As it had been doing lately, Emmett Worland's face flashed through her mind. But his disdainful words from the concert were also lodged there, repeating over and over. For far too many reasons, he was not an option. She could find someone else. He'd already refused the position, and she would not sink low enough to ask him for anything again, especially not where these ladies were concerned. If she couldn't manage them well, at least she could protect them.

Bea called the girls in and had them line up along the fence in their batting order with their starting pitcher, Anna Harvey, in place on the mound. Bea moved to stand behind Anna so she could see exactly how the girls were hitting.

They worked through the batting order in turn, with each girl getting the chance to hit five or six balls, even if it took her many missed swings. During that time, as often happened when they were on the field, several male students gathered to talk with the girls who were waiting their turn. Bea rolled her eyes at the distraction, but she knew from experience there was no way to stop it. At first, she'd asked the men to congregate farther away, but that forced her to cut their practices short because the girls kept sneaking off to follow wherever the young men went. She'd finally given up, although it still irked her to have so little control on the field.

But the presence of the male students reminded her of another reason including Emmett Worland in practices would be far more detrimental than any expertise he could bring. He was much better looking than any of the college boys. If they were enough to distract the girls, Mr. Worland would cause endless disruption.

So Bea ignored the flirtations as long as the girls came up to the plate when it was their turn to bat. Between hitters, Bea's position behind the pitcher's mound allowed her to notice Anna watching one young man in particular, a lanky fellow who looked charming enough. "Is that your beau, Anna?"

The girl turned with a shrug and a shy grin. "I hope soon enough he will be. I see him around campus, but he hasn't approached me yet."

"Why don't you approach him?"

The young woman gasped, a horrified expression crossing her face. "I couldn't. My mother would never let me out of the house again if she found out I did something so brazen."

Amusement and longing warred in Bea's chest as Anna threw a slightly off-center pitch to the next batter. Bea remembered the days when her parents' opinions weighed so heavily on her, determining her every action. Moving to Chicago to attend Northwestern University at eighteen had been difficult, and she still missed her family terribly. The money and time it took to travel to Iowa ensured she was only able to visit them on the occasional holiday. While there were times when she might trade a little of her independence for the chance to see her parents and sister more often—and especially her two young nieces—Bea had fought hard to forge a life where she got to make decisions without anyone pushing their opinions.

But that freedom had meant building up a resistance to what others thought about her. The walls that protected her from censure also made it quite difficult to make friends or even consider romantic notions.

And as much as Bea might know that she was better off without the attention of the kind of men she met in baseball, her heart didn't always acknowledge that truth.

Their time on the field was almost over when a group of four well-dressed men approached, far different from the boys who were there to get her team's attention. Bea instructed the girls to continue practicing while she left the field to greet the newcomers. As she got closer, she recognized the college chancellor, the men's gymnasium director, and one of the men from the school's financial department. But the fourth was a stranger.

Bea pasted on her brightest smile as she greeted the men. "Good afternoon. We're just about finished on the field."

The chancellor, Mr. Willis, responded. "We don't have any need for the field. I wanted to introduce you to the new head of the alumni association. Mr. Kendall, this is Miss Beatrice Curran, our women's baseball manager. Miss Curran, Aaron Kendall."

Bea reached out to shake hands with the newcomer, who offered her a disarming smile. Not too tall, the man nonetheless drew the eye of every woman in sight. His chiseled features and hazel eyes made a pleasing combination, and he was a man who took pride in his appearance, with not a single hair out of place or speck of dust on his fine suit.

As the leader of the alumni association, this man held a considerable amount of influence over the board of regents as well as over the process of raising money for any projects approved by them. Bea put on a professional air, praying she might be able to impress him in some way. "Welcome, Mr. Kendall. It's a pleasure to meet you."

"And you, Miss Curran." His voice rang with confidence and good breeding. So different from the rough baseball players she was used to.

Behind her, Bea felt the girls gathering at the edge of the field, their whispers reaching her ears, though not loud enough for her to make out their words. She'd better get this unexpected meeting finished, or they would get ideas about the attractive man. "If there's nothing else, I need to finish our practice."

Mr. Kendall stopped her with a light touch on her arm. There was nothing untoward about it, but Bea had to stifle a strange impulse to recoil. "Before I go, Miss Curran, I wanted to ask if you would be available for a meeting on Friday morning.

I'm trying to spend a few minutes with all the coaches and managers to get an understanding of their teams' needs. Will you be able to attend?"

Would anything cause her to miss a meeting with someone who seemed interested in her team that could also result in better funding? It was an answer to Bea's prayers. "Yes, certainly."

"Excellent. I'll see you Friday."

His gaze held hers longer than necessary, and a flush worked up her cheeks. She spent much of her time around men, but to most of them, she was either an oddity to be gawked at or a villain who made biased calls against their team. Other than the regular proposals that were thrown out as more of a practical joke than anything, she hadn't felt a spark of romantic interest from a man in a long time.

Except for Emmett Worland.

Her mind dredged up the memory of him hesitantly asking to escort her home after their first meeting and the disappointment in his eyes when she'd rejected him. But this man wasn't a baseball player, and he surely wouldn't have a reputation for pursuing every woman who crossed his path. Mr. Kendall was a professional man with a respectable career. So why did his lingering look feel...wrong?

Mr. Kendall finally turned back toward the athletic building with the others, but Mr. Willis paused, watching the women practicing for a moment. "Miss Curran, I've spoken with Miss King about her impending retirement. She might have hinted that you have an interest in taking over her job."

Bea's heart stuttered. She and Marjorie had discussed this at length, but since her friend wasn't retiring for several more months, Bea hadn't imagined her name would have been brought up already. "I do. I hope that's not too presumptuous of me."

Mr. Willis considered her for a moment, pursing his lips.

"Since your only involvement here at Western is with this team, your ability to help these students be successful will play a large role in the decision. You were hired with the expectation that you'll improve the women's baseball program, but you should remember that what you accomplish while leading this team is going to be the board of regents' basis for determining your suitability."

With a brief tip of his hat, Mr. Willis turned and followed the other men. Bea spun around to face her team, finding every last one of them had stopped to watch her. Bea shoved the rising worry deep down inside herself, clapping her hands once and putting on the guise of an experienced baseball team manager. "All right, girls. Two laps around the bases for everyone and then we'll clean up."

~

"Did you trick me into coming here?"

Emmett resisted the urge to press his palm to his aching head. Grandmother's driver guided her carriage along the narrow, well-kept lanes that wound through the Western College campus, rather than the scenic road bordering Lake Michigan that Emmett had expected them to be traversing. He glanced across the carriage in time to see Grandmother raise one slim shoulder in a careless gesture. "Would you have come to see Miss Curran's team any other way?"

Grandmother's support for Miss King's request that he help the college women's baseball team shocked him. He'd been pondering it since she first voiced her opinion the day after the concert, but he was no nearer to deciding her true motives two days later. It was so out of character for her that he couldn't help wondering if it was a test. Was she encouraging the idea of him spending his free time with a team of young ladies as a way to see if he would take her demands seriously? Did she still want him to refuse, or was the way she urged him to help Miss Curran genuine?

He couldn't decide which move would please her and which would disappoint.

So he'd intended to do nothing for the time being and claim he was considering it. But then he'd granted her request for an afternoon drive through the city, only to find himself at the college. And while her deception was infuriating and the headache that had returned once again was building to a nearly intolerable level, a rebellious part of his heart jumped at the chance to see Miss Curran again.

Which was ridiculous. The beautiful female umpire who danced through his daydreams wanted nothing to do with him. And the last thing he needed was to entangle himself and another woman in anything that could result in headlines.

The driver stopped the carriage outside the building that housed the college's athletic offices and gymnasium. Emmett helped Grandmother disembark while glancing around. It had been some time since he'd been to the campus, other than attending the recital on the other end of the property. The base-ball diamond and football field were new since his last visit, but the athletic building still had the same boxy frame and no-nonsense look that he remembered from trips with Grand-mother over the years.

Once on the sidewalk, Grandmother held her ground as a group of students split to pass on either side of her. Then she turned to Emmett with her lips curled up in disdain. "There's a reason I usually choose not to visit Marjorie here when classes are in session. But I do have an important matter to discuss with her."

The glass-paned door to the athletic building opened and Miss King herself emerged, greeting them both with a wide smile. "Good afternoon, Aileen. Emmett, it's been too long since you've visited the campus. The college has made many improvements and additions since you were here last."

Grandmother sniffed as if the mentioned improvements personally offended her. "I quite disagreed with the choice to build that science hall. The college should have used that money to add to the gymnasium. They haven't touched it in years, and the women are still stuffed into a small side room for their courses. Not to mention their limited access to the gymnasium."

Miss King accepted the protest with a cheerful smile. "Quite right, as always. But in the absence of having all the space we need, we're focusing on the future of our athletic training. Did you know Miss Curran is hoping to expand the college's course offerings into a professional physical education program? It will train teachers who can then take physical education classes to primary schools and other colleges or universities. They could even be hired by Young Men's or Young Women's Christian Associations."

With her lips pursed, Grandmother considered that news for a moment. Emmett did too. He could imagine Miss Curran would excel at coordinating such a program. But what did that mean for her umpiring career?

And why did he already feel the loss of her presence behind him on the pitcher's mound?

Moving on to discuss other changes coming to the college, the two women started toward the door to the building, which the driver hurried to open for them. Before going inside, Miss King glanced back at Emmett and waved toward the athletic fields. "You might like to see the new baseball field up close. The women's team will be finishing their practice any time now, and you're welcome to go explore it once they're done."

A sizzle of interest caught Emmett's attention. His grandmother barely let Miss King finish before she added, "I expect you to extend your help to Miss Curran for the summer,

Emmett. I see no reason you shouldn't do so. Supporting this college is a priority for our family."

Then the women disappeared into the building and Emmett was left alone, trying to decide what he was going to do. Grandmother's words had been direct enough. But still, he hesitated. The sharp ache in his skull intensified.

His feet started down the sidewalk toward the baseball diamond even as his mind mulled over the situation. Soon enough, he was standing near the fence, all but hiding behind a group of college men watching the ladies as they practiced. Or rather, distracting the ladies from their practice, it appeared. Flirtatious grins, meaningful winks, and excessive compliments flew faster than any of the pitches the women attempted to hit at home plate. No wonder Miss Curran needed help. It would be a difficult task for anyone to maintain control of the spectators while also directing the practice.

But that didn't mean he was the one who should step in.

The ladies continued batting, most of them missing many more pitches than they hit. From his vantage point, he could see how several of them were dipping the bat and swinging below the ball. Others moved too slowly, missing because the ball had already passed their bats by the time they were in full swing. Still others seemed afraid to step up to home plate, connecting with the tip of the bat and sending the ball over the foul line every time.

Emmett tried not to get invested, but his mind kept seeing ways he could improve the drills, refine batting stances, and especially fix the pitcher's form.

Another distraction soon arose, though, as if the male students weren't enough of one. Miss Curran left her spot behind the pitcher and strode across the field to greet several men who were certainly not there to flirt with the team. They were older and much better dressed than the college students gathered by the fence. And one of them, in particular, seemed quite taken with Miss Curran, judging from the way his eyes locked onto her and traveled up and down, perusing her form.

A burning in Emmett's chest joined the now-raging headache. He removed himself from the vicinity of the field, finding a wooden bench under a huge tree where he could still see the exchange but he wouldn't be noticed. Which was all well and good until the man placed his hand on Miss Curran's arm and she flinched ever so slightly. Emmett nearly leaped from the bench, restraining himself with the inward admonishment that his grandmother would hear of any indiscretions.

Not to mention, Miss Curran handled surly and amorous baseball players with ease every time she was on the field. She was more than a match for such a soft-looking fellow.

Emmett brought himself back under control while Miss Curran returned to her practice and the four men headed in Emmett's direction. He considered leaving before they reached his bench. The last thing he wanted was to face a man who had made Miss Curran so uncomfortable, considering the mood he was in. But the group had no business with Emmett. They would surely pass by with at most a simple pleasantry.

It wasn't until the group was directly in front of Emmett that one man stopped, causing the others to pause. The older man had a bearing that spoke of military service and he looked quite familiar to Emmett. Apparently, Emmett was familiar to him, as well. "Young man, I think we've met. You're Mrs. Buchanan's grandson?"

Emmett rose from the bench, nodding and holding out his hand to the man. Of course, most of the college staff would know his grandmother, and he'd spent enough time at her social events over the years to have met many of them too. "Yes, Emmett Worland."

The man returned his handshake. "Ben Turner. I run the gymnasium here."

Ah, yes. The man who'd started out running military drills

to keep the students fit and had then been recruited to oversee the gym. Emmett nodded his recognition. "Good to see you again, Mr. Turner."

Mr. Turner introduced Emmett to the others—the chancellor, the chairman of the financial department, and the younger man that Emmett already didn't like, Aaron Kendall, the new president of the alumni association.

After greeting Emmett with a slight frown, Mr. Kendall slid his hands into his trouser pockets, looking as comfortable as if he owned the school.

Mr. Turner addressed Emmett again. "What brings you to the campus today? I've heard you're on your way to becoming a big baseball star."

Emmett had to chuckle at that. "As much as I'd like to claim that distinction, I'm just the new man on a semi-pro city league team. I accompanied my grandmother to the campus today, and it was suggested that I should see the new baseball diamond. It's a very nice addition."

The chancellor looked pleased, and Mr. Turner nodded in agreement. But Mr. Kendall seemed unimpressed by Emmett's compliment, responding before the other men had a chance to speak. "It's a start, I suppose. Many universities the size of Western have more successful teams, which allows them a bigger budget for athletics. I'm hoping to address ways to put funding where it will bring the most attention to the college. We were just checking on the women's baseball team. From what I saw, that may be a short-lived program."

His scoffing tone assured Emmett of what he'd assumed. Aaron Kendall didn't value the women's team the way Miss Curran did. "On the contrary, their manager is a fine athlete in her own right and an excellent umpire. If anyone can help them prove themselves, it's Miss Curran. So I hardly think that quick dismissal is warranted."

Mr. Kendall's eyebrows arched, and he examined Emmett coolly. "And you know this because...?"

Emmett drew his shoulders back and raised his chin. "She referees in the city league I play for. I've seen her in action, and she's very talented. Not to mention the most trustworthy, honest, unbiased umpire I've seen in all my years playing."

Glancing back at the field, a calculating look crossed Mr. Kendall's face. "Well, I have a meeting with her Friday morning to discuss funding. I'll have to decide if a talented manager is a good enough reason to give her team any favors this year."

The comment held no warmth, so Emmett took it for what it was—a dismissal. Mr. Kendall was walking away with the other men trailing behind him before Emmett could have spoken a word, anyway.

Once they were out of sight, he clenched and unclenched his fists, releasing the tension Mr. Kendall's overbearing attitude brought out in him. He glanced toward the baseball field, where the women were packing up their gear. It rankled him to allow men like Aaron Kendall to assume women couldn't play sports as well as men. He'd seen proof of the opposite too many times to accept that phony belief.

And there was only one way Emmett could think of to prove it to Mr. Kendall and others like him.

He had to help Miss Curran make the women's baseball team into winners.

CHAPTER 6

The last person Bea expected to approach the field as she was cleaning up from practice was Emmett Worland.

But there he was, walking through the fence and bending to return a few balls to the basket before coming to stand by her. Goodness, he looked just as confident and sure of himself in simple brown trousers and a lightweight jacket as he did in his uniform or a formal suit. "Good afternoon, Mr. Worland. What brings you to Western today?"

He shuffled from one foot to the other before meeting her gaze. "My grandmother. She asked me to go for a drive with her, and we ended up here. As it turns out, she had an appointment with Miss King. Although I'm not convinced that wasn't a ploy to get me here to speak with you."

Humor rose in Bea's chest, but he looked uncomfortable enough about being tricked by his grandmother that she refused to let it show. It was like Marjorie to conjure up such a plan in hopes things would go the way she thought they should. It seemed his grandmother was willing to work as Marjorie's accomplice, for whatever reason.

But Mr. Worland's dismissive comments from the concert flitted through Bea's mind again, drawing all the amusement from the moment. "Go ahead, then. Give me an excuse for not helping with the team. I'll tell Marjorie and your grandmother that you had a good reason. Then we can be done with their meddling."

To her surprise, he shook his head. "I've...reconsidered. I saw some of your practice. There's potential here. Those ladies could play good baseball with the right direction."

"And you're the one to provide that, I suppose?"

He at least had the grace to look embarrassed for considering himself to be the solution to her problem. But then he raised his chin and leveled his confident blue eyes at her. "I can help, Miss Curran. That's all I want to do."

The words felt genuine—hopeful, even. And yet, she still heard his tone from the recital echoing in her thoughts, pricking her pride with its arrogance. Bea straightened her shoulders and tilted her chin up. "You do recognize that if you join the team, I'll still be the manager? Can you stand to work under the authority of a woman?"

His raised eyebrow and lopsided grin sent Bea's stomach floundering inside her. "You've met my grandmother. I'm used to women who take charge."

While she tried to understand why her body was reacting in such a ridiculous way to what some women might call his charms, Mr. Worland became serious. "I meant what I said, though. I want to help. Your team deserves a chance."

Bea dropped her gaze and turned to pick up a cap one of the girls had left behind. He seemed so sincere, so very different from the other night when he'd acted as if helping a women's team was far beneath him. So which man was he truly? The dismissive flirt or the honest, helpful gentleman?

Before she could figure out the puzzle of Emmett Worland, Marjorie called from the fence, where she stood with Mrs.

Buchanan. Mr. Worland caught Bea's attention again by brushing her shoulder with his fingertips. The light contact was similar to the way Mr. Kendall had touched her arm earlier, but her internal response was as different as night and day. "I apologize if I sound overly confident, Miss Curran, but it would benefit both of us for me to help you. I have plenty of experience navigating the world of fundraising. I can help you get the money you need for equipment, as well as support your efforts to improve the team's skill level."

As if proving his point, he held out a bat he'd picked up, one that was splintered and worn. They needed new equipment—she couldn't deny that. But could she trust this man to put aside his usual bravado and help her run her team? Would he take orders from her or fight her every step of the way? His place with the college would be temporary, but Bea had to prove that she could succeed here. Would accepting his help look like a good decision by a confident manager or like a woman doubting herself?

Bea needed to think. Without responding to him, she marched to the fence and faced the two waiting women. "Hello, Marjorie. Mrs. Buchanan, it's a pleasure to see you again."

The older woman sniffed, looking quite uncomfortable at the edge of the field. "I enjoy a good round of golf or hitting a tennis ball, but in this game, there's so much...dirt."

Bea pressed her lips together, stifling a giggle at her incredulous tone. "It might be hard to imagine, but the dirt is more of a benefit than a hindrance to the players. Haven't you been to any of your grandson's games?"

The mood around them shifted. Mrs. Buchanan's face went from puckered with incredulity to smooth and regal, as if the question offended her. "That is not pertinent to our visit. I trust my grandson offered his services to your team?"

She wished now that she'd been a bit kinder so that he might take pity on her and jump in with an excuse, but he stood silent, leaving her to explain. "He did. But I don't feel he would be the best influence on impressionable young ladies."

As soon as the words left her lips, Bea cringed. Mrs. Buchanan was certain to take offense at Bea's assessment of her grandson.

But to Bea's surprise, the woman nodded, all business again. "Quite right. I'm working hard to reform that image, my dear. I assure you, the moment he starts to behave inappropriately with any woman, he'll lose the career he cares so much about. You have my word that he will be on his best behavior."

The blunt words felt like a heavy insult to her grandson. Bea's heart softened toward Mr. Worland against her better judgment. He was a man, old enough to be responsible for himself. Yet his grandmother treated him like a naughty child who deserved punishment.

Was she behaving the same way by believing she'd need to protect the girls from him?

His words about helping her gain funding and pleas to believe he wanted to improve her team were difficult to ignore. The other three were all watching her, but Bea couldn't settle on a decision. She met Marjorie's eyes, silently communicating her doubts.

With a decisive nod, Marjorie took the choice from Bea. "Then we'll welcome his help, won't we, Bea? Emmett, can you be here for practice on Friday afternoon?"

At Bea's side, he straightened. "I heard there's a meeting about funding for the team on Friday morning. I'll be here for both."

The older two women both nodded in approval even as Bea's stomach began twisting into knots.

The knowledge that she now had to work with Mr. Worland hung over her head all week. She couldn't help thinking he was going to be a distraction to her team, and he was quite likely to undermine her at every turn, regardless of his claims. She umpired three games while worrying about it. She sat through meals with her boarding house companions with it weighing on her mind. She was only able to go through the motions of practicing the sports that usually relaxed her in her free time.

Finally, she showed up at the athletic department offices on Friday morning half hoping Mr. Worland would forget to join her. But she had barely reached the door when an arm stretched around from behind her to pull it open. She turned to meet the amused, confident, entirely too handsome gaze of Emmett Worland.

He held the door with his back, taking up too much space and forcing her to brush past him on the way through. He smelled of soap, a nice, light scent that she would appreciate on any other man. Now that she thought about it, he didn't tend to douse himself in strong-smelling pomade, as many men in pursuit of female attention did.

But that restraint didn't mean he wasn't exactly what the papers declared him to be.

He greeted her with a smile as she entered the building ahead of him. "Good morning, Miss Curran."

Rudeness would hardly be an auspicious start to this venture, so she responded over her shoulder without missing a step. "Good morning, Mr. Worland."

He skipped a few strides to catch up with her. "I was thinking this week that since we're going to work together, perhaps we could go by given names. You're welcome to call me Emmett."

He waited, obviously expecting her to reply in kind. Bea sighed. There was too much riding on this partnership to let herself behave the way she wanted to deep down. "And you may call me Bea."

His smile stretched into a full grin, sending an unwanted flutter through Bea's chest. No wonder it was so easy for him to get attention from women. He could be utterly charming without seeming to try at all.

Reaching the door to the meeting room Mr. Kendall was using, Bea rapped on the heavy wood with her knuckles, then stood back to wait for an answer. A muffled voice responded, "Just a moment."

They both moved a few feet away and stood in the hallway, awkward silence filling the space between them. Bea felt Emmett's gaze on her but had no desire to engage in small talk. Still, he spoke after a long moment. "What are your hopes for this meeting? What financial needs does the team have?"

That was not what she expected him to say. His interest in the team's needs was encouraging. "We need basic equipment, as you noticed. Bats, balls, gloves. The girls are resourceful and have made their own uniforms, but the men order theirs from a tailor, and I can't see why the women shouldn't have the same. My ultimate hope is that the team will be seen as a valuable asset to the college that deserves the same funding and field time as the men's team."

Would he laugh? Scoff, even? Bea hesitated to look at him, fearing his reaction would make her angry, a mood that wouldn't benefit her in the upcoming meeting. But she finally did and saw only open consideration written on his features. "That doesn't seem like too much to ask for. Be confident. Men like Aaron Kendall respond better to people who are sure of their worth."

His approval of her dreams for the team somehow warmed Bea. Maybe this partnership wouldn't be so bad. He believed in her ability to do what needed to be done, and it seemed he was capable of letting her continue leading the team, rather than taking over.

The door finally swung open, and Mr. Kendall motioned toward the empty chairs arranged around a small table. "Welcome. Please take a seat." He took a second glance when he noticed Emmett following her in. "And what brings you here, Mr. Worland?"

They were close enough together as they entered that Bea could feel Emmett stiffen at the question. "I'm joining Miss Curran as the assistant manager for the women's team. She invited me to sit in on this meeting."

Not exactly how things had happened, but she appreciated the way it sounded as though he was deferring to her as the manager. Once seated, Bea took charge, bolstered by Emmett's support. She slid a piece of paper across the table toward Mr. Kendall. "To begin, I've written out a list of equipment the women's team needs desperately, along with estimates of the cost for each item. Our current supplies are quite lacking."

Picking up the page, Mr. Kendall glanced over it. Then he set it back on the table and rubbed his nose with his thumb. "I'll be honest with you, Miss Curran. The alumni association has discouraged me from taking funding from the men's teams to give to the women. They don't feel that women's sports will draw the same crowds and attention to the college that the men's do. I'm not the one who determines where the school's funds get allocated, and I only have so much control over the alumni donations."

Bea's heart sank. All the girls' hard work was going to be for nothing. But then Mr. Kendall raised one finger and met her gaze. "But I do have the authority to support clubs or teams that want to raise money. So, while I can't hand out funds, I *can* help you figure out some ways to get the money you need for this equipment."

Bea's heart lifted. She wasn't afraid of a little hard work to help her girls. "Thank you. I wasn't certain how much help I could expect."

Next to her, Emmett shifted in his seat, clearing his throat as if to get her attention. She remembered his words from the hallway. This man would respond to confidence.

Raising her chin, Bea focused on the next step. "What kinds of fundraisers do you recommend?"

Mr. Kendall tilted his head to one side, pursing his lips. "I'll come up with a few options for you. We could meet again next week. Over dinner?"

The words hung in the air and Bea was suddenly having a hard time filling her lungs. Was this handsome, successful, man asking to spend time with her? Even though he knew of her involvement in athletics, which had driven off other men?

Bea should be excited about his willingness to help her and his potential interest in her personally. But Emmett's gaze boring into her created a strong urge to refuse the invitation that she had to tamp down. She needed to remain on Mr. Kendall's good side, for the team. "Yes, that would be fine. You can contact me at Mrs. Harmony's boarding house down the street."

A smooth smile spread across Mr. Kendall's face, bringing a flush to Bea's cheeks. She told herself that the meeting was all business. But would Mr. Kendall agree?

With a screech of wooden legs sliding on the floor, Emmett pushed up from his chair. Mr. Kendall followed suit, and they ended the meeting. But Bea was hardly aware of any of it, torn between feeling she'd done the right thing in agreeing and being certain she hadn't.

A fog of uncertainty surrounded her until she and Emmett reached the building exit and he pushed straight through, leaving the door to swing shut in her face. She caught it with one hand and then hurried to follow him outside. "Emmett? Is something wrong?"

Turning and throwing both hands in the air, he was suddenly not the charming, supportive man she'd walked in with. "What are you thinking, agreeing to dinner with a man like him?"

*E*mmett knew she didn't understand his reaction. He could see the confusion on her face as she blinked up at him. But he couldn't contain it. Mr. Kendall had been so smooth in there, putting off giving her details so he could convince her to see him outside of the meeting, without Emmett present. It was a familiar tactic, though one Emmett had never used himself. Because it was shady.

But the part that bothered him the most was that Bea fell for it. Genuine frustration filled her lovely features. "I was thinking that I'm grateful for any help in getting funding for the team. There's nothing wrong with doing business over dinner. We'll probably meet at the student dining hall and spend the entire time poring over fundraiser ideas."

"That's not the dinner he had in mind, Bea."

Her fists braced against her hips, brown eyes shooting sparks at him. "And how would you know that? He supports the women's team, and that's all I'm concerned about."

She started to march away down the sidewalk, fast enough Emmett had to rush to catch up to her. He needed to get control before his anger drove her into making a mistake. "At least let me go along. I've picked up plenty of fundraising ideas from my grandmother over the years. I know what rich socialites enjoy. I can help."

Halting in the middle of the sidewalk, her eyes narrowed as she examined him for a moment. Emmett took the opportunity to do the same, admiring the dark hair that framed her round face down to her pert nose and wide pink lips. For most people, her beauty was overshadowed by the novelty of her unusual choice of career and activities. But Emmett was always, always aware of it.

"And what would you do to get the money we need?"

Emmett's mind whirled, spinning through all the social

events his grandmother had planned and hosted over the years. He hadn't been to that many of them recently, but he'd been plenty aware of her calendar, and he remembered well all the things that took her time away from him as a child. One in particular seemed to be the most popular. "A ball."

Bea started strolling at a much more sedate speed. Emmett kept pace with her steps as the idea took root in his mind. But she didn't seem as confident in it. "A ball? As in, fancy gowns and difficult dances?"

"No, they've gotten much more relaxed these days. Supper and dancing. Open to anyone willing to pay. It's become popular. A nice meal at a big hall, then a popular band plays a few dancing tunes. Very modern, nothing stuffy."

He saw the moment the idea sank in for Bea. But she still seemed to hesitate. Her hands twisted together in the folds of her simple black skirt. "It's not a bad idea. But I hate formal events."

"Well, I doubt Mr. Kendall is going to give you anything more casual. The people with money like these sorts of occasions."

She tapped her lips with one finger, then glanced at an engraved pocket watch she pulled from her jacket. "I'll consider it. We best be getting to practice. With any luck, the girls are warming up already."

They started walking faster toward the field, where indeed, the ladies were swinging bats and tossing balls back and forth. But they didn't quite reach it before Bea settled her warm hand on his arm, stopping him. "There's one thing I want to say before we start this."

She hesitated, but he waited, giving her time to gather her thoughts. Finally, she drew a breath and spoke in a rush. "These girls are impressionable. They're already easily distracted by the male students who like to gather around the field at our practices. And you're an attractive, well-known older man. You're sure to catch their attention. Please promise me you won't lead on or compromise any of them."

As she finished the statement, she turned her face up toward his, eyes wide with earnest concern. A pang hit his heart harder than he would have expected. She didn't trust him. She believed he was the person he was trying to prove he wasn't.

And knowing she thought that of him was a blow like he'd never felt before.

Trying to let her see how serious he was, Emmett returned her steady gaze. "I promise. I'm here to help you and to redeem my reputation. No one seems to believe it, but none of what the papers have printed about me is true. I give you my word that I will not encourage any romance while I'm with your team."

She continued to search his face for a long pause. Then her shoulders relaxed, and she started toward the field again, throwing instructions over her shoulder. "Then let's begin practice. Pick a spot in the outfield, and I'll send the pitchers out so you can see what we're working with."

And thus began the worst practice Emmett had ever seen.

He'd spent years playing with a friend's company team, the starting point for most players. Those men hadn't had any training, any coaching, anything to help them. But they still exhibited more skill than most of the ladies on the Western College women's team.

There was some talent to work with in each position he observed. The three women who came out to practice pitching with him were strong and could throw hard. One had decent form but couldn't seem to grasp the impact of her finger place-ment on the type of pitch she was throwing. The outfielders caught what was thrown or hit to them about half the time, and several were good at getting the ball back to where it needed to go. Runners were fast, even if their batting needed some work.

However, the biggest problem was the lack of focus and

determination. The women didn't respond quickly or with much effort until young men started gathering at the edges of the field. And then the ladies were too distracted to play well, even if they were trying harder.

His first goal was to discourage the spectators.

He walked over to stand next to Bea. "Would you mind if I try to shoo our audience?"

She seemed startled by the question but nodded. Emmett immediately raised his voice and called the team to the pitcher's mound. Once all the women were gathered around, he spoke only for their ears. "After some observation, I've come to a conclusion about our biggest problem."

The team was all ears, their eyes glued to him, so Emmett continued. "You need complete focus to learn the basics, and that means no visitors during practice. Once you have the skills down, we can allow spectators. Does anyone have a problem with that?"

Several women in the back muttered to each other.

Emmett speared them with the type of stare that would make his grandmother proud. "Ladies? If you don't agree, you're welcome to get your things and leave."

Bea's gasp reminded Emmett that he'd promised not to undermine her authority. An assistant manager didn't have the right to dismiss players from the team. Cringing, he glanced over to see her eyes were once again shooting fire at him. He stepped toward her. "Bea, I'm—"

She raised a hand in front of her, holding him back. The words hung in the air, the entire team holding their breaths to see who would win this power struggle. Finally, Bea pursed her lips. "Mr. Worland is right. This can't continue."

The entire team released their breath at the same time. The two mutterers glanced at each other, then around at their teammates. Finally, the first baseman raised her chin and responded for them both. "Fine, if it has to be that way."

Murmurs of agreement came from the entire group then. Tension eased out of Emmett's shoulders. One hurdle out of the way. "Thank you, ladies. I'll go let the fellows know, but you'll be responsible for reminding them they aren't allowed for the time being. Think how impressed they'll be the next time they see you play, with new skills to show off."

The mood immediately shifted as the women started giggling together about what the men would say once they were better players. When Bea nodded, giving Emmett permission to continue, he smiled. Then he headed straight to the fence to deal with the men. "Good afternoon, gentlemen. While the ladies appreciate your support of their team, we're running spectator-free practices for the time being. I'm going to have to ask you all to leave for the next hour."

As expected, the men resisted more than the women did. Several complained loudly.

"What's the idea?"

"I have a right to spend time where I want."

"That's my girl. You can't stop me from watching her play."

Emmett had turned to walk away but spun back around at their comments. "All right, now, listen up. This is our policy, so if you insist on being here, we'll have to start putting you to work. You, in the back." He pointed to one of the tallest, biggest complainers. "There's a rake in the dugout. You can come smooth all the dirt so they'll have an even surface to run on."

The bravado visibly dropped from the group. As he'd thought, few of them wanted to do manual labor while the women played. The tall one put both hands out in surrender. "Fine, we'll go."

Emmett beamed as if thankful. "Excellent. I promise, as soon as the women are ready for spectators at practices, you'll be welcome back. If any of you show up again before then, I'll assume that means you're ready to work on the field for us."

In pairs and groups, the men slunk away.

Emmett returned to the pitcher's mound to find Bea watching them go with wide eyes.

"I've tried everything to get them to leave us alone. What did it?"

Emmett allowed himself a grin. "Threatening them with manual labor on the field."

Bea didn't respond at first. Emmett watched the words sink in. Then a laugh bubbled out of her, light and joyful. It was a sound he could listen to all day, a sound he longed to bring forth again.

Feeling lighter than he had in weeks, Emmett jogged to home plate, and they resumed practice with him making tweaks to the batters' stances and swings. This was going to work out better than he'd imagined when Miss King first broached the idea.

CHAPTER 7

*B*y the second practice with Emmett, Bea started to see the problem she'd been hoping wouldn't surface. With all the young men gone, the girls were much more focused on their new assistant manager. Which might have sounded like a good thing but certainly wasn't.

Because their attention consisted of batted eyelashes, shy grins, and giggles between themselves when he wasn't looking.

From her spot behind Anna, Bea watched Beth Marie Thorn ask too many questions about Emmett's advice for her batting stance. Beth Marie adjusted the bat over her right shoulder, her voice syrupy sweet. "Like this, Mr. Worland?"

Bea couldn't stop her eye roll.

Emmett, for his part, seemed oblivious, correcting Beth Marie from behind the plate. "Push the end up more. Then bring it around straight when you swing. No dropping the bat toward the plate."

Beth Marie tipped the bat but pushed the end down instead of up on her practice swing. "Is this better?"

Emmett was forced to step forward and move the bat for her, physically showing her what he meant while Beth Marie simpered under his attention. Bea gritted her teeth. "Figure it out, Beth Marie. Others need to bat too."

Glancing her way, Emmett raised one eyebrow, a grin teasing his lips.

Bea pulled off her cap and smoothed her hair. Hopefully, he would assume the flush rising on her face was due to the heat, not his smile.

Emmett stepped back. In front of Bea, Anna might have chuckled before launching the ball toward the bat. Beth Marie swung hard, and for once, her bat connected with the sphere, sending it flying toward third base. Then she repeated the move with the next four pitches. Bea could only stare. Such a simple adjustment, but it had changed the way Beth Marie batted.

Having Emmett there might be what her team needed, after all. Maybe it wasn't so terrible if the girls were infatuated with him. When they were vying for his attention, at least they were trying harder than usual. As long as he didn't pursue any of them, the arrangement might work.

The rest of the practice went much the same way. Emmett made corrections, the girls adjusted, and by the end, they looked like a decent ball team. After releasing the girls for that day, Bea made her way around the field, gathering any overlooked equipment as she went. She'd assumed Emmett would feel that picking up was beneath him, but there he was, going around the opposite side without even being asked.

When they met back at home plate with a bat and several balls, Bea offered Emmett a smile. "I have to admit, I was hesitant to bring in help. But in this short time, you've started transforming this team. Thank you, Emmett."

His lips tipped up in a crooked smile that sent a flutter through her chest. "It's my pleasure. You've got a group with potential. They just need to make a few adjustments. I know their first few games were hard losses, but I can't wait to see how they do against another team now. When's our next game?"

The way he included himself as part of their team so soon made Bea's pulse quicken. She both loved it and battled uncertainty. Maybe the team would be better off without her. Maybe they'd rather Emmett take her place.

He waited for her response, so Bea swallowed the lump rising in her throat. "Next Saturday. Do you think we can get them ready by then?"

Confidence oozing from him, Emmett nodded, effortlessly twirling the bat he held. "I do. They'll be a whole new team by then. I'll help you get this equipment put away if you'd like."

Bea nodded, unaccustomed to having help. In silence, they gathered everything and carried it all to the nearby athletic building, where she had a space to store their bats, balls, and gloves.

Once the equipment was packed away, Emmett followed her back outside but didn't leave immediately. "Are you working the Lincoln Parks' game today?"

Again, all Bea could manage was a nod. She was starting to understand the girls' response to Emmett. He was charming in the most genuine way, not at all what she'd expected from the type of ladies' man he was said to be. Every word he spoke was bathed in real kindness, as if he cared about her responses because he respected her as a person, not because he had a selfish angle.

It was enthralling.

Emmett grinned at her affirmation, tipping his hat as he started backing away with his gaze glued to her. "Then I'll see you in an hour or so."

He didn't just walk away. He sauntered down the sidewalk with a jaunty step that she couldn't help but watch. He was such a lighthearted person, especially when compared with his dour grandmother. It raised questions. What had his childhood been like with such an intimidating woman as his caregiver? How had he grown to be so cheerful? And would Bea ever have a reason to find out the answers to those queries?

Out of nowhere, a snippet from that morning's issue of the *Chicago Eagle* popped into her mind. *New territory provides Lincoln Parks' pitcher Emmett Worland opportunities for conquests.* The brief social editorial said that Emmett was often seen encouraging the attention of various women before he joined the Lincoln Parks, including a Miss Charlotte Ford. There had only been a few lines printed, but it was enough to speculate that their sudden parting of ways meant Emmett had abandoned Miss Ford once he was hired by a semi-professional team.

The warmth fled from Bea's heart. No matter how well he coached her team, no matter how kind he might appear, Emmett Worland was a baseball player through and through. She'd seen his over-confidence firsthand. On the field, he acted as if he was the star of every play. He'd spent enough time flirting with women that his own grandmother was ready to disown him because of the shame it brought to her name.

Resolve settled over Bea as she returned to the athletic building and made her way to the women's changing room to get her bag before heading to the Lincoln Parks' field for the afternoon game. She would have to guard herself against Emmett's obvious charm. Getting involved with any player was a bad idea. And with Emmett Worland, it was an even worse one. If the Lord was going to put a man in her life, it certainly wouldn't be a baseball player.

She had a career to focus on, a goal that was almost within reach. Losing her umpiring job because of biased behavior would cast her in a negative light with the board of regents, endangering her opportunity to take over for Marjorie.

She was so close. No romantic entanglement was worth

giving up her dream. Especially an entanglement with a man who couldn't possibly be God's best for her.

With that established in her mind, Bea felt ready to face Emmett again by the time she walked onto the Lincoln Park field an hour later. She refused to even look at Emmett. Word would soon get around that he was helping her team, and that would be more than enough to raise questions about her impartiality. She could not allow anything to make their connection more of an issue than it was.

Because there was no relationship.

And that was exactly how she wanted it.

As the teams warmed up and the start time grew closer, everyone on the field became aware of heavy, dark clouds gathering overhead. A cooler breeze rose, a welcome respite from the June heat but also bringing the fresh scent of rain. Bea had been waiting near the away team's dugout, but when a rumble of thunder broke through the chatter of the spectators and players, she moved to join both teams' managers at home plate.

Jet Anders, the Lincoln Parks' manager, turned his attention to her. His intensely dark eyes and hair must have drawn attention from female fans, even if he was shorter than most of his team. With that stocky build, he'd likely been a catcher for the Lincoln Parks before becoming their manager. "Should we delay, Miss Curran?"

Bea tipped her head back to examine the clouds. A spray of raindrops fell on her face. "Yes, I suppose we should before everyone gets soaked. The clouds are moving fast, so let's hope it will pass soon and we can start in a bit."

The managers jumped into action getting their players into the dugouts while Bea went to inform the field manager, who would in turn have his staff explain to the crowd. Many spectators left as soon as the word spread, and the rest rushed to find cover underneath the upper bleachers before the heavens opened. Soon enough, the thunder increased, lightning joining it, and then a torrent of rain was unleashed on the field.

Bea waited out the storm in the press box with the field staff and a few reporters, watching the downpour from the large openings that allowed those in the box to see all the action on the field. The stands cleared out more with every passing minute. The announcer grimaced as he addressed her. "We're not going to get this game in, are we?"

It was a shame to make that call so soon, but she could already see the field conditions wouldn't support the teams playing. The rain fell in heavy sheets that had created a muddy mess. "I'm afraid not."

It rained for another half hour while the remaining spectators and the teams and staff waited for the storm to let up before they left. Finally, the drops slowed, and the sky lightened. Bea made her way out with the others to assess the field condition, which was just as bad as she'd assumed from the press box.

The players all poured from the dugouts, seeming reluctant to leave without playing, as they compulsively started tossing balls back and forth, milling around the field together without regard for what team they were with. Bea leaned against the low wall by the stands and watched the men begin a contest to see who could throw the farthest. While every field was different, the distance from home plate to the outer wall at Lincoln Park was four hundred feet, a considerable distance for anyone to hit a ball, much less throw one. But the men all tried valiantly to see who could get it closest to the wall.

One of the men jogged to the outfield and paced out how far from the wall the balls landed, shouting the distances back to the group.

"253!"

"228!"

"267!"

It went on as the men all cheered and jeered, good-natured taunts flying back and forth.

Eventually, Emmett walked up to the plate and lined himself up to pitch. At the last second, before stepping back to raise his arm, he glanced her way. The eye contact was brief but plenty warm enough to cause a flutter in her chest.

Several men near her chuckled. One even declared, "Miss Ump, better watch out. They say ladies can't resist Worland's smile."

Heat burned across Bea's cheeks and neck. One shared look and her credibility was at risk. She might as well be one of the women who attended games just to catch the attention of a player. Bea bit her bottom lip as Emmett's ball flew straight and fast toward the outfield wall. The man calling distances shouted, "271!"

Emmett laughingly accepted a taunt from the man waiting to take his place, then jogged over to join Bea, a grin splitting his face. "That's the farthest I've ever thrown. Think it'll hold as the best distance of the day?"

What she needed to quell the rumors that were going to start surfacing was a distraction. And she knew the perfect way to provide it. "I'm not sure any of these men can beat it. But I can."

❧

When Bea issued her challenge, a hush instantly fell over the field. Emmett's pride in his accomplishment wobbled. His teammates would never let him live it down if a woman beat his distance in a throwing contest.

But he couldn't exactly stop her.

And part of him didn't want to. Could she do it?

Before anyone could react, Bea was marching toward home plate, stooping on the way to grab a ball from the basket. She positioned her feet in the mud and windmilled her arms a few times, stretching her muscles in preparation. Then she got into an excellent pitching stance.

Every breath froze in anticipation that was almost palpable in the damp air. Emmett watched, fascinated as she pulled her arm back and released the ball in a perfect pitch that sent it sailing straight forward. All eyes followed the sphere as it flew across the field and landed very near to where Emmett thought his had fallen.

Hank, who'd been using his steps to measure the distance, counted twice to be sure before picking up the ball and holding it aloft. "279!"

Cheers erupted from the men on both teams. Despite the embarrassment he probably should feel, Emmett's chest swelled, and a grin stretched his lips. Bea had a way of winning people to her side that she didn't even seem to be aware of. People liked to root for her. And she'd accomplished a feat these men would be talking about the rest of their lives.

She was stunning.

Emmett moved to intercept her as she walked away from home plate, standing close so she was the only one who could hear his words. "Bea, that was amazing. How did you learn to throw like that?"

She shrugged, and he tamped down the urge to grab her shoulders and make her see the truth. She was completely unaware of how remarkable she was. There should be someone in her life who could show her that she was more than just a great umpire. She was a beautiful, kind, encouraging, smart, and capable woman. Emmett longed to make sure she knew she was nothing short of incredible. But he had a feeling that compliments coming from him would only solidify her belief that he was an unrepentant womanizer.

And that knowledge sent a chill through him, extinguishing the thrill of pride.

He was far more invested in spending time with Bea Curran than he ought to be. He enjoyed her company too much. His entire future playing baseball was at stake. If Grandmother refused to support him while he built his career, he wouldn't be able to devote the necessary time to what he loved. He might never work his way up to reach the major league. And he wanted to play there more than anything he could imagine. That was the only way he could show his grandmother that playing baseball was not only his passion but his talent, something she could be proud of him for.

A sharp pain shot through Emmett's skull as he watched Bea leave the field. He sucked a breath through gritted teeth, trying to look as normal as possible. The headaches had been coming more often since the season started. Emmett refused to let them hinder him, though. He was strong enough to play through some pain. His dream was worth it.

It took a few minutes of standing still, forcing himself to breathe in and out in a steady rhythm before the agony subsided. The visiting team members were leaving the field, and the Lincoln Parks were gathering their equipment while storm clouds rolled back in. Emmett helped as much as he could with the pain still pounding in his head, then retreated to the locker room with the others as the rain started again.

As the familiar locker room chaos surrounded them, Boot stopped right next to Emmett, his voice low. "Are you sick? You're pale as my mama's white bedsheets, and you all but limped back here."

Emmett must not be hiding the pain as well as he thought. "I'm feeling a little off, but I'm sure a good night's sleep will fix it."

Boot dropped onto a bench and leaned over to unlace his shoes. "It had better. Word is there will be some important visitors from the major league teams here sometime soon. They're looking for some new talent for next year."

Emmett's heart raced, pumping enough blood through his veins to wash away any remnant of the headache. "Really?"

"That's what Jet told me. Said not to spread it around, but you're the one they're most likely to be impressed with. I figure you got a right to be prepared."

Was his chance finally here? Emmett thanked Boot for the tip, then rushed through changing and stuffed all his gear into his bag, leaving the room before any of the others. He had a stop to make.

Aileen Buchanan wasn't a particularly religious woman, but she understood the power of a good image, and she did have a soft spot for charity work. So every Sunday from the time his mother died until he started traveling for baseball, his grandmother had insisted Emmett join her in the Buchanan pew at the Chicago Avenue Church.

Driven by the thrill of facing a career-changing opportunity, Emmett followed a whim and soon found himself standing in front of the sprawling red-brick building. The corner tower built over the arched entrance drew many appreciative gazes as people strolled past along the busy street. But for Emmett, the familiar sight brought a wave of comfort. He'd always liked attending the church, with its fiery ministers who sometimes shouted and other times spoke low and gentle. He'd only stopped going out of spite for his grandmother's rules.

But today it wasn't preaching he was after. He wasn't sure what brought him to the church, but walking into the dim interior, with soaring ceilings and the same smooth wooden pews, allowed Emmett to draw a deeper breath than he'd been able to for several months.

He settled into Grandmother's usual pew, memories flooding his mind from all the years he spent attending Sunday services and Wednesday hymn sings and the favorite type of meeting of church founder Mr. Moody—Sunday School classes. The recollections brought a certain warmth, even if he'd never gotten much out of attending.

A shuffle at the end of the center aisle caught his attention. Emmett turned to see an older man shambling toward the pew. He'd hoped not to meet anyone but now steeled himself to answer the inevitable questions about his presence there on a Saturday afternoon.

The man finally reached Emmett's seat and lowered himself down a few feet away. "Good afternoon, young man. I'm Henry Parker, building caretaker and longtime member here."

Mr. Parker held out his hand expectantly, so Emmett returned the introduction. "Emmett Worland. I used to attend here with my grandmother, Mrs. Buchanan."

A hint of amusement crossed Mr. Parker's wrinkled face. "Ah, yes. Mrs. Buchanan is a force in this world, is she not? She's mentioned you on occasion."

That wasn't what Emmett would have expected. "I'm surprised. She's been rather ashamed of me the last few years."

The man shook his head. "Oh, no. She's concerned about you more than anything. There's pride in her voice when she talks about your baseball career."

Emmett couldn't form a reply to that. Mr. Parker had to be placating him. Grandmother had never shown one shred of pride over anything Emmett had chosen to do.

But the man was likely trying to be kind and encouraging, so Emmett didn't argue. Instead, he shifted, starting to rise from his seat. "I won't keep you any longer, Mr. Parker. I'm not sure why I stopped in here, but I suppose I should be going."

Mr. Parker stretched out a hand, pausing Emmett's escape. "There's no rush. You take all the time you need. I won't bother you. But is there anything I can pray about for you before I go?"

Had anyone ever offered to pray for Emmett? People had extended many condolences after his mother's death, but they'd been perfunctory and often insincere. Most people had been there to watch the disaster his mother created detonate. She'd brought it on herself, they said. As if a young woman whose only crime was falling in love with the wrong man deserved to die young from a ravaging disease. It was hardly her fault his father had run off, never to be heard from again.

But this kind man likely didn't know any of that. It had been enough years that most of society didn't think of it anymore and wouldn't dare bring it up for fear his grandmother would exact some kind of social revenge. Mr. Parker's offer to pray for him must be genuine, and that was touching.

Emmett thought for a moment. The upcoming visit from major league managers was exciting. But his biggest concern was something more difficult to put into words. "You know I'm a baseball player. My career means everything to me, but it's very physical. I have to be in perfect health. I've been having these headaches." He touched the side of his head, which was still tender. "I wasn't worried at first, but they're getting worse."

Mr. Parker immediately scooted closer, holding out one hand as if to touch Emmett while hesitating with a question on his face. "May I?"

Emmett nodded, and Mr. Parker rested his hand lightly on Emmett's shoulder. The older man closed his eyes as he started to pray, so Emmett did the same. "Lord, thank You for bringing Emmett here today. He may not know what's going on in his body, but You do. I ask You to heal the source of this pain. Don't let it interfere with his baseball career. Help him find the path You have planned for him going forward. In Jesus's name, amen."

The simple prayer lodged in Emmett's mind as Mr. Parker leaned back, removing his hand and opening his eyes. Usually, the minister's prayers went on and on, eloquent and filled with flowery words that Emmett had never imagined he'd be capable of putting together. So he rarely prayed. But if he could just *talk* to God like that...

Mr. Parker slapped both hands on his knees and rose with a bit of difficulty. "You're welcome to stay as long as you like, Emmett. I'll leave you to it. But I'll continue praying for you. Please stop by anytime."

Emmett watched the man shuffle back up the aisle to the back, where he disappeared through a door that Emmett knew led to a hallway filled with offices and classrooms. Silence fell in the sanctuary, but being alone there made him restless. He left the church, feeling for the first time in a long time that he might return for the service the next morning.

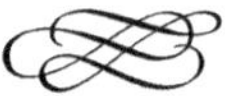

Bea walked into the college dining hall with high hopes. Her meeting with Mr. Kendall was going to result in funding for the women's team. Thinking otherwise only made sweat break out around the high lace collar of the white shirtwaist she wore under a blue-checked jacket.

The dining hall was almost empty at eight o'clock, well after the dinner service was complete. Only a few students occupied scattered tables, nursing coffee or tea while studying for their summer courses. Mr. Kendall sat at a table next to the floor-to-ceiling windows, reading a newspaper. When she approached, he glanced up and greeted her with a smile. "Miss Curran, I'm glad you could make it. Please, have a seat. It's a shame you weren't able to join me earlier so we could enjoy a meal together. Allow me to see if anyone is in the kitchen and have them prepare you something."

Emmett's suspicions about Mr. Kendall's purpose had stuck in her mind, against her better judgment, and she'd decided to err on the safe side and keep the meeting as businesslike as possible. When she'd attempted to set the appointment during the day, Mr. Kendall had insisted he couldn't get away from his work until the dinner hour. At the time, it had seemed as if meeting afterward might be less conspicuous, but now the intimacy of an empty dining hall was proving her wrong.

Bea chose the chair across from him and placed the notebook she'd brought along on the table in front of her. "No, thank you. I'd rather focus on fundraising plans, not on eating."

For a moment, she worried he would take offense at her blunt response. It might have been better to temper her words, to claim she wasn't hungry or some other feminine nonsense.

But a gleam of approval lit Mr. Kendall's eyes, and he nodded. "Very good. Let's begin."

Bea took up her pencil, prepared to take notes on his suggestions.

Mr. Kendall leaned back in his chair, crossing one ankle over the other knee. "I've taken the liberty of scheduling an exhibition game for you. There aren't many women's teams nearby that aren't already on your schedule, so I had to search rather far for an opponent that might be free on short notice. But the women from the University of Iowa have agreed to come play your team on Saturday."

The words didn't immediately make any sense to Bea. She blinked a few times, trying to comprehend all he was saying. "Your plan to raise money for our team is an exhibition game? That you've already planned? Before we have the equipment or skill to win such a contest?"

"You make it sound as if I've overstepped, Miss Curran. I'm sure your team is perfectly capable of putting on a good show. Their family and friends will pay to attend, and I'm sure many others will turn out to see the novelty of women playing baseball. You'll get the equipment you need before the season is over. There's nothing for you to worry about."

To him, the words probably sounded like confident support. But she'd assumed they would work out a fundraising plan together. His implication that the women were a novelty rather than a skilled team that could gain an audience on their own merit was frustrating, to say the least. "I would like to come up with a few options. We could try several ideas and see what brings the most money in. An exhibition game for a women's team with such a terrible record in their first few games might not be the best-attended event."

Mr. Kendall's clean-cut jaw clenched. "You don't trust me to know the best way to raise money? I've been entrusted with managing the fundraising for the alumni association, Miss Curran. This is my job. I didn't get it by throwing out wild ideas. These alumni are always looking for places to give their money to make them feel as if they've accomplished some good. Why shouldn't it be an unfortunate team instead of the next building project?"

His tone remained even, but tension laced it. This man was Bea's best option for raising money to help the girls improve. She had to temper her expectations. He was right, after all. It was his job to fundraise for the athletic teams and clubs at the college that the alumni supported. He must have some idea what he was doing. "I'll have the ladies as ready to play as I can get them Saturday."

Sinking back into the chair again, he smiled, and the layer of friction dropped from the air. "That's good to hear. Now, allow me to have the kitchen bring out some coffee, and we can talk for a while."

Emmett's implications about Mr. Kendall inviting her to talk over dinner flitted through her mind again. Mr. Kendall was handsome and charming—although overbearing when it came to his work, she was learning. Even if she enjoyed his company—which she couldn't quite claim—she had a reputation to uphold, especially if she was going to join the staff in the fall. It wouldn't do to overlap her business with Mr. Kendall with anything that could be seen as romantic. "No, thank you. I need to be going."

She started to push her chair back from the table, but he moved faster, sliding into the empty chair next to her and placing his hand on her arm. "I insist. Stay a few moments."

His touch was warm, and his eyes softened with their nearness. He leaned in close to her, intent on her face. "You're quite beautiful, you know."

Was the flush in her cheeks obvious? Did he know that she rarely heard those words uttered with any kind of authenticity? Even now, she wasn't certain if he meant what he said or if he, like so many of the baseball players, was looking for a prize to win in the form of the lady umpire.

Bea examined his features, finding no flaw in his straight nose, bright blue eyes, or wide lips. She was caught for a moment in his piercing gaze. What would it be like to let a man see her true self, the woman she couldn't be on the field? Would Mr. Kendall be able to look past her strong, tough shield? And was he the kind of man she'd want to do so?

And that, of course, was how Marjorie found them—tucked close together at a quiet table in the nearly empty dining hall, staring at each other with Mr. Kendall touching her arm. Bea jumped when her friend's voice split the air. "Good evening, Bea. Mr. Kendall. What brings the two of you to the dining hall, of all places?"

Thankfully, Mr. Kendall removed his hand and put a few inches of space between them. "We were discussing my plan for an upcoming women's baseball fundraiser. We're holding an exhibition game on Saturday. I hope you'll attend, Miss King."

Marjorie arched her eyebrow. "An exhibition game? You're sure that's the best way to raise money for the girls right now?"

A bit of weight lifted from Bea's shoulders. At least she wasn't the only one concerned this idea wasn't going to be the most profitable.

Mr. Kendall, on the other hand, was put off by being questioned again. He slapped both hands onto the table and pushed up. "If you want the fundraising support of the alumni, this is the plan. The game is scheduled for ten o'clock. If your team doesn't show up, I'll have to refund any money raised, so it would benefit them to at least try."

Marjorie leveled another pointed glare at him. "And was this your idea, or did Miss Curran get to have any input? It's her team, after all."

Seeing the standoff that was about to begin, Bea rose and stretched a hand toward each of them. "There's no need for an argument. Marjorie, we're going to try the exhibition game. It won't hurt. It might be good for the girls to see what it feels like to have a real crowd at one of their games, not just their friends and a few family members."

Both of her companions backed down, a hesitant truce settling around them. Bea took advantage of Marjorie's interruption to escape the dining hall, needing to think about Mr. Kendall's obvious advances. "Good night, Mr. Kendall. Thank you for the meeting. I'm going to walk with Miss King, as we have some matters to discuss."

This time, he let her go without stalling, offering a pleasant good night to her and a tip of his chin to Marjorie as if no harsh words had been exchanged.

As soon as they were out of sight of the dining room, Marjorie speared her with a glance. "What on earth is going on, Bea? That was a rather intimate moment for a meeting about college business."

Bea let her head fall back to look at the expanse of twilit sky that stretched over Lake Michigan behind the college buildings. The brilliant sunset colors would normally enchant her, but tonight they paled under the weight of her situation. "I don't know, Marjorie. Emmett warned me Mr. Kendall had unspoken intentions when he invited me to meet over supper. I didn't believe him, but I did try to keep it professional, requesting that we meet here well past mealtime. But then Mr.

Kendall told me I'm beautiful, and he looked at me so warmly…"

Her voice trailed off, but Marjorie understood the words she couldn't speak. "And now you wonder if he's the kind of man you might want to pursue you?"

A nod was all Bea could muster without releasing tears that suddenly pooled in her eyes. Marjorie slid her arm around Bea's waist, the touch comforting in the exact way she needed right then. "Ah, my dear girl. I knew you weren't as impervious to men as you try to let on with the players and fans. You'll have to decide for yourself as you get to know Mr. Kendall whether he's worthy of your attention or not. But don't ever feel you have to settle for a man who isn't worthy simply because he's the one who's there. The Lord will guide your steps. Don't rush."

With a lighter heart, Bea bid her friend good night and returned to Mrs. Harmony's boarding house, putting thoughts of romance out of her mind for the time being. She had a busy week ahead if she was going to prepare her team for an exhibition game. She had no time to worry about men and their intentions.

∼

*E*mmett no sooner reached the Western College campus for the scheduled practice on Thursday afternoon than he was met by Miss King, who appeared more flustered than Emmett had ever seen her. "Mr. Worland, I'm glad you're finally here. I fear Bea's done something that could be a terrible mistake for the baseball team."

A chill washed over him despite the warm breeze across the lake. "What is it?"

Miss King wrung her hands, her fingers twisting together, showing uncharacteristic worry. "She's agreed that the girls will put on an exhibition game as a fundraiser. You know as well as

I do that they aren't ready for something like that. They'll be humiliated."

An exhibition game? "That's ludicrous." Emmett flinched. He hadn't meant to say that out loud.

But Miss King was undeterred by his breach of etiquette. "My thoughts exactly. You must try to talk her out of it. Those girls will be demoralized if it goes as badly as I imagine it will."

They made their way across the campus as his mind raced through the possibilities. "I can't believe Bea came up with that idea."

Miss King shook her head so hard the feathers on her hat threatened to take flight. "Of course not. It was Mr. Kendall. They met last night, and he somehow convinced her it couldn't hurt. But it can, if it's an abysmal failure."

"Which it will be." Emmett's fingers curled into fists at the part of Miss King's news that was more concerning to him. Bea went ahead and had dinner with Mr. Kendall after Emmett told her what the man's underlying intention was. Had she... enjoyed his company?

They walked in silence for a few minutes. Emmett managed to pull his thoughts back to the matter that was upsetting Miss King. The game was a terrible idea. But what could he do if Bea had made up her mind? It seemed she wasn't interested in taking his advice to heart. "I'm only her assistant, and not one she values very highly. If she's set on something, I doubt I can talk her out of it."

Pausing within sight of the ball field to rest her gloved hand on his arm, Miss King offered a slight smile. "I think you'll find you have more sway than you believe. Please, try to talk her out of it."

Though reluctant, he nodded, and the woman grinned in return. She took her leave with a cheerful wave while Emmett stood in the middle of the path, watching the baseball team gathering at the field for practice. Was Miss King correct? Did he have any influence over Bea's choices?

Her choice to have dinner with Mr. Kendall was strong proof that she wasn't going to change her plans based on Emmett's opinion. But he'd promised to try, so he walked the last stretch of sidewalk to the field and joined Bea and the women.

Bea started practice before he could ask about the game. She had the team run the bases to warm up. Then she had them line up to one side of home plate. While they did so, she tossed a ball Emmett's way, grinning when he fumbled and nearly dropped it.

"I wasn't ready," he protested.

"You better get a handle on that so you can pitch to the girls." The laughing glance she threw over her shoulder as she walked away made his heart pound in his ears. He was used to women flirting with him. Even if he didn't respond, they liked to find him before or after games and make all sorts of silly, vain, or suggestive comments to try to get his attention.

Bea had never done any such thing before now.

So why was she the only one who made him long to chase after her and give her the kind of kiss a look like that made a man think about?

Instead, Emmett placed his feet in just the right spots on the pitcher's mound, ready to pitch for batting practice. One after another, the women stepped up to the plate, where he and Bea both offered suggestions to help them find the perfect form. Then he threw a few pitches to each one. Not his hardest, fastest throws, which could be challenging even for the semi-pro men, but hard enough to make the ladies work for hits.

They went through the entire rotation twice. By then, Emmett was sweating in the intense late-afternoon sun. Out of the corner of his eye, he caught sight of movement next to one of the dugouts. A young man, most likely one of those who used to gather and distract the ladies.

As soon as Bea had the team take a break to cool off, Emmett made his way to the lone spectator. "You were here when I explained the team's new policy on visitors at practice?"

The tall, lanky fellow nodded once. Emmett waited, but no explanation for his presence came. "And you understand that being here means I'll assume you want to work?"

To Emmett's surprise, the man nodded again.

Emmett took a step closer to him. "Are you sweet on one of these women?"

Finally, the visitor spoke. He had a quiet voice, which Emmett had to strain to hear, but the words had a refined tone. "Yes, sir. Luella Stevens. But I'd like to help the team too. I'm here to volunteer."

Huh. Emmett hadn't expected any of the college men to choose to help with field maintenance. "What's your name?"

The young man straightened, his eyes glowing with more confidence when Emmett didn't immediately send him away. "James Laramie, sir."

Emmett stuck out his hand, pleased when James returned his shake firmly. "All right, then. I'm Emmett Worland. Come back after practice, and I'll show you how to rake the dirt and put down chalk lines. You can be responsible for that at our game on Saturday."

A smile lit James's face. "Yes, sir."

Bea had gathered the team around her, so Emmett joined them in time to hear her announce the upcoming fundraiser. "Ladies, I want to work especially hard for the rest of our practice today because we have an opportunity to play in an exhibition game against a team from the University of Iowa on Saturday. It will be a way to raise funds for our program so we can replace this old equipment we inherited from the men's team last year." She paused, eyes wide in expectation, waiting for a reaction from the team.

The women glanced around at each other and shifted on their feet until Miss Thorn raised her hand. "Miss Curran, we can hardly get spectators besides our beaus and family at our regular games. Who's going to come to watch us play against a team no one knows from out of state? Their spectators won't be here."

It was all Emmett could do not to wince. Bea was trying to build up excitement in the team, and it was failing miserably. When he shot her a questioning look, she raised her shoulders in a brief shrug.

Emmett stepped forward. "I know it sounds like a stretch, ladies. But you're better players than you realize. Miss Curran and I will do all we can to get supporters of college athletics here if you focus on playing the best game possible. Give them a show that makes them want to donate to our program. Then it won't matter if you win or lose, or even if there are very many here."

Finally, excited whispers started to rise from the women. Emmett backed up, yielding their attention to Bea again. Before starting with the team, he'd imagined it would be difficult to find a balance between allowing her to lead her team while also instituting changes that he knew would help them. But working alongside Bea was going remarkably well. It was natural to step in and support her when she needed it, then let her take over again.

But there was still the fact that he needed to address her choice to collaborate with Mr. Kendall. Could he do so without making her think he was undermining her?

Bea walked the team through how the exhibition would go and then assigned them several drills to work on. The ladies scattered to different locations on the field to do as requested, and Emmett stayed busy for the next hour working with the two pitchers.

Once practice was over, Emmett found Bea gathering balls that had hit the backstop behind home plate. He stooped to pick up an errant one on the way, reaching out to hand it to her as he approached. He knew what he needed to bring up, but instead, he addressed James's presence. "We had a visitor to practice today."

She nodded. "I saw him. And I saw that you handled it. Thank you. The girls are much more focused when their suitors aren't gawking."

"Actually, this one was here for a different reason. He wants to work with us, to help care for the field. I hope you don't mind that I told him I'd teach him how to rake the dirt and measure out the lines."

Her head tilted to one side. "I suppose that's acceptable. As long as he doesn't cause a distraction."

"As soon as he does, I'll send him on his way."

A smile played around her lips at that response. He'd approached her to follow through on his agreement to help Miss King talk her out of the exhibition game. But he couldn't bring himself to erase that smile from her lips any more than he could have let her be disappointed with the team's response to the news of the exhibition. The game was already happening. His best option now was to do what he could to help it succeed, rather than upset Bea.

Bea's eyebrows inched upward. She'd been waiting for him to continue, and now he looked like a fool, standing there staring at her. Shoving both hands in his trouser pockets, Emmett backed away a few steps as he responded in a rush. "I suppose I'll see you at the game on Saturday. I need to see about training our new field help."

CHAPTER 9

*H*olding Emmett's gaze, Bea tried to make sense of what had changed. The conversation had somehow turned stilted, and she didn't know why. For most of the afternoon, there had been an easy camaraderie between them, one she'd very much enjoyed. Then before she knew it, they were in danger of resorting to discussing the weather.

All while he watched her with such an intense expression.

Bea finally nodded in response to his parting statement. "Please get here as early as you can Saturday so we can get the field ready and the team warmed up."

His gaze didn't waver as he took a few more steps backward toward the benches where their new helper waited. "I'll be here whenever you need me, Bea."

His voice was low and rough, something in his tone making her throat go dry. Bea tried to swallow, to dampen her mouth again, but her body wouldn't cooperate. Emmett turned and strode to the fence while James jumped up and joined him. Now she was the one who was staring. Which wouldn't have been so bad if Emmett hadn't chosen to glance back at her, a slow grin drawing up his lips when he caught her.

Bea twirled around, grabbed the basket of balls and two stray bats, and marched to the athletic building without looking back. Emmett Worland was an insufferable rake. She'd known that from the moment she saw his name in print. It had been more than confirmed at their first meeting.

But a small corner of her heart argued that that wasn't *all* he was. He'd been kind and supportive of her. He was encouraging with the team while remaining professional with all the ladies. And the only woman she'd ever personally known him to flirt with...was her.

That realization distracted Bea from worrying about the exhibition game until Saturday morning when reality hit as she walked across the campus with the early sun glinting off the dewy grass. She took determined steps, but her heart fluttered with concern about how the girls would do. Marjorie had made her opinion about this event clear over the last few days, and Emmett, while he hadn't voiced doubt, also hadn't given the impression he was confident this was a good idea.

The arguments against the event echoed in Bea's mind while she pulled the bats and balls from the equipment storage cabinets in the athletic building and dragged them to the field. Once everything was placed in the dugout, she stopped to watch Emmett and his new helper, who had arrived and started working on the field. James tugged a long-handled rake through the dirt, smoothing out the infield with slow, straight strokes. Meanwhile, Emmett was pouring chalk dust from a paper sack into the metal line marker that would lay it down as he walked between the bases.

Bea allowed herself a moment to sit on the bench in the home dugout and think about the game to come. It had to go well. She tried to hold on to the belief that God wouldn't let her fail, since He'd given this opportunity in the first place. Why would He grant her the chance to prove herself and then not help her through?

It was clear from the last few practices that the girls *could* play an excellent game if they focused and remembered all the things they'd been working on. But *would* they? They'd already lost all four of the games in their regular season against other Illinois and Wisconsin college teams. Sure, there weren't many women's teams to compare themselves to, but a losing record was never encouraging.

As he passed her spot while using his footsteps to measure the distance of the foul line, Emmett sent Bea a grin and a wave. But by then, her heart was heavy enough that she couldn't return his greeting. Jumping up from the bench, Bea busied herself digging through the basket to find the balls that were in the best condition for a game, ending up with a pitifully small pile once she finished.

At the sound of shoes scuffing in the dirt, Bea straightened and turned around to find Emmett approaching, brushing chalk off his hands with a handkerchief. "Good morning, Bea. Are you ready for the game?" His voice was soft as if he didn't want to disturb the peaceful, still summer morning any more than she did.

Ready? Possibly. Wanting to go through with it? No. "As ready as I can be."

But he saw through her words. Emmett stepped into the dugout, stopping close beside her. Awareness of his height, his scent, and his warmth surrounded Bea in a cloud of comfort that brought the oddest urge to stay at his side all day. "Bea, it's understandable if you're worried about how this will go. The team needs that money. But even more, they need the confidence that they can win."

Unbidden, tears rose in her eyes. Bea blinked them back, refusing to allow emotion to overtake her. "And can they?"

Confidence radiated from the smile that stretched across Emmett's face. "I know they're capable of it. It's up to them to play the way we've been teaching them."

The words released the well of pressure that had built in Bea's chest. She couldn't determine how the team played that day. She and Emmett had given them the knowledge they needed. Now the girls had to choose if they would use it. "Thank you, Emmett. For everything. I must admit, I thought having you around would be a problem rather than helpful. But you've proven me wrong."

His warm chuckle mixed with the sound of feminine voices as the girls arrived at the field in groups. Their matching dark skirts and shirtwaists with hand-embroidered *W*s near one shoulder weren't impressive as far as uniforms went, but they were clean and neat. Every one of them had tightly secured braids and twists in their hair so it wouldn't come loose and get in their way. They looked the part of a decent baseball team.

Bea instructed the girls to begin warming up at the same time that their competition arrived, walking across the campus in a large, intimidating cluster. As they got closer, it became clear that while the Iowa team had more players than Bea's team, they weren't that much better outfitted. They also had some worn equipment and handmade uniforms. Bea's spirits lifted.

Preparations for the game went as usual. Mr. Kendall appeared and met the Iowa team, showing them to the visitor dugout and generally being hospitable. A smattering of spectators gathered in the stands, mostly family and friends of her girls, as Marjorie had speculated. The umpire made his way to home plate to await the start of the game.

But then a procession of well-dressed ladies and gentlemen came down the sidewalk. Bea watched them as she tossed balls to the outfield, only half of which the girls were able to stop before they rolled to the back fence. But Bea hardly noticed that. The group stopped by the field as if they were there to attend the game. Bea recognized the regal form of Mrs.

Buchanan in the lead, as well as a few other faces that were well-known in Chicago.

Emmett left his warmup with the pitchers to greet his grandmother, then went down the line of the entire group, welcoming each with a handshake or polite nod. Bea's heart warmed. He'd done this. He'd made a promise to her team and then followed through, making sure there would be potential supporters at the game. He'd enlisted his grandmother—despite the tension between them—and possibly saved the day.

Now if only the team could pull out a win and prove to these influential people that the girls deserved their donations.

As the start time drew closer, Bea's confidence rose a little at a time. While both teams continued warming up, she walked across the field to greet the other team's manager, a burly man who looked rather disgruntled. Was he unhappy to be playing them? "Welcome to Western College. I'm Bea Curran, the women's baseball coach."

Reluctantly, the other coach returned her handshake. "Bill Warner. We're used to bigger facilities. This is...quaint."

Bea pursed her lips to hold back a snide retort, then mustered a smile once she'd composed herself. "I'm sure you are. We're trying to build a new program here—thus, the need for a fundraiser."

Mr. Warner shrugged. "As long as we get to play a good game, I guess it'll do."

Then he turned and went back to his dugout, gathering his team as he went. Bea licked her dry lips and did the same. It was time to see what her girls could do.

~

*E*mmett leaned against the wood plank wall in the shadow behind the home team's dugout. He pressed one hand into his head, wishing the pressure was enough to ease the pain. Why did it have to return today? Why right now, when the game was starting and Bea and the team needed him? He'd missed the beginning of the game and could only hope Bea hadn't noticed his sudden disappearance. The last thing he wanted to do was disappoint her on such an important day.

A prayer formed in his mind, pleading for God to take away the pain so he could continue with what he needed to do. Drawing a few deep breaths to release the tension the sudden burst of pain caused, he dropped his hand and tried to walk back into the dugout without letting on that anything was wrong. He didn't need Bea to be distracted by worrying about him. Or his grandmother trying to sniff out the weakness he refused to accept.

Emmett glanced at the spectators. His grandmother fanned herself in the heat, her forehead furrowed as she watched the action on the field. To the right of her and the group she'd brought, Mr. Kendall sat with his body turned toward the alumni, clearly not even attempting to pay attention to the game. Thankfully, no one in the stands seemed to notice if Emmett looked pale or was sweating an odd amount. If anyone did, maybe they would think it was nerves.

The Western College women were up to bat. Miss Thorn had made it to first, with Bea standing next to her, coaching from the base. Their second batter had just been struck out by the visiting pitcher. Emmett leaned on the fence that separated the dugout from the field, focusing on listening for the crack of the bat meeting the ball rather than the pulsing pain filling his skull.

But that exciting sound didn't come. The visiting pitcher struck out the next two women without much difficulty, and Miss Thorn had to return to the dugout from second base, the farthest she was able to advance on the field.

Emmett stopped Anna Harvey, their starting pitcher, on her way out onto the field for the start of the second inning. "Miss

Harvey, you know what to do. Remember the stance we worked on."

The young woman nodded, but she didn't look as confident as she should. She could be an excellent pitcher if she stopped doubting herself and let her skill take over.

Emmett welcomed Bea's presence as she returned to the side of the field by their dugout while the visiting team's coach took the spot by first base. She glanced at Emmett as their opponent's first batter walked to the plate. "I would feel much better if we'd gotten a run in the first inning."

Despite his pain, Emmett couldn't hold back a grin at the way she shuffled from one foot to another. "Have patience. Even the major league teams struggle to score in the first inning sometimes. They'll get warmed up and comfortable enough to earn runs soon—I'm sure of it."

Her attention shifted to the batter at home plate and Miss Harvey, who had settled into her starting position on the pitcher's mound. Emmett traced the path of her motions with his eyes, watching as she performed every step with precision. Three times she threw perfectly, and three times the batter swung and missed.

A burst of pride surprised Emmett. He'd helped the young woman learn how to do that. He'd never envisioned himself being an effective manager, with all the strategy involved in determining the batting order and fitting players into the right field positions. But helping others achieve success in the game he loved was more fulfilling than he'd expected. Maybe the coordinating would come naturally, too, if he ever tried it.

The first batter returned to the visitor dugout as hope rose on the Western College side. As much as Emmett wished the matchup was close to even and Bea's team had a chance, it was soon evident that was not the case. While Miss Harvey pitched well, the women from Iowa were very good batters and managed to fill the bases with only two outs. Miss Harvey closed the inning before the other team scored, but only because the final batter was not one of their best.

The bottom of the second inning saw three quick outs for the Western College team. Miss Harvey allowed a run, and then another in the third inning. Emmett started warming up their relief pitcher, but the discouragement in the home dugout was obvious.

The women continued limping along through the game, growing more frustrated and allowing the other team to play better. But as much as he wanted to help Bea and the women, Emmett was fighting his own battle. The headache was almost unbearable by the middle of the fifth inning when Bea called Miss Harvey out of the game and replaced her with their second pitcher. It was all Emmett could do to return to the dugout without staggering like a drunk man.

He collapsed on the bench, unable to keep from rubbing his forehead, pushing hard against it in hopes of alleviating the agony. Once again, he tried offering a prayer, but his hope of it helping his situation waned. God didn't seem to care that he was in agony.

Returning to the bench, Miss Harvey took notice of his condition. "Mr. Worland, are you well?"

As much as he wanted to wave off her concern, he shook his head. Immediately, the other two women remaining in the dugout jumped into action. One handed him a metal cup filled with somewhat cool water. The other hand shoved a wet cloth at him, which he used to wipe away the sweat now pouring down his neck and forehead.

But he couldn't let them become distracted from the game. "Thank you. I'm fine now. Don't lose focus. You can still come back and win."

He might have heard one of them harrumph in doubt, but Emmett chose to ignore it. However, when he caught sight of Bea after the sixth inning, he couldn't ignore the anguish on her face. The Western College team was down three to zero, and the players were all trudging along, dejected.

Emmett gathered every bit of strength in his body to rise and move to the dugout entrance, forcing himself to stand straight and wiping the sweat away again before catching her attention. "Bea."

She looked at him, shoulders slumped.

Emmett leveled a serious, confident look at her. "Call a time-out and rally the team. You can lift their spirits and help them turn this around, I know it. There's still time to score enough runs to win."

Her beautiful blue eyes held his gaze as she considered his words. Then her lips lifted slightly, and she waved toward the umpire, calling for a pause in the game. While she gathered the women around her and tried to encourage them, Emmett returned to the bench, glad she was busy because he was unable to stand a moment longer.

James found him there, nearly doubled over in pain. "Mr. Worland, you need a doctor. There's a clinic on the campus. Can I help you get there?"

Although it was the last thing he wanted to do, Emmett nodded. He let James help him to his feet, and together they shuffled away from the field. Bea and the team would be too busy to notice his departure. Hopefully, his grandmother wouldn't notice his disappearance either. Having her poking around in this business was not something he could handle.

Progress was slow, so it took some time, but James finally delivered Emmett to the clinic across the campus. Before the young man left, Emmett grabbed his arm. "Tell Miss Curran I'm sorry. But please don't tell her I'm sick."

James hesitated. "She should know why you left."

If she knew he was sick, she'd be worried about him. That worry would be obvious, and before long, the team would know. Bea might even ask his grandmother about his health.

Word would get out, and the Lincoln Parks' leadership might get wind of it. Emmett couldn't take that chance.

So Emmett shook his head as forcefully as he could. "No. Just make sure she knows how sorry I am to miss the end of the game."

Still looking uncomfortable with the request, James nevertheless nodded and left Emmett to the doctor's attention.

The older man had a gentle but matter-of-fact way about him when he spoke to Emmett after his examination. "Mr. Worland, have you had an injury to the head recently?"

That was the question he hadn't wanted to face, holding out hope that something else—something easily curable—was causing the headaches. "I was hit by a baseball during a game last fall. But the doctor employed by my new team said there were no lasting effects from that."

The doctor smoothed back the thinning hair on the top of his head. "There is evidence that the effects of a head injury can be delayed, even for months or years. It's my opinion that these symptoms are related to that injury. I'm giving you something for the pain when it's unbearable, but you'll need to start restricting strenuous physical activity. Let your body heal."

Emmett's heart plunged. "For how long?"

The doctor nodded his head to one side. "As long as it takes, I'm afraid. With constant management, you'll be able to live with the symptoms. But if they worsen...well, you certainly won't be playing baseball at that point."

The world spun around Emmett. He gripped the edge of the examination table he still sat on, trying to let the words sink in without the truth drowning him. He could either give up baseball in favor of resting and managing the pain, or he could keep playing and take the chance that the symptoms would grow bad enough to take the game from him.

There was no choice at all.

Paying the doctor for his services, Emmett left the clinic in a fog. He couldn't stop by the field now to see how the game ended. He was far too shaken by the news.

If word got out, he would be pitied. Looked down on. Treated as an invalid. Most likely, fired.

Emmett walked along the edge of the campus that bordered Lake Michigan, listening to the waves gently lapping the rocky shore. Resolve threaded through him, giving him the strength to push through the pain that lingered even after taking one of the tablets the doctor had given him. He'd lived with the symptoms this long. If the medicine could take off the edge, he could handle the rest and continue living his dream.

He would make it to the major league, have a long and rich career, and impress his grandmother with his success. He would not give up and waste away in bed, a disappointment to his grandmother and a charity case to those who knew him.

Or he would die trying.

CHAPTER 10

Bea didn't notice the moment when Emmett left the field. But the emptiness in her chest when she realized he was gone caught her by surprise.

As the girls came in from the eighth inning—dejected despite her efforts to inspire them—she asked each one if they'd seen where he went. Beth Marie slumped on the bench, hardly looking at Bea as she replied, "He was sick with discouragement earlier. He tried to be reassuring, but maybe the game was too awful for him to watch."

The other girls murmured amongst themselves at Beth Marie's pronouncement, and Bea's heart broke for them. This was her fault. "I know this isn't easy. But play the best last inning that you can. Give our spectators a great ending to the game. That was the point of this, anyway, right? For the crowd to enjoy a few hours watching baseball."

Luella Stevens let out a harsh laugh. "Calling that handful of people a crowd is generous. No one wanted to pay money to watch us lose to a team from another state."

She was right, of course. Bea had known it when Mr. Kendall brought up the idea, but what could she have done?

He'd been so set on it, with arrangements already made. She hadn't believed it would hurt the girls as much as Marjorie had tried to tell her it would.

But looking around at their frustrated, angry, miserable faces now, it was clear how wrong she'd been.

Bea clapped her hands together, getting the attention of all her players. "Even so, we have a game to finish. Mr. Kendall and a group of prominent alumni are in those stands, waiting to watch you play your best. Raise your chins, and let's lose with as much grace as any bunch of women ever did."

The ladies brightened somewhat, enough to start the inning with a bit more energy in their movements. But Bea could no longer focus on the game. Emmett had gotten so discouraged that he'd abandoned them. He'd left without even telling her.

She hated that this moment confirmed what she'd been trying to tell herself for weeks. He was the exact sort of rake she'd assumed, a man who wouldn't remain committed to something that didn't serve his need for attention or pride. And she would be left to deal with the results of this embarrassing loss alone.

So why did a small part of her, deep down in the recesses of her heart, still wish he was there?

The game ended with a final score of five to zero. The Western College women congratulated the winners with poise and dignity, but Bea could see their less positive emotions simmering under the surface. She had plenty of work to do if she was going to bolster their spirits enough to get through their upcoming regular season games without losing every single one.

Bea encouraged her team to leave right away after the game, to go enjoy the rest of the day and not dwell on the loss. She prayed they wouldn't overhear any negative comments on the way out that would reinforce the frustration in their minds.

Once they'd all gathered their things and left the dugout, Bea walked out to face the spectators and the other team.

Alone, thanks to Emmett.

At least Marjorie was there, though. Her friend met her at the entrance to the dugout, her face creased with worry. "Bea, dear, I'm so sorry. That was...difficult."

That was a kind way to put it. "It was mortifying, and you know it. But then, you warned me it would be. I'm sorry I didn't listen to you."

Marjorie slid her arm around Bea's waist. "You're learning the difficulty in balancing the ideas of those above you with what you know in your heart will or won't benefit your team. It's something you'd have to face sooner or later. Mr. Kendall may have risen to a prestigious position, but that doesn't mean he's qualified to make decisions for everyone. Learning to stand your ground now will help you when you're running the physical education program."

Bea's heart ached. Marjorie always spoke about Bea taking over for her as if it was already decided, but the truth remained that Bea had yet to prove herself to those who would make that decision. And a mistake like this game would certainly be a stain on her record.

As they rounded the dugout and walked toward the spectator benches, Mr. Kendall himself stood regaling the society guests and Emmett's grandmother with some kind of tale that he clearly believed they were fascinated with, missing the very obvious signs that they would do anything to stop his prattling. Bea pursed her lips. He could be quite charming. What made him turn into such an insufferable snob at times?

Seeing Bea and Marjorie, Mrs. Buchanan pounced on the chance to break into Mr. Kendall's story, raising her voice to address the entire group she'd brought along. "Ah, there are the ladies in charge. You all know Miss King, but let me introduce you to Miss Beatrice Curran."

Bea tried to commit all the names to memory during the introductions, but only a few stood out. She'd been far too busy building her career since coming to Chicago to pay much attention to socialites and the upper crust, although it was hard to miss the ones who were mentioned in every single newspaper. And many of those people were now standing before her, having watched the team she was responsible for fail miserably.

Marjorie moved among the group with ease, used to interacting with them. In comparison, Bea felt like an unexperienced batter reaching too hard for the ball. It didn't help that they all looked at her with either pity over the hard loss or the fascination of viewing a side show oddity.

She thought she'd gotten used to that, but evidently not.

Still hurt over Emmett's disappearance, Bea worked her way to Mrs. Buchanan's side. "Emmett left at some point, and no one knows where he went. Do you know what happened?" Bea kept her voice low, not wanting to expose Emmett or Mrs. Buchanan to unwanted gossip.

The matron straightened at Bea's question, her thin lips pressed into a tight line. "I do not. Every time I think that young man will settle down and fulfill his obligations, he does something like this. Probably off trying to impress a woman or some such nonsense."

The thought that he'd abandoned them for a woman's attention hadn't even crossed Bea's mind. But now that it had been suggested, she couldn't dislodge the vision of Emmett leaning down to whisper sweet words into a pretty girl's ear, chuckling warmly at her response. The girl would be far more traditional than Bea, excelling at embroidery and painting, probably dressed in a beautiful frock that had never once had a speck of ballpark dirt on it.

Bea had to forcibly shake herself to end the torment. "I'm sure he had a reason. When you do see him..." Her words trailed off. She had no right to ask him to explain himself. Yes, she relied on his help during practices, but leading the team was her responsibility. If he chose not to follow through, she would have to move forward without him. "Never mind. I hope you enjoyed the game, despite the loss."

Mrs. Buchanan's sharp gaze and pursed lips made Bea want to squirm. Could the woman see the turmoil in Bea's heart? Thankfully, a change of subject took the pressure off Bea. "It was still quite enjoyable. Loss is part of any competition, isn't it? Even if this particular game was likely ill-advised."

Everyone except Bea must have come to that same conclusion before the game even began. Bea drew a breath but was saved from responding when Mr. Kendall appeared at her side. "Mrs. Buchanan, I can't tell you how pleased we are to have you and your friends in attendance today. Even though the women lost, I'm sure you'll agree there's a great deal of potential for their future."

With a skeptical brow arched, Mrs. Buchanan nonetheless answered with impeccable manners. "Yes, much potential. I do hope future fundraising efforts will focus more on their strengths than weaknesses, however. These ladies deserve much better than what you've given them today."

Turning away without waiting for him to answer, Mrs. Buchanan gathered her companions, and Marjorie escorted them toward the street and their waiting vehicles.

Mr. Kendall sighed as they departed. "I never expected interest from so much old money. Maybe there are some benefits to having Emmett Worland helping you, after all."

Ire burned through Bea's chest. "Do you have so little faith in me and my team? I thought you believed in us."

He turned a warm, assuring gaze toward her, but it felt flat. "Oh, I didn't mean you couldn't do it without him. Only that every connection we can leverage helps."

He rested one hand on Bea's elbow, drawing her to walk

alongside him toward the athletic building, although all she wanted was a moment alone to recover from the humiliation. "We should debrief this event, go over what went well and what we could improve upon. Then we can make a plan to move forward. Would you join me tonight at the dining hall again?"

A check in Bea's heart gave her pause. Was it wise to continue meeting with him that way? The more times it happened, the more it would look as if there was something besides fundraising talk going on. But was that such a terrible thing? Why shouldn't she be allowed to enjoy a man's attention and company? He was respectable, and they were always in public places. In fact, spending time with Aaron Kendall on campus was much more socially acceptable than any of the time she spent on baseball fields.

Bea felt Mr. Kendall's eyes on her as she hesitated. It wasn't the worst feeling, knowing he had an interest in her that went beyond the novelty of meeting a female umpire. She could get used to spending time with a man who had no ties to baseball whatsoever.

So why was a little corner of her heart yelling *danger*? Compared to the warm, safe sensation Emmett's watchfulness brought, having Aaron Kendall stare at her sent an unpleasant shiver up her spine. "I'd prefer to meet some other time when Mr. Worland can be included. As my assistant manager, he should be present to contribute to the discussion."

Mr. Kendall's expression darkened, confirming that she'd made the right choice. Marjorie had told her she would learn if he was right for her as she got to know him. It was clear at that moment that this man did not have her best interests at heart. But the last thing Bea needed after the morning she'd had was to confront his intentions. So she bid him goodbye before he could speak and rushed to enter the athletic building. At least he didn't follow her.

*E*mmett had once again been summoned.

He walked downstairs to Grandmother's parlor at exactly seven o'clock on Saturday evening, as her message—delivered earlier by a footman—had demanded. Not asked, of course. It didn't matter that he might have had plans to go out that evening, or whether he *wanted* to visit with her. Would she even have cared if she'd known about the immense amount of pain he'd been in all day? She likely still would have required his presence.

Standing outside the room, staring at the familiar grand hallway, part of him considered turning around and ignoring the summons. If he couldn't play baseball, anyway, he would have to find regular employment and would no longer need her financial support in order to chase his dream. There were no other repercussions for offending her that he couldn't handle.

But she was the only family he had. She hadn't been a good surrogate parent, but he still held a soft spot in his heart for her. After all, she'd lost her only child when Emmett's mother died. He hadn't been the only one mourning that great loss. The way her reaction to the grief hurt him during his formative years wasn't easy to forgive, but Emmett had decided long ago not to live in bitterness.

So he straightened his shoulders and strode into the parlor, making every effort to hide the throbbing ache that lingered despite the medicine the doctor had given him. When his grandmother glanced up from the book she held, an unfamiliar emotion flitted across her face. But that must have been a trick of the electric lights she'd had installed and not real concern for him.

Emmett took his usual seat in a comfortable leather chair that sat next to Grandmother's upholstered one. She closed her book and set it on the small table next to her. "Emmett, why did you leave the game today? Miss Curran was rather distressed."

At least she got right to the point. His chest tightened at the confirmation that his actions had caused Bea to worry. "A...situation arose."

She folded her hands in her lap and speared him with a straightforward glare. "You will explain yourself at once. In as much detail as possible. What situation?"

He knew that scowl. She would not let it go until she had answers. She would hound him day and night. What was the point in resisting? He would have to tell her eventually. It might even be nice to have someone who knew the truth and could help him if the pain grew too great and began effecting his daily life. "In a game last fall, I was hit by a ball, hard enough to require several stitches in my forehead. I thought it was fine once the cut healed. The Lincoln Parks' doctor cleared me to play and said there was no long-term damage. But I've been having worsening headaches and dizziness for the last few months. Today it grew unbearable. A student helped me get to the clinic on campus, and the doctor there told me it's delayed symptoms from a concussion I must have gotten with that injury."

When Emmett finished, silence lingered, punctuated by the tick of Grandmother's beloved green enamel Cartier desk clock, which sat on the table next to her. Finally, she offered a decisive nod. "Well, that does explain it. What did the doctor suggest you should do about the pain?"

If he'd bothered to hope for sympathy, he would have been disappointed. Luckily, he hadn't. "Rest. He believes I should stop playing baseball."

One delicate eyebrow arched. "And will you?"

"Not unless it becomes unavoidable."

"And why didn't you explain this to Miss Curran after the game?" Her voice was unusually soft as if she cared more than he'd thought and was bothered by the news of his health. But of course, that couldn't be the reason.

Emmett ran one hand through his hair. "I don't want anyone to know. If this information gets out, my manager could decide not to take the risk that I'll be able to continue playing. It would be in his rights to fire me. I've worked too hard for this to let it be taken from me now."

His grandmother stretched her arm across the gap between their chairs to rest her wrinkled hand on his. It had been years since she'd touched him. Emmett wasn't even sure he remembered the last time. "I am sorry, Emmett. I may wish you'd stop wasting your time trying to earn a living with a game that makes a better hobby, but that doesn't mean I can't admire your commitment and passion for it. It must be difficult to learn your time playing is limited."

The resolve that had been growing in him strengthened into certainty at her assumption that the doctor was correct. He stood, channeling his restlessness into pacing toward the tall windows lining one side of the room. A warm evening breeze stirring the curtains did nothing to cool his burst of temper. "It doesn't have to be. I'll find a way to keep going."

"Oh, Emmett, don't be stubborn. That time will come, we both know it. Baseball isn't a lifelong career for someone in good health. Even if this illness doesn't force you to, one day you'll have to stop playing and take your place as the heir to your grandfather's company. I can't keep running it forever."

"I've told you before that I don't intend to become the sort of man who sits at the Chicago Club all day making deals to increase my personal wealth while contributing nothing to this world. I want to make a name for myself, not thrive off yours."

Grandmother massaged one temple with her fingertips. She never moved inelegantly, but her motions started to show signs of losing patience with the conversation. "It's impossible to reason with you about this—I've known that for years. I won't tell anyone about your illness, but I want your promise that you won't push yourself into an early grave over this game. I..." She cleared her throat. "I can't lose another person I care about who should far outlive me."

Emmett's heart plunged at the allusion to his mother. He had no memories of her face, but her image from the portrait Grandmother kept by her bed sprang to mind. Lucy Buchanan had possessed beautiful blond curls and delicate features. On the rare occasions when Grandmother mentioned Emmett's father, she always told Emmett that's where his rougher looks had come from. Not that anyone would ever be able to confirm it. The lowly steelworker Lucy had fallen in love with had disappeared before Emmett was even born, leaving no trace of his presence except an unwanted son.

Shaking off such thoughts, Emmett examined his grandmother. Her cheeks were blotchy, and her eyes held the sheen of restrained tears. Showing emotion like this was unusual for her. Had the revelation of his illness made more of an impact on her than he ever would have thought?

More likely, it was the memory of his mother. She'd never gotten over the loss of her beloved Lucy, a fact she made sure Emmett was aware of each day of his life.

"I'm not dying, Grandmother, and these symptoms won't kill me. I just have to face a great deal of pain at times. Your heir is still going to live to a ripe old age while suffering through every year of it."

Her head tilted at the bitterness that crept into his tone unintended. "Emmett, these kinds of injuries are unpredictable. I may not follow baseball, but even I know about players losing their minds, becoming irrational, or even violent after being struck too many times. Adhere to the doctor's recommendations and perhaps your body will heal enough you can enjoy your remaining years."

He could only shake his head. She might pursue fashionable sports with her friends, even going so far as to be an influential leader of the Chicago Woman's Athletic Club. But she'd never understood his drive to forge a career of his own, much less in one as strenuous as baseball. He wasn't going to try to convince her again. "I'll consider it. But until I decide my health is really at risk, I'm going to continue living my life."

Emmett strode toward the door, hesitating as he passed her, the urge to rest his hand on her shoulder flaring up. But they'd never had the type of relationship where they comforted one another, and she likely wouldn't welcome the change to one now. So he offered wishes for a good night on his way out and returned to his room upstairs, where only the questions about the future he'd envisioned kept him company.

CHAPTER 11

*B*ea tugged on the tie she'd knotted a bit too tight that morning, trying to imitate the relaxed style of the other female golfers entering the Chicago Golf Club. As comfortable as she usually was in athletic situations, she felt out of place at an upscale, exclusive golf club like this one. If not for Marjorie's insistence that Bea round out the foursome Mrs. Buchanan was putting together, she wouldn't have mustered the courage to be standing in front of the elegant clubhouse.

But Marjorie *had* insisted, and Bea had agreed to play with the two older women. Before she'd known Emmett would also be joining them, unfortunately. Refusing to let his actions ruin another day, she raised her chin and did her best to look as though she belonged there as she marched up the stone steps and into the cool, dark interior.

Emmett was the first to see her across the lobby. He raised his hand in a wave, but it was the way he searched her face that almost made her pause mid-step. Was he concerned that she might be upset after he abandoned the team on Saturday? Had he lived with guilt or regret over it for the last four days?

Because he certainly should have.

Not ready to forgive him until she had some answers for his behavior, Bea offered the briefest nod to Emmett and then focused her attention on the ladies. "Good morning, Mrs. Buchanan, Marjorie. Thank you for including me in your outing."

Mrs. Buchanan waved to get the attention of a young caddy standing nearby. "We've already had this young man prepare clubs for us. I had him get some of the sets the club keeps on hand for you and Emmett to use. So I believe we're ready to start."

They followed Mrs. Buchanan through the tasteful lobby and out a set of double doors in the middle of a wall of windows that displayed the immaculate greens behind the building. The morning air was already heavy with the promise of a hot afternoon, making Bea grateful for the trend toward more relaxed golf attire. She loosened her tie a bit more as Mrs. Buchanan and Marjorie stopped at the first tee, discussing which clubs they planned to start with.

Next to Bea, Emmett leaned closer, his voice low. "Grandmother has convinced me to join her a few times in recent years, but I've never excelled at golf. Are you any good?"

"I've never played so I have no idea."

He took her cold tone for the discouragement it was and dropped back a pace while Bea moved closer to the other women and pulled a club from one of the bags the caddy had set down. "What benefits are there to the different clubs?"

Marjorie and Mrs. King gave Bea a thorough explanation of what each club was best suited for, then watched as she chose a heavy-ended driver to try first. Mrs. Buchanan nodded. "Very good choice, Miss Curran. Now watch Marjorie and I and try to replicate our form. Then you'll be on your way to an excellent first drive."

Bea watched closely and was very pleased when she not

only hit the ball off the wooden tee on her first try but also managed to send it flying halfway down the green. Not as far as the other two women, but it seemed a respectable enough hit.

Emmett had claimed the last turn in their foursome, so he placed his ball on the tee next. He positioned his feet with as much care as he did on the pitcher's mound, lined up his club, and then swung it back in a wide arc. Despite his claim of not excelling at the sport, his drive was perfect, muscles flexing under his linen shirt, sending the ball on a beautiful flight far past hers.

Before Bea could look away from the intoxicatingly masculine sight, he glanced back and caught her watching. Bea turned to examine the clubs in the borrowed bag, but she couldn't stop the flaming heat burning its way up her neck due to the knowing glint in his eyes.

The game progressed, but Bea grew worse after her decent first shot. She started to understand the frustration many golfers spoke of, particularly when her ball disappeared into the trees lining the edges of the course more than once. The first time, she spent several minutes searching, but it was hopeless. The next time, she took the extra strokes added to her score and didn't even bother.

By the sixth tee, Marjorie and Mrs. Buchanan had run out of advice to give. Mrs. Buchanan released a heavy sigh. "I know you have the ability, Miss Curran. I fear I'm not the best teacher. Emmett, you seem good enough at teaching those young women to play baseball. Perhaps you can help Miss Curran correct her swing."

The last thing Bea wanted was Emmett watching her movements, inspecting the way she held her body. Yet a part of her longed to see where this would go. She silenced that part. "That's not necessary. I'm sure I simply need practice, and I'll be much improved after playing a few more times."

But Mrs. Buchanan waved her protests away. "He's humble

about it, but Emmett is very good. Let him see if there are any tips he can give to help you improve going forward. Marjorie and I are going to wait in that bit of shade over there. This heat is going to drain me before we reach the next hole otherwise."

When she found herself alone with Emmett, Bea commanded her heart to stop beating so fast. *Alone?* He was the one who left her and the team alone. It would benefit her to remember that.

"Stand over here away from the tee and swing a few times, and let me see if I can find the problem." His voice was low and gentle as if he knew he was on shaky ground with her and wanted to change that fact.

And her heart betrayed her by softening in response.

Bea positioned her feet as she'd seen the others do, then lined up the head of the club perpendicular to where she wanted the ball to go and gave it a few tiny practice movements. Then she pulled it up over her shoulder and brought it back down, twisting at the waist while keeping her feet in place.

She held the pose for a brief moment, as she would if she was watching the ball sail down the fairway. Then she repeated the entire process twice more. Finally, she dropped the end of the club back toward the ground and turned to gauge Emmett's reaction. "How was that?"

With his head tilted to one side, he paused before respond-ing. Was she so terrible at golf that he had to hide his true thoughts?

He moved closer to her, near enough that she could feel warmth emanating from him. "It wasn't the worst swing I've ever seen. Get back into your starting position, and I'll see if we can improve it."

Bea once again placed her feet and the club as if she were going to hit an imaginary ball. The touch of Emmett's rough fingers on her hands, moving her grip on the club, caught Bea off guard. She instinctively glanced up into his face, which was so very close to hers. There were flecks of green in his blue eyes that she'd never been close enough to notice before. And his lips looked softer than she would have imagined.

His gaze held hers while his hands moved from the club to her shoulders. He ever so gently turned her to a better angle. Then he rested one hand on her cheek, turning her face away from him. "Line your entire body up facing the ball like this. Relax your shoulders. Don't move your head as you bring the club down. That's how you get the right angle to hit the ball straight."

His breath tickled the hair that had come loose around her face in the heat. Bea had to remind her lungs to draw in a breath so she wouldn't faint. But that possibility brought on a curiosity to know what it would feel like if he caught her, if his strong arms wrapped around her and supported her.

Support. He hadn't seemed concerned about supporting her when she needed him at the baseball game. She had to stop this line of thought immediately before she embarrassed herself. Emmett Worland was so used to women throwing themselves at him that he probably thought a few touches would make Bea forgive any slight. Well, he'd learn that she was not a woman to be trifled with.

Even if teaching that lesson was the hardest thing Bea ever had to do.

～

*E*mmett stood back and watched Bea execute a much-improved swing, but his mind hardly noticed it. All he could think about was how close he'd been to wrapping his arms around her. And how much he'd wanted to.

But he needed to convince his grandmother—and the rest of the world—that he was not the rake they assumed him to be.

Embracing a beautiful woman on a public golf course

would not aid him in achieving that goal. Even if holding Bea had become one of the things he most longed for in life, something he dreamed about regularly.

Emmett drew one of his clubs from the bag the young caddy held out for him and took his shot, pleased when it soared down the fairway and landed near the green. He hadn't lied when he told Bea he didn't excel at golf. This game was just going better than usual.

Until the dizziness began.

Grandmother and Miss King had rejoined them, and they were all moving along down the course now, with Bea not needing to chase after her ball so often. On the ninth and final tee of their short game, the now-familiar swirling started in his skull. Emmett used the club he held as a support, hoping the feeling would pass and not grow as unbearable as it had been before. He managed a halfway decent drive, willing himself to remain standing as he waited for the women to putt.

Somehow, he made it through the last hole, then followed the women back to the clubhouse, where his grandmother insisted that they all have lunch together. The dining room was much cooler than outside, thanks to a shaded interior and the light breeze that swept through open windows. It was a relief for Emmett to finally sit down. He was still lightheaded, but at least in a chair, he wasn't in danger of falling and looking as if he'd imbibed in something stronger than lemonade.

While they ate the vegetable soup and roasted turkey that were on the menu for the day, Emmett snuck one of the pills the campus doctor had given him. Before long, he was able to relax in his seat as the world stopped spinning around him and awareness of his surroundings returned. His companions must have been talking about the women's baseball team. Grandmother was looking at Bea with one eyebrow arched. "And were the funds raised by the exhibition game sufficient for your needs?"

Bea sighed, the heavy sound sending a pang straight through Emmett's heart. "I was able to order some new balls to replace those that are too worn to use. But we still need money for bats and gloves." He hated the resignation in her voice. "I was hoping we could even purchase hats to match their uniforms instead of the men's old cast-offs. Mr. Kendall has mentioned trying again, and I intend to work with him to come up with a plan that's better suited to the team this time."

Emmett managed to hold back a harsh laugh, but his face must have shown his skepticism.

Grandmother tilted her head, her gaze leveled in his direction. "Do you have a better idea for Miss Curran, Emmett?"

"Actually, I already told her my better idea. She chose to go with Mr. Kendall's instead."

Silence fell over the table. Emmett let his eyes drift shut for a moment. He'd spoken without thinking, and now it was going to cause a scene. When he looked again, Bea's cheeks were marred by red splotches, and her lips were set in a tight line. "I had little choice but to go with the plan the Alumni Association president suggested. If you still think your idea will work, why don't you explain it to your grandmother and Marjorie?"

All three sets of feminine eyes locked on him, and the weight of their expectations threatened to bring on a headache to go along with the dizzy spell. He realized his leg was bouncing against the table and forced it to be still. "I...I thought, perhaps..." Words wouldn't come to his mind. What had he suggested before?

His gaze fell on Bea, waiting with a challenge written all over her face.

He swallowed and pushed the words out in a rush. "A ball. A charity ball, like the ones you've thrown so many times, Grandmother. I've seen the proceeds from those events, and we could more than cover what the team needs. If you think your society friends would be interested in attending such an event for a women's baseball team instead of for the church or Ladies' Aid Society, that is."

Grandmother's stern look melted into thoughtful approval. "That's not a bad idea, Emmett. We could include the Woman's Athletic Club. They would be enthusiastic about supporting young female athletes, don't you think, Marjorie?"

"Oh yes. That's a much more suitable plan than Mr. Kendall's. Bea, I hope you haven't already agreed to meet with him again. Especially after what happened the last time."

A chill raced across Emmett's skin, dispelling the flush that always accompanied his concussion symptoms. "What happened last time?"

Bea refused to meet his gaze, instead pushing a bit of roasted potato around her plate. "Nothing untoward, so you needn't be concerned on my behalf. And I can handle myself just fine, Marjorie."

But Emmett couldn't let it go. He gripped the edge of his chair, hoping his voice wouldn't betray the temper rising in his chest at the idea that Mr. Kendall might have hurt or compromised her in any way. "What did he do, Bea?"

She finally shot a glare at Miss King and relented, her chin rising as she met Emmett's gaze. "He complimented me. And expressed romantic interest. He was more respectful than many of the baseball players who propose to me, so there was no harm done."

Miss King pursed her lips. "I'd hardly call him respectful. He looked far more comfortable telling you what to do than you're letting on. I don't like the idea of you meeting with him alone."

"Neither do I." Emmett didn't have a right to tell her how to comport herself, but he couldn't stop the words from flying from his lips. "Mr. Kendall puts on a charming façade, but I'm willing to bet he isn't as respectable as you seem to think."

His grandmother raised both hands, staving off any more discussion. "Miss Curran, Marjorie and I will help you plan the event as part of our activities with the Woman's Athletic Club. You can send word to Mr. Kendall that we volunteered to support your team, so there will be no need to ask for anything from the alumni at the moment. Will that solve this problem?"

The urge to hug his grandmother was unexpectedly strong. Since he'd been traveling for baseball, it had been years since he'd spent this much time around her, and he was finding she was kinder than he remembered. Or perhaps he was seeing a side of her that she hadn't allowed him to see before. She was more willing to get involved in his life. Helpful, even. He could get used to having someone supportive around.

Bea nodded in acceptance of the plan, and the older two women began discussing what would need to be done.

Emmett leaned closer to Bea, keeping his voice low for only her to hear. "Does that mean you won't go to dinner with Mr. Kendall?"

Her chin lifted and her shoulders squared. "I don't see how what I do with my time is any concern of yours. He's a successful, handsome man who enjoys my company. If that's a reason for me to avoid him in your mind, I would say the problem lies with you."

Emmett's chest burned. Words swirled through his mind, but none of them would cool her temper, only inflame it. Still, he couldn't sit by and watch her make a mistake that could bring her harm. "He may be handsome, and he plays the part of a decent man, but be careful, Bea. Please. I've met many people like him. Deep down, he's only out to get whatever he wants. He won't care who he hurts in the process."

The spark of anger in her eyes melted into confusion as her gaze strayed back to her plate.

Emmett let the matter drop. Perhaps she would at least

consider his words. And while she did, Emmett would hunt for any way he could find to keep her from being alone with Aaron Kendall again.

CHAPTER 12

$\mathcal{B}$ea followed Emmett, Mrs. Buchanan, and Marjorie out of the golf club after lunch with an ache growing in her chest. Emmett hadn't said a word about leaving her and the team on Saturday, and it appeared he didn't intend to. No apology. No regret. No concern at all for the unexpected amount of hurt his actions had caused her.

She hadn't realized how much she'd hoped he would apologize and give a genuine, reasonable explanation for his disappearance. At some point, she must have come to believe he was more than a womanizing, arrogant baseball player because his failure to do the right thing left her more disappointed than she ought to be. Instead of an apology, he'd acted as if he had the right to give her advice on the relationships she chose to pursue.

Which he did not have.

Still, his unease over thinking she would meet with Mr. Kendall again stuck in the back of her mind as the group waited outside the golf club for Mrs. Buchanan's carriage. She'd already decided it wasn't wise to be alone with the man, but the confirmation that all those closest to her felt the same helped her release the last vestiges of worry that remained about the choice. Even if the last thing she wanted to do right then was agree with Emmett.

Near the wide stairs, the two older women were discussing ideas for where to hold the charity ball, so Bea was left to stand with Emmett, neither of them speaking, both shuffling from one foot to the other. But no matter how uncomfortable the situation, she refused to bring up his behavior. He should rise to the occasion and show contrition for his actions without being told.

"Are we following the usual practice schedule this week?" Emmett glanced up and down the street, watching for the carriage rather than looking at her as he spoke, and his careless attitude suddenly became too much for Bea.

Despite her resolve to make him own up to his mistake, Bea found herself saying the first words that came to her mind. "Why? Are you planning to *be* there for practice, unlike the end of the game on Saturday?"

His gaze darted to hers as his head jerked back. Then a shadow crossed his face, and he looked away. "I should have apologized for that before now, Bea. I'm sorry. There was an... unavoidable situation that I had to tend to."

He didn't elaborate. Bea waited until the silence grew uncomfortable again, her heart dropping farther toward the bluestone sidewalk under her feet with each passing second. He wasn't going to tell her the truth about what had happened. He thought she was stupid enough to accept such a superficial excuse without question. "I'm not sure we'll need you at practices any longer, then. You can use that time to attend to your unavoidable business instead."

Their companions, unfortunately, fell silent at that moment, and the two women quickly looked their way. Mrs. Buchanan leaned past Marjorie to address Bea. "Miss Curran, I implore you to give Emmett one more chance. He is trying to redeem himself, after all. He might not be perfect at it, but I assure you, he won't repeat that mistake. Will you, Emmett?"

Her pointed look was enough to make anyone cower, but Emmett didn't hang his head. Instead, he nodded with a burst of enthusiasm. "I will certainly not repeat it. Bea, I'll be present for every practice and game remaining in the season that doesn't conflict with the Lincoln Parks' schedule."

When Bea hesitated, Emmett turned his body to block the view of the others. "Please, forgive me, Bea." His voice was lower, intimate even, and there was no way she could deny—or ignore—the sincerity in his eyes. "And know that helping your team has become more important to me than I imagined. Allow me to prove myself."

Against her will, Bea's heart thumped in her chest, thrilled by his closeness. While her pride still wanted to say no and put him in his place, her determination weakened. She needed Mrs. Buchanan's support. And helping her grandson redeem his reputation seemed to be part of the package. "Then I better see you at four o'clock tomorrow afternoon for practice. I know your game is at noon and it won't take four hours. There will be no acceptable excuse if you miss practice."

The man dared to grin at her as if all was forgiven.

And her heart dared to long to do just that.

Bea started to shake her head, but Mrs. Buchanan's carriage arrived at that moment, and a flurry of activity ensued. After saying their goodbyes, Emmett got his grandmother settled inside, then climbed in after her. Bea watched the vehicle disappear down the street with her stomach tightening into knots. She'd been so determined not to trust Emmett Worland, and now here she was forgiving him for all sorts of behavior.

Marjorie linked arms with Bea and pulled her into motion, heading north toward the train station that would take them back to her neighborhood. "Do you have some time this afternoon to sit and talk about this ball? Aileen and I came up with a few ideas, but I don't want to leave you out of the process. It's for your team, after all."

If only Mr. Kendall had said the same about the exhibition game, Bea wouldn't have been forced to agree to this event, which was entirely out of her element. "Marjorie, I don't know anything about a society ball. Decisions like the most fashionable gowns and the best flower arrangements elude me. You and Mrs. Buchanan should go ahead with whatever you think is best."

"Now, Bea. You'll never learn if you don't try. If you're going to run my department when I retire, you'll have to be able to handle occasions like this. Fundraising is part of the job. You'll have to get comfortable with social events and asking for money from those with more of it than they know what to do with."

So Bea ended up in the small parlor of Marjorie's second-floor apartment with a sheet of paper on the table next to her chair, writing down ideas for a ball. Marjorie consulted her own list, which she'd started when they first sat down, speaking without even looking up. "And what do you think about dessert? Ice cream? Cake, of course. Oh, I had the most delicious macaroons at the new Marshall Field's tearoom the other day, and it would be a delightful treat to have them at the ball."

Bea jumped from the tufted chair she'd been occupying and paced to the other side of the room. "I don't know, Marjorie. Why can't you make the decisions? I'm not qualified to do this."

Her friend dropped the list on top of the other notes she'd taken and joined Bea by the window. "You're usually one to face a challenge or new experience with confidence. Why are you so reluctant to participate this time?"

Bea had been asking herself that for the last two hours. "This isn't something I can learn by trying, like throwing a basketball or swinging a bat. There are rules, trends, expectations. None of which I have any idea about because I don't move in society circles. Any misstep will be gossip fodder for the rest of my career. I'm an umpire. I play sports. Nothing about a society ball fits any skill or knowledge I have."

"Is that all there is to it? It's nothing more than thinking you can't learn this?"

Marjorie was far too perceptive. Bea could see from Marjorie's eyes that she was not going to let the question go without a thorough answer. So Bea cleared her throat and forced the words out. "When I was young, I dreamed of parties and dancing and romance, like most girls do. But God gave me the ability to play sports and play them well. Since women are rarely allowed into the world of professional sports, much less invited, I've had to hold back the part of myself that wanted things like lovely gowns and romantic gestures in favor of showing that I'm strong and capable of working in a man's world. I worry now that if I give those longings any space in my life, I'll want things I'm simply not intended to have."

"Oh, my dear. Come here." Marjorie sat on the sofa next to the chairs they'd occupied earlier and patted the open space beside her.

Bea sank onto the plush cushion, uncertain how to feel about revealing her deepest feelings. As good a friend as Marjorie had been to her during her years in Chicago, sharing this much of herself still wasn't comfortable.

A soft smile accompanied Marjorie's understanding expression. "You know I've faced many of the same battles you have. I had to fight for my right to work at the college. Ten years ago, the men were much more resistant to letting a woman even be on the faculty, much less run the department. I gave up dreams of marriage and children long ago. But being strong enough to face the world alone never meant I had to deny my feminine side. It looks nothing like I thought it would when I was younger, but God has shaped the desires of my heart."

Thinking back on their years of friendship, it was clear Marjorie had succeeded in being her true self while remaining strong enough to face the hurdles life threw at her. Bea had often envied Marjorie's graceful yet practical style, her ability to maintain her feminine interests while also living in the male-dominated world of the college, and the way she moved easily through both the halls of higher education and the dance floors of society.

But that didn't mean Bea was capable of the same. "No, you've done well at being yourself even as you fight for women to be allowed where men don't want them. But I've never been as feminine as you to begin with. And I certainly didn't grow up in society as you did. I wouldn't know where to begin preparing for a ball like this."

A gleam lit Marjorie's eyes, and she thrust one finger into the air. "That's why you need me. I know exactly where to start when preparing for a ball."

Bea drew back in surprise. "And where is that?"

Marjorie broke out into a wide grin. That mischievous look did not bode well. "A shopping trip."

*It might have taken every ounce of strength Emmett possessed, but he'd pushed through the pain and dizziness for the last two weeks and made sure he attended every practice and game for the women's team, as well as playing the best he could for the Lincoln Parks.

But he was beginning to think he might not be able to do it all for much longer. The train rides to different colleges and city league fields for games were starting to wear on him, each one eliciting headaches of increasing intensity, not to mention the strain of trying to do his best for all the people who were depending on him. The symptoms had gotten bad enough that he often had to excuse himself to sit down for a few minutes, making the situation far more noticeable than he'd prefer.

While the women were warming up for a game against their rival, the University of Chicago, Emmett had escaped the view of the college's very expensive-looking baseball field by hiding in a stand of trees behind the home dugout. Despite taking several of the pain tablets, he struggled to stand up straight. But a glimpse of Bea walking across the field strengthened his resolve to push forward. He couldn't let her down. Not again.

In the weeks since she'd agreed to let him continue helping the team, she must have forgiven his disappearance at the exhibition game. She'd been pleasant during practices, relied on him during games, and had even smiled at him when she umpired for the Lincoln Parks.

It was impossible to consider disappointing her that way again. The state of his heart had become irrevocably tied to her happiness. He lived for those slight smiles that were all for him on the baseball field. With the charity ball happening the next night, he couldn't hurt her today and still expect her to want his company at the ball. And he desired nothing more than to be at her side while she enjoyed the party.

So Emmett drew several deep breaths and straightened his spine a little at a time. Once he had control again, he returned to the visiting team dugout in time to see the women taking the field.

The starting pitcher, Miss Harvey, paused at his side before she left the dugout. "Do you think we have a chance to win? This team beat us by a significant margin when we played them for our first game of the year."

Emmett offered a confident smile to bolster her. "I know you have a chance. Since the exhibition game, you've been striking out far more batters than you've allowed to hit. That's a vast improvement from when the season started. Get out there and show them how much better you are now than the last time they saw you."

Miss Harvey beamed and nodded, then headed out to the pitcher's mound with a bounce in her step.

Coming up next to Emmett, Bea rested her arms on top of the fence surrounding the field. "You've been good for our team, Emmett."

Her rare praise warmed every inch of Emmett's body, but he couldn't tell her that. Working with the women had been more beneficial for him than it had been for them. Learning the balance between supporting Bea's leadership and doing what he knew would help the team had taken some time. But once he had figured it out, Emmett found he enjoyed teaching the ladies the finer points of the game. It had become natural enough that he could imagine a future as a manager—after building a successful professional baseball career of his own, of course.

Bea's shoulder pressed against his, the contact bringing visions to Emmett's mind of entwining his fingers with hers and then tugging her close. He'd been dreaming of such things far more often in the last two weeks, but with the full knowledge that they could only remain daydreams. The uncertainty in his future and the reality that his every interaction with a woman would be scrutinized and judged by the entire city made the idea of pursuing Bea too risky. He would never forgive himself if he damaged her chance at achieving her dream.

Unaware of the turmoil in Emmett's heart, Bea graced him with one of those gentle smiles he craved. "They're playing so well, Emmett. I have to give you a little credit for that, whether you want to accept it or not."

There was a teasing lilt to her voice that took some practice to recognize, but now that he was aware of it, Emmett loved to hear it. "A little? I'll take any credit I can get." He let a grin tilt his lips up to show her his retort was in jest, as well.

Companionable silence hung between them as they stood side by side at the fence whenever Bea wasn't at first base. The teams were better matched in skill level than anyone might have expected. By the eighth inning, neither team had scored and Emmett began to fear they would have to go into extra innings. He was managing to hide it, but there was almost no chance he'd be able to withstand the headache for much longer.

When an opposing batter hit the ball solidly toward left field in the bottom of the inning, Bea tensed, straightening as she watched the sphere fly along with the players and spectators. Emmett, however, only watched Bea. While she seemed stoic upon first meeting, it turned out her expressions were quite telling. Interpreting them wasn't difficult if one knew what to look for. A faint twitch in her cheek proved she was clenching her jaw, and the slight wrinkle of her brow revealed her concern that the Western outfielders wouldn't stop the ball fast enough and the other team would score.

When Luella Stevens caught the ball with ease and tossed it to get an out at third, Bea's shoulders drooped a mere inch, but it was enough that he read her relief. Emmett nudged her. "That play wouldn't have happened before you started working with her. She's improved a great deal."

A smile tugged at her lips as Bea elbowed him in the side. "Only because you freed up my time to help the outfielders more."

As much as he enjoyed trading compliments with her, Emmett had to stop talking for a few moments as a wave of dizziness caused sweat to break out on his brow. At least the hot, sunny summer day would disguise the reason for the dampness.

But wouldn't it be easier if she knew?

It wasn't the first time he'd had such an outlandish thought. It *was* getting harder to ignore them, though. A part of him longed to confide in her, to explain why he sometimes disappeared for a few minutes, why he'd left the exhibition game.

But if she knew, she might handle him as if he were damaged or fragile. Someone would notice her special treatment and wonder at the reason. He of all people knew how easily rumors could start, and if anyone thought he might be in less than perfect health, his career would be in jeopardy. Not to mention the damage to her spotless reputation if word got around that the lady umpire was showing preferential treatment toward Emmett Worland, famed womanizer of the Chicago City League.

He couldn't bear to fail now. Not when he'd worked so hard. Not when major league scouts were visiting games, looking for talented players to call up. The baseball field was the only place he'd ever felt accepted and at home. He couldn't lose his chance to keep playing.

The outfielders returned to the dugout, their chatter bringing Emmett's mind back to the game. He watched as Bea rallied the women, bolstering their confidence before heading to her spot next to first base.

Miss Thorn was their first batter up in the ninth inning. With no runs scored yet, Emmett hardly dared to hope that she would hit the ball, but she did look determined. She lined her feet up in the grooves that were worn into the dirt next to home plate. She angled the bat up past her shoulder. She adjusted her stance a few times. Then she leaned into her swing as the opposing pitcher released the ball.

The crack of the bat connecting with the ball echoed across the field. The entire dugout watched with bated breath as the ball sailed toward the outfield and Miss Thorn ran as fast as she could toward first base. To everyone's surprise, the center fielder missed the ball, and it rolled to the fence, sending the outfielders scrambling.

Miss Thorn made it all the way to third base before the ball was returned to the infield while the entire Western team jumped to their feet and shouted encouragement. The mood in the dugout shifted palpably. Emmett grinned at the women lined up on the bench despite the pain in his head. "There you go, ladies. Miss Thorn got you started. Now help her bring it home."

The next Western batter hit the ball only hard enough to reach the shortstop. That woman threw the ball in a perfect arc to first base in time to get the batter out, but the play allowed Miss Thorn to run hard and slide into home, earning a run. The Western College team erupted in cheers.

The opposing pitcher got herself together and struck out the next two Western batters. It felt as if the entire field and all the spectators held their breaths through the final half of the last inning. Confirming Emmett's confidence in her, Miss Harvey pitched one of the best innings he'd seen from her yet, getting three outs in quick succession to leave the Western team with their first win of the season.

The stands emptied while Emmett helped Bea and the women gather their equipment. As a group, they walked two blocks to the train station to ride back to the eastern side of town. Emmett snagged the seat next to Bea before anyone else could. She glanced up at him and smiled so brightly it could have lit a baseball field enough to play in the middle of the darkest night.

The loose hairs framing her face and cheeks pink from the sun made such a charming picture that he forgot himself for a moment. Before he could stop them, the words that had been on the tip of his tongue for two weeks slipped out, even though he knew they shouldn't. "Bea, could I escort you to the ball tomorrow night?"

Her expression sobered and she bit her bottom lip. "Oh, Emmett, I don't think that would be appropriate. I'll still be umpiring games for your team for the rest of the season. If any accusation of me having romantic inclinations toward you were to spread..."

She trailed off, but Emmett knew she was right before she even started speaking. It had been reckless of him to take the chance. Impulsive. He had his own reputation and secret to guard. If only his chest would loosen and his throat relax so he could swallow. "You're right, of course. I do hope you'll allow me a dance, though."

She softened, leaning closer until their shoulders pressed together again. Her nearness was almost worth the sting of rejection. "I wouldn't dream of denying you one."

CHAPTER 13

Bea fluffed the skirt of the gown Marjorie had helped her purchase, but she was nearly ready to take it off and find something less conspicuous. "It has a train, for goodness' sake. I can't spend the entire evening in this. I'll trip. I'll get tangled in it and knock over an entire table of food or fall into the mayor and spill punch on his very expensive jacket."

Smoothing a few tendrils of Bea's hair back into the loose pompadour they'd fashioned, Marjorie chuckled. "You will not. You're one of the most dexterous women I know. If you can jump or duck to avoid a baseball hurtling toward you faster than a runaway horse, you can walk around a ballroom with a train and not cause mass damage."

Taking another look at herself in the tall mirror in Marjorie's guest room, where she'd been invited to dress for the evening, Bea had to admit the effect of the gown was unexpectedly lovely. She was swathed in brilliant blue satin covered with a soft layer of silver tulle. The gown cinched at her waist with a lovely sash embroidered in black thread, and billowing lace sleeves created a fashionable silhouette.

If only she could do it justice.

For two weeks, while the older women planned and arranged, Bea had tried to involve herself. She'd learned more about chic supper choices and which flowers set the right tone for a ball than she'd ever dreamed possible.

But learning how to plan a charity ball wasn't the hard part. She'd always been a quick study with facts. Roses were better than daisies for the centerpieces. A common cake wouldn't do. What she couldn't grasp was how she was going to behave perfectly the entire night without making a fool of herself. There was so much she still *didn't* know about how to act around the rich that she was certain to make some unintended faux pas that shocked and horrified a ballroom full of guests from the highest echelons of society.

Turning to Marjorie before tears of worry could spring to her eyes again, Bea tried to unclench her fists. "Am I ready?"

Marjorie's face softened into a motherly smile as she placed her hands on Bea's bare shoulders. "You look stunning. Be yourself. Don't worry about impressing certain people or doing just the right thing. Aileen and I will take care of encouraging donors. You dance with the gentlemen. Talk to people. Have fun."

Bea's throat nearly closed up. Marjorie was trying to be encouraging, but dancing and making small talk were far more worrisome for Bea than the other woman could imagine. She was committed to this now, though, so she fixed a smile on her face and let a deep breath fortify her as they left Marjorie's apartment and climbed into the hired carriage that awaited them outside.

The ball was being held in the reception room at the Chicago Woman's Athletic Club, which Mrs. Buchanan had declared was the only suitable place for the occasion. The first three floors of the Michigan Avenue building had been converted into a gymnasium with a running gallery surrounding it, a library, tea rooms, a swimming pool, Turkish baths, and even bowling alleys. Mrs. Phillip Armour, the founder of the club, had strived to ensure the country's first women's athletic club was a paragon of modern respectability. The club's popularity proved she'd succeeded.

When two footmen pulled open the wide double doors of the reception room for Bea and Marjorie, Bea's breath caught, this time in delight. While the space was beautiful to begin with, the club members had transformed it into a magnificent wonderland. Fabric draped the corners of the room, and the electric lights gave off a warm, bright glow, making the fine dishes and silver sparkle. But the most breathtaking element was the flowers that were *everywhere*. Bea was relatively certain large sprays of them had even been nailed onto the walls.

Marjorie was immediately caught up by one of the young women who'd helped put the event together, gasping something about a problem with the punch in a panicked tone. With a distracted wave toward Bea, Marjorie followed the woman into the crowd, their departure leaving Bea standing by the doors with no idea what to do next.

Within a few moments, a strong hand cupped her elbow. Bea turned, relieved when she saw Emmett and not a strange gentleman whom she'd have to ask to kindly unhand her. His eyes—the same blue as a delicate forget-me-not—warmed when he looked over her attire, sending a flutter of butterflies cascading through her stomach. "You are breathtaking, Bea. My grandmother will be quite impressed."

The rock in her chest started to dissolve at his words and admiring expression. "Should I go say hello to her? I'm afraid I'm not sure of all the etiquette here."

Stepping back, he held out his crooked arm with a half bow. "Allow me to escort you, then. I happen to have been to more of these events than any man would like and am an expert at what's expected. Stick with me, and I'll sneak you hints when you need them."

The idea of spending the next few hours on Emmett's arm was not at all unappealing. Bea rested her hand in the bend of his elbow, and he led her across the room, steering her around and through the throngs of attendees. The crowd was a great deal larger than she would have guessed. "I'm amazed there are so many people here. Your grandmother is a determined woman, but how did she do this? It's a fundraiser for a mediocre women's college baseball team most of these people have probably never heard of."

Emmett's grimace was not the response she'd expected. "She's more than determined. All of society is afraid of her. Not one of them would dare to miss an event she planned and sanctioned. It seems they all brought any acquaintances they could dig up, as well."

Whether or not the methods were questionable, Bea appreciated Mrs. Buchanan's habit of getting things done. "This is going to bring so many opportunities to the team."

When Emmett's gaze locked on her, his expression soft, awareness shot through Bea. Her breath quickened and she looked away. As much as she appreciated his help and company, wasn't this the exact situation she'd spent half the summer trying to avoid?

They reached the spot at the front of the room where Mrs. Buchanan was holding court, surrounded by guests flocking to make their presence known to her. Bea was thankful for Emmett, who pushed his way through the crowd to reach his grandmother's side, allowing Bea to follow in his wake. The older woman nodded at Emmett but beamed when she saw Bea. "My dear, Marjorie did an excellent job with you. That gown was the perfect choice. The effect is stunning."

Bea's heart warmed, although the same sentiment had meant a great deal more coming from Emmett. She couldn't help peeking in his direction, finding him still staring at her. It was all she could do to keep breathing as his expression—now more heated than before—sent tendrils of longing through her.

For the years while she'd focused on building her career, Bea had disciplined herself to ignore any hints of wanting anything else in her life. She'd missed her family but had turned that loneliness into hours spent practicing various sports. Any time she longed for companionship, she went to the campus gymnasium and interacted with those who were like-minded. She'd developed friendships with women like Marjorie. Yes, on occasion, she'd found herself watching a mother with young children at a baseball game and experienced a pang of desire for a family of her own. Or imagined herself in the place of a young couple on campus walking arm in arm with adoring expressions. Once reality sank back in, those moments only ever served to remind her how unsuitable the selfish, arrogant men around her would be as potential husbands.

But Emmett...as much as she wanted to place him in the same box as the other players she knew, Bea couldn't do so any longer. He wasn't like them, no matter what the newspapers claimed. He'd proven himself to be kind and compassionate, caring toward those around him, even selfless. It couldn't be easy for him to let a woman tell him what to do on the baseball field, but he accepted his place as her assistant manager with grace. He treated her with respect and as an equal.

And her heart had noticed all of it.

Bea turned away from his searching eyes and forced her attention toward the guests vying to get Mrs. Buchanan's approval. Just because Emmett was different than she'd expected didn't mean she had any reason to start imagining things she could never have. All the other women who worked at the college had quit when they married. Perhaps they chose to focus on their husbands and future children. Perhaps their husbands asked it of them. Perhaps the chancellor or board of regents convinced them to do so.

The reasons didn't matter. In the end, if she wanted to join the staff and stay there long enough to build a professional physical education program, marriage was going to be an obstruction for some time to come. Maybe forever.

Not to mention that Emmett's presence was temporary. He would very soon move on to play for a major league team—she was sure of it. Even if he played for a Chicago team, the travel involved would make the chances of her seeing him far less likely. Her life would be on the Western College campus, and his would be wherever baseball took him.

Even as she tried to believe that was for the best, Bea found her heart crying out to God to help her resist the warm feelings building in her chest. She wasn't strong enough on her own to deny Emmett if he expressed romantic intentions toward her, no matter how much she wanted to accomplish her dreams. And judging by the look in his eyes, romantic intentions were looming as strongly in his mind as they were in hers.

∼

*E*mmett couldn't look away.

Bea was always beautiful. He saw it in every plane of her face, every word she spoke, every graceful movement. But usually, that beauty was overshadowed by the aloof facade she put on or undermined by her serviceable, practical wardrobe.

The sight of her standing out from the crowd of society women in the most intriguing gown he'd ever seen—with a soft vulnerability wreathing her face—would now be burned into his mind forever.

She was a vision.

And she had no idea.

There had been uncertainty in her eyes from the moment she walked in with Miss King, but he couldn't understand why. She shone among the other women in the room. She had every reason to be completely confident in herself. He'd seen her adapt to situations most ladies would never dream of even going near. A ballroom should be the least of her worries.

But she'd looked up at him with those magnificent brown eyes brimming with doubt, and nothing could have dragged him from her side.

The crush around his grandmother was getting more overwhelming by the second, so Emmett tapped Bea's arm. Her face tilted up toward his, and he had an impulse to lean down and press his lips to hers.

An absolutely foolish idea.

He pushed the thought as far into the recesses of his mind as possible. "Could I interest you in a dance?"

She nodded, thankfully unaware of the direction his imagination had turned. Taking her arm again, he pushed through the guests still waiting to try to impress his grandmother until finally, they emerged at the edge of the dance floor. Emmett slid one arm around Bea's back and took her hand with the other, then he moved in familiar steps as the music swelled around them.

They glided across the dance floor in silence for the first half of the song. Bea watched the people dancing and standing off to the sides, and Emmett watched her gaze darting around the room. Finally, she looked up to meet his eyes, and he smiled. "You dance beautifully. Someone taught you well."

A pretty flush spread across her cheeks, making her even more appealing, if such a thing was possible. "My mother insisted. She knew me well enough to say it was a physical activity like any sport and I should treat it as such. My youthful mind liked that comparison and made it into a competition with my sister."

Emmett chuckled, enchanted by the image of a younger Bea attempting to out-dance her sister. "And who won this competition?"

A smirk tilted her lips upward as her eyes lit with humor. "I did, of course. How could you doubt it?"

Air was suddenly impossible to come by. All humor left Emmett in a rush as his heartbeat increased to the kind of pace that usually accompanied a sprint around the bases. This woman was changing him in ways he never would have imagined.

And he enjoyed it very much.

Before he could respond, the music trailed off, and the dancers began shuffling partners for the next song. A young man appeared at Emmett's side, hand outstretched to Bea. She glanced at Emmett with a question in her eyes. He stepped back and offered a gallant bow. Not because he wanted to surrender her to another man, though. That, in fact, was the last thing he wanted to do.

But he needed a few moments to clear his mind and think about how he could continue a professional relationship with Bea when all he wanted to do was kiss her.

And oh, how he wanted to.

Instead, he stood at the side of the dance floor and watched her spin between couples with the young man leading her. She looked bored with her partner's chatter, which lifted his heart. At least she wasn't enjoying another man's company more than his.

The evening continued with Bea turning out to be a sought-after dance partner. She was hardly ever without a man at her side. And at some point, it all got to be a bit much for Emmett. He escaped the hot, crowded room and found a secluded chair in the lobby of the building.

He hadn't spent enough time alone when the sound of heels tapping on the stone stairs alerted him to another's presence. He tried to melt into the shadows of the hall, but the electric fixture on the wall cast too much light for that. Miss King appeared, heading straight toward him. "Emmett, there you are. Bea seems a bit lost without you."

"She was fine dancing with every other man present when I left." He cringed at how petty that sounded. As if he hadn't been the one to encourage her to dance with another partner. Would she have stayed at his side all night instead, if he'd asked?

Miss King shifted her feet in a way that looked as if they were sore, causing Emmett to rise and offer her the chair. She sank onto it with a sigh of relief. "She was very worried about this ball, you know. I felt terrible for leaving her as soon as we arrived, so I rushed back and saw the moment you found her in there. She came alive."

Emmett dropped his head back against the wall he was leaning against. "I didn't need to hear that," he mumbled, hoping the words were muffled enough Miss King wouldn't hear them.

Maddeningly, her laughter rang through the air. "Oh, Emmett, that's the whole point. You need to know the effect you have on her. I've never seen her react that way to anyone, certainly not a baseball player."

"Not even Aaron Kendall?"

Her jaw tightened and her eyes flashed. "No, definitely not Mr. Kendall. He runs right over her with no regard for her opinion or feelings. I'm glad she chose not to see him again."

He hadn't meant for the question about Mr. Kendall to slip out, but Miss King's immediate change in attitude made him glad it had. At least he wasn't the only one who disliked the man. And he could rest easy in the knowledge that Bea must have realized the truth about him too. She was as smart as he'd believed.

A few moments of silence stretched out before Miss King

sighed and pushed herself up from the chair with stiff movements. Emmett stepped forward to help her, but she waved him off. "I might be retiring soon, but I'm not a feeble matron yet. Only sore from all the preparations and dancing. I should return, though, and make sure there aren't any more problems that need solving. Go find Bea. I imagine she would appreciate a familiar face by this point."

Despite Miss King's certainty, Emmett doubted Bea had even noticed his absence. But he needed a glimpse of Bea like parched dirt needed rain. He searched the dance floor first, with no success. He slipped through the group of people still vying for his grandmother's attention, but she wasn't there. Finally, he caught a glimpse of the train of her blue and silver gown and made his way toward her.

As if summoned by his conversation with Miss King, Bea stood near a corner, pressed close to none other than Aaron Kendall. Emmett paused. Would she welcome his presence, after all? It looked like the sort of intimate moment he'd wanted to have with her himself.

Wasn't that all the more reason to step in?

But Mr. Kendall's rising voice caught his attention before he could decide what to do. "Miss Curran, I don't like it. You can't go behind my back like this."

Emmett couldn't hear Bea's response, but Mr. Kendall looked angry enough to spur Emmett into action. Marching over, he grabbed the other man's shoulder and pulled him away from Bea. "There's no need to speak to her like that, Kendall."

Mr. Kendall's expression grew dark, his lips pressed into a tight line. "Get your hand off me. Miss Curran has undermined my efforts on her team's behalf, and I was discussing that with her. You have no business here."

Pushing himself between Mr. Kendall and Bea, Emmett reached his hand back toward her, relieved when she wrapped her fingers around his. He nudged her farther behind him as he backed away from Aaron. "That isn't the way a respectable man conducts business or treats a lady, and you know it. Leave her alone, or I'll go to the alumni association about your behavior. I happen to have a bit of sway with their most important member, so I have no doubt they'll take my words quite seriously."

Mr. Kendall's face turned ashen as Emmett's words registered. He backed up several steps but offered a parting shot directed at Bea. "Miss Curran, I'd take care if I were you. I've met a woman who was damaged by his wayward behavior. Miss Charlotte Ford would have a great deal to say to you if she saw the direction you're heading."

Then he spun on his heel, stomped across the room, and pushed through the doors without pausing. While the guests in his wake stared and whispered about what had happened, Emmett pulled Bea toward a side door he'd noticed while trying not to watch men flirt with her earlier.

As soon as the door closed behind them, Bea leaned against the wall of what he realized was the empty, darkened gymnasium. She drew several deep breaths, regaining her composure a bit more with each one. The cool air in the large space offered a welcome relief from the crowded reception room and the heated exchange they'd just endured. But it did nothing to cool the fire in Emmett's chest or relax his clenched fists. As much as he'd always wanted to believe he could leave his past behind him, it seemed he'd been terribly wrong. Mr. Kendall had thrown Charlotte's name at Bea like shooting a bullet from a gun. Her expression at the moment of impact had been just as painful to see.

Bea tilted her face back to look up at him, highlighted by the dim light of a single electric fixture across the room. Now there was vulnerability etched in every curve of her features rather than the confusion from Mr. Kendall's accusation. "Thank you for stepping in. He was being so unreasonable. I have no idea why a ball that had nothing to do with him made him that angry."

Emmett dropped back against the wall next to her, their shoulders pressed together, hands so close he could twitch his fingers and feel her soft skin. This was his chance to remind her that spending any more time with the other man would be a terrible idea. Dangerous, even, given the behavior he'd exhibited.

But instead, Emmett's mind was crowded with an overpowering urge to lean down and press his lips to hers. It had been on his mind all night, but now, alone in the dim light with the woman he'd come to care about intensely, all the reasons he'd had for not doing so fled, leaving him with the single, instinctual desire to show her how much she meant to him.

CHAPTER 14

Emmett didn't immediately respond to her thanks for saving her from Mr. Kendall, but Bea was rather distracted, anyway. He angled his body toward her, which placed his face so close that when she turned in response, she could see flecks of green in his blue eyes. Eyes that lowered to look at her lips for a moment before rising to meet her gaze again.

Bea swallowed hard. His brazen glance at her lips made her curious about what his would feel like. She'd never been kissed on the lips before, although several bolder men over the years had dared to kiss her hand or cheek even though she gave their advances no encouragement.

Now she couldn't help imagining Emmett being the first to really kiss her.

Unfortunately, Mr. Kendall had done more than simply irritate her with his aggression. His words churned in her mind, threatening to ruin the moment with the memory of how Emmett's face had paled at the mention of Miss Ford. What had she meant to him? Did she still hold a place in his heart?

And what had gone so wrong that an entire reputation had been formed for him based on it?

Emmett finally spoke, breaking into the endless questions rolling through her thoughts. "Aaron Kendall is the kind of man who takes a little power far too seriously. Since he's in a position to make decisions for the alumni association, he feels all fundraising should be done his way. He'll react that way to any efforts that don't revolve around him, and that's his only real objection to this ball. Because other than that, it's a very nice event and has drawn a good crowd. At a dollar per ticket, this night will pay for all the equipment the team could want."

Pushing aside all thoughts of Miss Ford and Mr. Kendall, Bea focused on that truth. She'd been so concerned about behaving the right way—about impressing the society guests inside—that she'd almost forgotten the purpose of all this. Her heart lightened with the reminder. "It is a success, isn't it? I'm glad the three of you talked me into this...now."

He caught her teasing tone and replied with a slow smile. As their eyes met again, he reached out and entwined his fingers with hers. His thumb slid back and forth across the back of her hand. Bea swallowed hard. Unlike when other players took liberties and touched her, Emmett's caress sent rivulets of warmth coursing over her skin. How nice it would be if he would keep doing that forever.

All too soon, though, the movement stopped as he spoke. "Bea, I know what you think of me. You've believed from the moment we met that I'm the flirtatious rake the papers have called me. I've been hopeful that I could prove the truth about myself to you, as well as to everyone watching me. But I'm not sure I'm succeeding. Because all I want to do right now is kiss you."

Bea's heart thumped so hard in her chest that she wondered if he could hear it. A rake wouldn't have spoken with such honesty, would he? The words were so genuine and raw. He couldn't have said the same to other women. To Miss Ford. Could he?

Then a response she never planned to say escaped her lips. "Then maybe you should."

The air between them grew heavy, leaving Bea feeling as though she couldn't draw a full breath. She couldn't look away from Emmett's warm gaze, either, instead standing frozen, waiting for his next move.

As her words sank in, he finally acted. Leaning forward, he closed the inches between their faces and pressed his lips to hers. They were warm and softer than she'd expected. Then he shifted to face her more and slid his arm around her waist, pulling her against him.

Bea lost all awareness of her surroundings. The entire world was only Emmett's lips on hers, his arm holding her, his hand resting on her back. If only the moment could last forever, she would be content.

But all too soon, he broke the contact of their lips. His arm remained around her, and they were still touching from chest to knees as he examined her face. "Bea..."

He seemed at a loss for words, another first. Bea gave in to the urge to run her fingers down his arm, feeling well-defined muscles through his formal coat. "That was lovely, Emmett."

If only that statement carried the full truth of what his kiss had felt like. But she was unable to put that into coherent speech, so the trite description would have to do.

Before she was ready, Emmett stepped back, separating them. When he ran his fingers through his hair, tousling the previously impeccable style, a chill ran through her. "Bea..." he repeated, a tortured expression twisting his face.

In an instant, the reality of what was happening crashed down on Bea's happiness.

He regretted kissing her.

She'd enjoyed the moment more than she ever would have

dreamed possible. His kiss had shifted her entire world. But here he was, about to apologize and rip away the shreds of warmth that still lingered for her. She didn't want to hear it, couldn't hear it. "Of course, you needn't worry that I expect anything to change because of one kiss. I still have goals for my career, and you have your reputation to think about. And kissing in the shadows at a fundraiser for the baseball team doesn't benefit either of those things. We can pretend it never happened."

He finally looked straight at her again, searching her face. Bea forced aside the part of her that screamed she shouldn't lie to him and made her expression as sincere as she could. No matter how good her acting was in that moment, though, she would have to put some space between them soon, or she would no longer be able to hold back the tears that threatened to fall.

Seeming to accept her charade, Emmett let his gaze linger a moment more before he gave one sharp nod. "Then we'll forget it."

Except she never would.

Bea accepted his outstretched arm to return to the ball, glad for the first time that there were so many people there to distract her. But before they got to the crowded areas of the reception room, there was one issue she couldn't let go of. She needed to hear what he would say. So she pulled him to a stop near the gymnasium door. "Emmett, tell me about Miss Ford."

From his side, she could see the way he blanched and his broad shoulders drooped. "It's in the past. I...I don't want to speak ill of a lady."

"Giving me some idea of what happened with her isn't besmirching her character. It seems everyone in Chicago except me already knows about it, anyway."

When he swung around to face her, there was such anguish in his eyes. He kept his voice low. "It's where all my trouble began. I was new to the experience of women paying attention to me because of baseball. I let a young woman kiss me after a game, and I knew at once that I'd made a mistake. It was impulsive and shouldn't have happened. But she wouldn't listen to me, wouldn't believe that I didn't feel the same way she did. And neither would anyone else once the papers reported it with our names. I tried to stay away from her, but it took me making a very public scene for her to finally see that I didn't return those feelings."

Bea tried to accept his explanation for what it was. But all she could think was that it sounded horribly similar to what had just happened between them. An impulsive moment. A kiss that he instantly regretted. Was she no better than that young woman who'd been swept off her feet by a handsome baseball player, imagining reciprocated feelings where they didn't exist?

Emmett started to move closer to Bea. Then, as if he realized all over again that being near her was a mistake, he immediately stepped back. He licked his lips, his gaze imploring her to understand. Whether that was referring to the situation with Miss Ford or their own, she wasn't sure. "I seem to always end up in improper situations. It's no wonder I can't prove to my grandmother that I didn't string anyone along."

That confirmed his feelings with a harsh blow to Bea's heart. She was now part of an improper situation he didn't want to be in. The kiss that had tilted her world on its axis was nothing but a regret to Emmett. With nothing left to say, she allowed him to walk with her back to the more crowded area next to the dance floor. But as soon as possible, she extricated herself from his side and found Marjorie, who was entertaining a group of acquaintances with a story about some of her students. It was both a relief to put space between herself and Emmett and torture not to be by his side, showing just how much of a fool she was.

Once Marjorie was done with her tale and the conversation had moved on to another topic, she leaned close to whisper to Bea. "Aileen wanted to see you. She looked very excited about whatever she had to say. Shall we go together?"

Bea nodded, then followed Marjorie to the spot Mrs. Buchanan still occupied, although at least it was quieter around her now. As Marjorie had claimed, the older woman lit up with enthusiasm when she spotted Bea. "Ah, Miss Curran. Please come close. I had the most marvelous idea."

Moving to her side, Bea prayed it had nothing to do with Emmett. How she was going to continue spending time with him at baseball practice and games was already eluding her. She couldn't possibly stand to have him present in more of her life after what had happened.

Mrs. Buchanan's expression bordered on gleeful as she began telling Bea her idea. "I believe it would benefit your career to be more involved with the Woman's Athletic Club. The club is as much about making the right connections as the enjoyment of sports, you know. And you could use a few advantageous associations."

"That's a fine idea, Mrs. Buchanan. But I'm afraid I don't earn enough to join an exclusive club of that nature. Especially since I'll be ending my umpire career when this season is through."

Mrs. Buchanan waved her hand in dismissal of Bea's argument. "Of course not. That's why it occurred to me to become your sponsor. I'll pay your dues and recommend you for membership."

"You would do that for me?"

The older woman nodded as if it was decided. "It would be my pleasure. We need young ladies like yourself to help us continue the club into the next generation. You're passionate about athletics, talented, smart, and driven to succeed. The perfect fit."

Having the positive regard of a woman like Aileen Montrose Buchanan had its benefits. Being part of such a club could only improve Bea's chances of securing funding for both her team and any needs her program at the college might have in the future. She was learning to put aside any personal pride and take advantage of an opportunity when it arose. "When you put it that way, I couldn't refuse. Thank you."

Looking completely satisfied with herself, Mrs. Buchanan patted Bea's hand. "Wonderful. I'll start the process and let you know when the membership committee wants to meet with you."

Bea tried to show the excitement that Mrs. Buchanan expected. It wasn't that Bea didn't feel it. The thrill was there, deep inside. But it was overshadowed completely by a glimpse of Emmett across the room, dancing with a beautiful young lady who obviously fit in better at a society function than Bea did.

With her heart aching, Bea had no choice but to stand and watch. Or try not to watch, which was what occupied her for the rest of the evening. But it was impossible to keep from catching sight of him now and then, often either talking to or dancing with one of the many lovely women in the room. It had taken him no time at all to recover from their clandestine kiss. Pain tore at her heart at that thought. Despite what she'd started to believe before that night, maybe he *was* the rake he was said to be. Maybe he'd worked all that time to trick her into thinking he was kind, generous, and supportive when all he wanted was another conquest.

And maybe she was a fool for still wishing he would come look at her that way again.

$\mathcal{E}$mmett did everything he could to avoid Bea for the rest of the ball, but every second away from her was torture.

Her miserable expression was visible from across the room, making him want nothing more than to run over, take her in his arms, and continue what he'd started in the gymnasium.

That kiss. The moments that would be imprinted in his brain and relived over and over. Her soft skin and lips. Her sweet smile when he'd lifted his head.

Why had he gone and ruined it?

The now ever-present pain in his head was why. Pausing for a moment in a concealed nook at the back of the room, Emmett pressed his hand to the tender spot, willing the pain to cease, wishing his repeated prayers for relief would be answered. In the moments after kissing Bea, all he'd been able to think about was what she would do when he had to reveal his illness to her. If they continued to grow closer, he would have to do so. And he could only imagine one way a strong, independent, ambitious woman could respond to a man who was about to lose his career and succumb to a simple injury. She would lose all respect for him.

In the best case, Bea might show kindness. She was a compassionate person. But it would always be laced with either pity for what he'd lost or fear for his life. In the worst case, she would dismiss him immediately, repulsed by his weakness and the likely failure of his baseball career.

He couldn't live with any of those scenarios.

And as if the awareness of his limited options wasn't bad enough, the image of Bea's distraught face when he'd had to explain Charlotte was burned into his mind.

Bea might have thought she was covering her feelings well, but he saw the moment her respect for him slipped, replaced by dismay. She'd listened to his story and returned to the same conclusion as everyone else. Emmett Worland was an irredeemable womanizer.

It was better for both of them if he kept his desires at bay and never repeated those moments he'd recklessly let himself have with Bea in his arms.

Even if doing so felt more likely to kill him than his injury.

∾

The days that followed the fundraiser ball took on a miserable routine. Emmett played and practiced baseball, pushing himself to continue through the pain and dizziness. He made certain to be at every practice and game for the women's team as well, refusing to let them or Bea suffer because of his problems. And every night, he begged God to keep him strong enough to deny his longing for Bea's company.

It had been two weeks, and being on the baseball field with her was still the most difficult time to keep his distance. He'd always understood why so many players thought they should try to gain the attention of the lady umpire when they saw her on the field. Passion radiated from her when a game was going on around her, and she was clearly at her most comfortable with herself in that environment.

The problem was that it was all Emmett could do not to be one of those players.

The shouts of his teammates taunting the opposing team's batter pulled Emmett's thoughts away from the beautiful woman behind him and back to the game he was pitching. Their opponents, the Negro League Leland Giants, were far too good for Emmett to be so distracted. They'd won over forty straight games in each of the last two seasons. And he'd heard excellent reports about the players they'd picked up in the off-season, including their new manager and pitcher, Rube Foster.

Emmett moved into his stance and then paused to take a

deep breath, letting the field settle around him and the anticipation build. The batter shifted back and forth, preparing for his swing. Emmett pulled his arm back to let the ball fly.

But a wave of dizziness hit him right before the release, causing him to falter as the ball left his hand. He gasped at both the way the world spun around him and at how far askew the ball went. The entire field and stadium of spectators watched in shock as the ball tumbled, falling to the ground twenty feet from home plate.

The batter was the first to gather his wits. Jumping back from the plate, he waved wildly to his teammates. Emmett swiveled to see the runner on second sprinting to third with his eyes locked on home plate.

Realizing what was happening, Boot leaped up from his catcher's crouch, lunging for the ball. But his valiant effort wasn't enough. The runner slid across the plate a single second before Boot reached out and touched him with the ball.

Bea's voice trembled as she called from behind Emmett, "Safe!"

The crowd roared, the boos and grumbles of Lincoln Parks' fans mingling with the cheers of the Giants' fans. When jeers reached his ears, Emmett's chest tightened. He yanked his cap off and ran a hand through his hair, an excuse to compose himself. As he plopped the cap back on his head, he risked a glance at Bea.

Sure enough, worry widened her eyes. "Emmett, is everything all right?"

They were only five feet away from each other, so he could keep his voice low enough that none of the other men would hear. "I'm fine. Everyone has a bad throw now and then."

"That wasn't just a fluke throw. You looked as though you were about to fall to the ground. And you're pale as can be now."

He'd have to do a better job of hiding the symptoms if they

were going to be this bad. She looked ready to pull him off the field, and if he made another mistake like that, Jet would be too. "Nothing's wrong. It was an unfortunate error."

Emmett turned his back before she had time to respond. Facing the batter again, he forced his body through the motions of the perfect pitch, breathing easier when the ball went past the bat exactly where he'd been aiming it. It landed in Boot's heavy catcher's glove with a satisfying *thunk*.

He managed to repeat solid pitches enough times to end the inning without another run. But he returned to the dugout to see Jet frowning, his arms crossed as he waited for Emmett. "What was that, Worland?"

At least Jet would be easier to convince than Bea. As long as his players were performing how they should be, he didn't usually pry into their personal lives. "I was off balance, and it affected that one throw. Won't happen again. You saw the rest of those pitches. They were perfect."

"But safe. It isn't like you to risk a win by throwing easy pitches. I'm putting the new kid in for the rest of this game."

Emmett's heart plunged to his feet. "You don't have to do that. I'll step up." He tried not to sound desperate, but he could hear the panic in his voice as well as Jet could.

Jet shook his head, sticking a wad of chew deep into his cheek before responding. "Just take a break. It's not permanent. You'll be starting again next time."

There was no use in arguing. It would only irritate Jet and raise the chances Emmett wouldn't start next time, after all. So he dropped onto the bench with his teammates and watched the rest of the game in silence, never once letting himself look in Bea's direction. He couldn't bear to see pity or revulsion in her eyes.

Back in the locker room, no one was happy about the loss they ended up with. Emmett tried to keep to himself in a corner, certain the others would all blame him.

Sure enough, Hank barged in after the rest of the players and strode straight over to Emmett. "What's wrong with you, Worland?"

Emmett pushed away the thick finger Hank jabbed toward his chest. "Don't blame me. I got taken out of the game. You had the rest of it to fix my one mistake."

Hank's face turned so red, it was almost purple. His eyes bulged. "That was more than a mistake. Something is wrong with you. We've all seen how distracted you are. It's that lady umpire, isn't it? We know you're seeing her outside of games."

A chill washed over Emmett. If players started thinking Bea was treating him preferentially, the consequences for her would be much worse than they would be for him. "She doesn't consort with players. Haven't you seen how many men try and fail?"

"But none of the others let her boss them around on a college baseball field."

The entire team had stilled, watching the drama unfold. Emmett could turn the tide of this conversation away from his failings and protect himself from losing more dignity in his teammates' eyes. But he would endure any ridicule to protect Bea's reputation and keep them from hurting her. "I can't deny that. It's my penance for the way I've treated other women. Learn from my mistakes and be more respectful."

Boot stepped up beside him, clapping Emmett on the shoulder with a wild laugh. "This fella's grandmama is punishing him for flirting with the ladies. Believe me, Miss Curran hates having him on the field with her. There's no love lost between those two."

The air in the room immediately relaxed. Hank glared at Emmett but stalked away without pushing the matter while most of the others chuckled amongst themselves about Emmett being henpecked by his grandmother and a lady umpire.

Emmett turned to Boot. "Thanks. You didn't have to make me look like that much of a fool, though."

Boot grinned and knelt to tie his worn boots. "You know I did. I like Miss Curran and don't want to see her fired any more than you do. Watch yourself so you don't go messing things up for her."

The words struck a chord in Emmett's heart. Boot spoke more truth than he realized. Emmett had been walking a very thin line between what he wished could happen and the reality of his life. He'd let it go so far that he'd even kissed her.

The memory of her face as they pulled apart after that kiss flashed in his mind. She'd been as awestruck by it as he had. She'd been vulnerable, open to caring for him. But that wasn't something that could happen. He couldn't let his desires destroy her reputation before she got a chance to follow her dream at the college. And he wouldn't lead her heart into feelings he might share but couldn't act on. Because of his condition, the only future he could offer a woman involved pain, struggle, and likely either a decline into poverty or an early death.

For her sake, he would have to let Bea hurt a bit now so she wouldn't be devastated later.

CHAPTER 15

Bea hated the way Emmett was acting.

In the weeks since the fundraiser, he'd been distant. At first, she'd wallowed in the hurt he'd caused at the ball. She'd compared herself to Miss Ford, feeling like a fool for thinking he had romantic intentions toward her.

But her grip on her emotions returned after a few days, and she realized her initial response was shrouded in lies she'd been telling herself. She'd seen the way he looked at her the moment after they separated, before reality returned and he decided it had been a mistake.

He'd enjoyed kissing her as much as she had him.

So it was only circumstances that brought regret to his features. It was chivalry that made him put deliberate emotional distance between them whenever they were in the same place. They both had reputations to protect, and he didn't want to repeat what had happened with Miss Ford.

But this wasn't the same situation, and chivalry wasn't a good enough reason for Bea anymore.

He'd pushed his way into her life against her will, and he

would need to have a better justification than what other people thought if he was going to vanish from it.

From her spot next to first base, Bea tried to concentrate on the flow of the game and how the girls were playing. But her gaze kept straying to Emmett, leaning against the fence by the dugout, down to his shirtsleeves in the August heat.

And if the sight of him was terribly distracting, the memory of his kiss was even worse.

Bea tried to turn her attention to Luella Stevens after she walked up to the plate, tapping one of their new bats against the ground a few times before getting into her stance. It was still difficult to believe how much money the ball had raised for the team, but the new matching uniforms and fresh bats, balls, and gloves were wonderful proof that Emmett had been right.

The equipment—and the knowledge that people in Chicago were willing to support them—had boosted the girls' confidence. They looked serious and ready to play in the uniforms they'd chosen—white blouses, navy ties, and shortened skirts with wide navy and white stripes that lent them the look of men's pinstripe uniforms. Along with Emmett's instruction, the elements had all combined to vault the team to a winning record with three weeks left in the season. Bea was so proud of them.

Glancing at the full stands, she couldn't help smiling. The college had started promoting the team, and that led to more spectators at their games. On a fine, clear day like this one, the seats were filled, and many more observers stood around the edges of the field to watch. The teams—both the Western College ladies and their opponents—thrived on the energy from all those fans, making for a thrilling game.

Once her team had secured another win and the players left the field, Bea took a moment to greet some of their spectators. With a genuine smile, she approached Mrs. Buchanan, who sat with several women Bea was starting to recognize as members of the athletic club. Mrs. Buchanan's brusque attitude might deter many from enjoying her company, but underneath, she was a lovely person, and Bea appreciated her support.

As soon as she was within earshot, Mrs. Buchanan waved Bea closer. "Miss Curran, come join us."

Bea took a spot at the end of the wooden bench, relieved to sit down for a few minutes after being on her feet for the entire two-hour game. "Thank you for coming to see the game, Mrs. Buchanan. And for bringing guests, as well."

Mrs. Buchanan offered a quick nod before getting to the point with a gleam in her eyes. "I received word from the membership committee at the club. They want you to come in and meet with them so they can get to know you. I'll send word about when you can stop by."

Four months ago, the moment would have filled Bea's heart to the brim with joy. Now it was bittersweet. She wanted to share the good news with Emmett, but he would likely remain as distant and unenthused as he'd been about everything recently.

This step could help the women's team in the future, though, as well as provide a source of support for any needs that arose if she took over Marjorie's post. The women she would meet at the club were the kind who could boost her career at the college. So she summoned a bright smile and tried to express enough excitement to match Mrs. Buchanan's.

Without quite meaning to, Bea shot a glance over her shoulder, her eyes seeking out Emmett. He and James were packing the bats into the canvas bags they stored them in, ready to return them to the athletic building. When she turned back to the women, she found only Mrs. Buchanan remained while the others walked over to talk to several of the Western players. The older woman's expression was far too shrewd for Bea's liking. "My grandson is having a rather difficult time right now, as I'm sure you noticed."

Would she reveal why he'd been so distant? Why he'd retreated from her so quickly after a kiss Bea knew he'd enjoyed? Why he refused to let her get close to him again?

Bea nodded, and they sat in silence for a few moments, watching the students who milled around the campus enjoying the fine weather. Mrs. Buchanan didn't offer anything more, but Bea couldn't let the moment pass without trying. "Is there anything I can do to help him? He's been such a benefit to the team, I would like to find a way to show my appreciation."

Several of Bea's players walking past stopping to great Mrs. Buchanan, who spoke with them briefly. While she did, Bea risked another glance behind her at the field but didn't see Emmett or James this time. They must have still been putting the equipment away in the athletic building.

The two women left, and Bea took the opportunity to ensure the conversation didn't veer away from Emmett. "Please, tell me what I can do for him. What would make the situation easier?"

Mrs. Buchanan's eyes shifted, the hedging unusual for a woman who tended to be blunt and shrewd. "I shouldn't have mentioned the subject. Don't feel you need to do anything. I'm sure he feels quite appreciated."

Bea leaned closer to her, trying to not plead too hard but desperate to know what was going on. "Are the hours spent with the team too much for him? The women have improved enough that he could stop by once a week to work on minor issues and that would be sufficient, rather than attending every practice and game."

A shadow fell over Bea, and she and Mrs. Buchanan both looked up to find Emmett standing over them. Bea's heart lurched at the way his eyes were blazing, and his brow furrowed as he glared at his grandmother. "You told her? I asked you not to reveal my condition, and you did, anyway? I was beginning to believe you might have more concern for me than I felt as a child, but I see I was wrong. Please stay out of my business from now on. And if that causes you to stop supporting me so I can play baseball, so be it."

Emmett strode past them, heading toward the road that ran through the campus. Mrs. Buchanan sputtered, trying to call his name and explain at the same time, resulting in a jumble of words. When Emmett didn't even glance back at them, she slumped back onto the bench and sighed. "Well, we made a mess of that, didn't we?"

"*We?* All I want is to know what's going on. You didn't have to be so secretive."

Mrs. Buchanan responded with a hard look at Bea, one eyebrow arched sharply and her lips pursed tight together. Any other time, it would likely have been quite intimidating, but Bea was so worried for Emmett that she would face any amount of disapproval from his grandmother if she could just know what was happening.

When Bea didn't back down, Mrs. Buchanan rose and held out her arm. "Walk with me. You saw how much it hurt him to believe I told you his secret, so I won't reveal it and make things worse. But I can tell you a bit about him."

Curiosity got the better of Bea, and she rose, taking the older woman's arm as they walked. As she tended to, Mrs. Buchanan got right to the point. "When Emmett's mother, my dear daughter Lucy, came to me and told me she was marrying Edward Worland, well, naturally, I was horrified. The man had hardly a penny to his name and no prospects at all. He wasn't even from Chicago but a Canadian, for goodness' sake."

Under normal circumstances, Bea might have giggled at Mrs. Buchanan's appalled tone, but she was far too interested in the story to risk interrupting. So she kept silent and let Mrs. Buchanan continue. "But Lucy had her heart set on him, so I relented. I was young and in love once, too, believe it or not. I still remember how it felt like the world ended every time Laurance and I were apart."

She paused as if memories played in her mind before squaring her shoulders and continuing. "But Lucy's choice wasn't as wise as mine. Edward left her to seek his fortune with a shipping company on the Great Lakes and was lost in a storm not long after. Of course, I didn't hold it against her but welcomed her home with open arms. Unfortunately, the grief weakened her, and Emmett's birth was difficult. Too difficult. I was so consumed by the pain after losing both my husband and my only child that I know I neglected Emmett for several years. Lucy was all I'd had for so long. I didn't know what to do without her."

Bea couldn't help herself, breaking in quietly. "But Emmett needed you. *You* were all *he* had."

When Mrs. Buchanan glanced over, the sheen of tears in her eyes drew an ache in Bea's heart. "By the time I realized that, I had no idea how to connect with the boy he'd grown into. He was all wild energy and impetuous adventures all the time. It was wrong, but I allowed myself to believe he was better off being raised by the staff."

Emmett's frustration with his grandmother, the way he held her at arm's length, made more sense in that light. He'd never known his grandmother as a family member, only seeing a distant, aloof benefactor instead of someone who loved him. "It's not too late to bridge that gap and build a relationship with him now. There's plenty of time."

A single tear escaped the older woman's eyes and ran down her wrinkled cheek. Mrs. Buchanan swiped it away. "We never know that for sure. I'm doing all I can to prove to him that I care and will continue to as long as the Lord gives me that chance. But I can't count on unlimited time."

It sounded very much like the sort of thing an aging person might say as they looked back on their life and thought about how little time they might have left. But Bea got the distinct impression that she wasn't talking about herself. An uneasy knot formed in her stomach. Combined with Emmett's mention of a condition, the words were a confirmation that she was right to worry. Bea didn't quite grasp what it all meant, but she had a sinking feeling that the truth could change her future when she finally learned it.

～

*E*mmett had planned on not appearing for his standing weekly lunch with his grandmother. But after attending the Sunday morning church service with her and listening to a very good sermon on forgiveness, it had been impossible to follow through on the impulse. No matter how betrayed he felt, her actions were nothing compared to the treachery Jesus had faced. And if Jesus could forgive people who had put him to death, Emmett would do his best to forgive his grandmother.

But that didn't mean he wasn't still upset. The way Bea had been trying to lessen his time on the field—as if he wasn't strong enough to help anymore—said everything he needed to know about what she thought of him now. It was good that he'd already seen reason and separated himself from Bea since their kiss at the ball because it would have been that much more painful to do so now if he hadn't.

Not that it wasn't already heart-rending to stay away from her.

The table in the large dining room was empty, much to Emmett's surprise. He and Grandmother usually sat together at the head of it, even if silence tended to fill the rest of the room. But today, the butler, Hugh, gestured Emmett into the drawing room.

There, a smaller table had been moved from the library and

contained two place settings of Grandmother's favorite china and several serving platters steaming with fragrant ham and flaky meat pies, one of Emmett's favorite foods, along with vegetables and bread.

He froze in the doorway, looking around the room and trying to comprehend what was happening. It was their typical Sunday lunch fare, but he'd never seen his grandmother eat a meal in the drawing room. Ever.

From her seat in one of the two chairs, Grandmother waved him in. "I know what you're thinking, Emmett. It's all over your face. This isn't a practical joke. It's high time we grew closer, and that isn't going to happen in a stuffy, oversized dining room. Please, sit down and eat with me."

Still not sure he understood her purpose, he made his way to the table and sat down, sliding the expensive linen napkin onto his lap by habit. Grandmother leaned across the table and reached out a hand to him, which he reluctantly took in his. "Would you give thanks for our meal, please?"

Another change. Usually she recited a solemn, rote prayer over their meals together, one that hardly meant anything because they'd both heard it so often. Emmett bowed his head and spoke a brief, genuine prayer of thanks, something he never would have felt comfortable doing until these last few months. If nothing else good came from his injury, at least he had rediscovered his faith.

Once he was finished, his grandmother immediately gestured to one of the footmen—a new one Emmett was unfamiliar with—who came forward and started serving food onto their plates. "While we eat, Emmett, I want to explain this to you a bit more. I know you're upset with me for what you believe happened at the college game on Wednesday. But I assure you, it wasn't what you think."

Anger burned in his chest at her bold lie, but Emmett tried to muster a God-honoring response instead of letting his feelings run loose. "Then what was it? Because it appeared to be you and Bea discussing my ability to continue helping her team without my input. The only way that would have come up is if my health was in question."

Undeterred by the hints of temper that leaked out in his words, Grandmother calmly spread butter on a roll before looking up at him. "While I did start the conversation by mentioning that you've had some things on your mind recently, Miss Curran had already noticed that you haven't been yourself. It was her concern that spending so much time with her team has stretched you too thin. She thought if she asked less of you, that might lighten your load and let you enjoy your life a bit more."

Emmett searched her face for any sign of deception, but she looked and sounded completely sincere. The angry heat inside him fizzled out, replaced by both warmth at Bea's worry for him and discomfort that he was the cause of her feeling that way. "So she doesn't know about my injury?"

Grandmother paused with her fork in the air and shot him a meaningful look. "She does not. But I think that should change."

"What good would it do for me to tell her? She pities me enough as it is. Even without knowing why, she was looking for ways to make adjustments for me, to oblige my weakness." The thought sent a spike of panic through Emmett.

"Maybe it wouldn't improve your situation, but it can't hurt for you to have someone else who would support you. Miss Curran is invested in your life. There's no pity, only sincere caring. She's the sort of woman who would help you pursue the best for your future, whether that involves playing baseball or not."

Before she even finished, Emmett was shaking his head. "No. I can't tell anyone. It would be admitting to inevitable failure. And I refuse to fail." Emmett clamped his mouth shut after the words slid out without his permission.

Grandmother's eyes widened, then her features settled into an understanding expression. "I'm certain that response is my fault. I know how I must have seemed throughout your childhood. You must have believed I didn't care about you unless I could show you off. Emmett, I didn't set up this lunch simply to explain what happened with Miss Curran. I also want to apologize, and now seems as good a time as any."

In all his years growing up in her home, Emmett had never heard his grandmother apologize. The mere idea froze him in his tracks.

She set down her fork and dabbed her lips with her napkin before placing it on the table. "I've known for many years that I didn't do the right things when you were young. There's so much I wish I could change about your upbringing. I don't believe your mother would have been very happy with me."

The mention of his mother brought a pall to the room. To his surprise, a sniffle from his generally unemotional grandmother broke through the silence before she drew a breath and continued. "I was wrong to leave you alone so often. And wrong to be so demanding. I know you needed love and acceptance from me, and I didn't provide that. I'm sorry and I hope you'll forgive me. But please, don't let my failure lead you to believe all women are the same. Miss Curran is a much better woman than I am. She would never reject you over an illness, even if it does end your career."

Emmett couldn't wrap his mind around the words. But something in his heart released, allowing him to reach across the table and take her hand again. "I forgive you. You've always tried in your own way to show you care. It was just hard for me to see for quite some time."

She responded with another sniffle and the warmest smile he'd ever received from her. His injury was most definitely not a good thing, but now he was seeing good coming from it in several areas of his life. He'd spent hours questioning why God had cursed him with these symptoms when his career was on the verge of success, but maybe there were good reasons, after all.

They returned to their meal, this time with the atmosphere feeling more comfortable than usual. Emmett even tried making small talk, pointing out interesting things he'd seen at the church service that morning. For possibly the first time, he returned to his room after a meal with his grandmother feeling that he'd enjoyed being with her.

But as much as her apology and being able to forgive her lightened his spirit, it was her words about Bea that stuck with him for days. A deep part of him longed to tell her the truth, especially now that she knew there was something he'd been keeping from her, anyway. He went so far as to plan out what he might say to her. But his resolve always wavered when his mind returned to one persistent question.

Was he strong enough to face Bea's rejection if she didn't care about him the way he hoped?

CHAPTER 16

$\mathcal{B}$ea sat in one of the chairs that were pushed against the wall to make space for a large conference table in a room almost too small for it. Did the board of regents enjoy making visitors feel unwelcome in the space where they held their meetings, or was it a coincidence that they were always scheduled in this tight room?

A little discomfort would not get the best of her, though. This meeting was for the board to review the budget for every department for the upcoming school year. The board members read requests from each department in turn. Any staff member in attendance could then stand and discuss the requests with the board, so it was rather surprising more weren't there.

Then again, sitting through the drone of financial details about departments that had nothing to do with you was enough to bring a person to tears of boredom. And when it was combined with the rising heat in the stuffy room, it wasn't hard to see why many chose to send their requests in writing.

But Bea was prepared to show that, as part of the college, she would take an active role in planning for the future. Although her possible employment in Marjorie's place wouldn't be reviewed until later in the fall, Bea was still able to attend the meetings since she was employed as a team manager.

So she made her best effort to appear attentive through all the tedious details.

Mr. Willis, the chancellor, leaned back in his chair, eliciting a squeal from the worn wood. Many of the other men shifted, several stretching, one fanning himself with a sheaf of papers. Finally, Mr. Willis straightened and shuffled to the next page in his stack. "Physical training department, including the men's and women's gymnasium programs. Page eighteen."

Bea perked up, a knot forming in her stomach. It was time. She'd prepared for three days for this meeting. She'd practiced her requests with Marjorie, who she wished was there to offer a supportive smile. But when a schedule conflict had arisen for Marjorie, they'd agreed that Bea could do this on her own, to show the men in charge that she was capable and confident.

If only she could feel a bit of those qualities now.

The board worked through requests from the men's side of the department. Then it was time for the women's.

Bea swallowed hard as Mr. Willis read several written requests from Mr. Turner, the gymnasium director, regarding allowing more time for the women's use of the facilities. Then he sent a glance around the room, settling on Bea when he saw the other three staff members present had nothing to do with physical education. "And do we have any staff requests?"

Rising from her seat, Bea cleared her throat. But she hadn't pushed out a single word when the familiar voice of Aaron Kendall cut through the room. "I have a request. Or rather, a concern. On behalf of the alumni who financially support this fine institution."

Spinning, she saw him lounging in an insolent pose in the open doorway. As the board members craned their necks to see who had spoken, Mr. Kendall sauntered into the room, taking his time.

Mr. Willis waved one hand. "Well, go on, Mr. Kendall. We have much left to cover."

Mr. Kendall slid a glance her way, appearing to be aware that he'd stopped her from speaking. Had he done it on purpose? Her pulse pumped hard in her ears. Mr. Kendall had been quite angry with her at the ball, but that had been a month ago. She hadn't seen him since, and he hadn't tried to contact her again. She'd let herself believe Emmett had put him in his place.

But she was wrong. He'd been biding his time.

With her heart in her throat, Bea listened as Mr. Kendall finally explained himself. "The young lady over there, Miss Beatrice Curran, is employed by the college as the manager for the women's baseball team. She's also been making plans to apply for the position of head of the women's physical training upon Miss Marjorie King's upcoming retirement."

Every head in the room swiveled to look at Bea. She forced her chin up and offered the most confident smile she could manage, although it might appear arrogant instead when Mr. Kendall got to whatever point he intended to make.

The men looked back at Mr. Kendall as he continued. "I've been working with Miss Curran this summer to raise money for the women's baseball team to supplement what the college budget has allowed. And this has brought grave concerns to my mind over her suitability as a full-time member of the college staff."

Bea's heart plummeted, and she longed to wipe away the sweat beading along her collar. Mr. Kendall had indeed come to ruin this for her.

Mr. Willis regarded Bea once again, then turned back to Mr. Kendall. "Enlighten us, already. What concerns do you have, and why have you brought them now, when we're not even discussing her employment?"

Mr. Kendall nodded with a serious expression. "I bring this up now because she's here to make requests on Miss King's behalf, and I thought it prudent that you fine gentlemen know her...character faults...before coming to any decisions about her vision for the physical training program."

Bea's chest burned and her heart raced. It was all she could do to remain seated while waiting to see what exactly he was accusing her of. But jumping up and shouting at him like a hysterical female wouldn't help these men to trust her word over Mr. Kendall's. So she gripped the edges of the wooden chair until her fingernails nearly splintered in an effort to stay where she was while Mr. Kendall went on.

"As for my concerns, you know training our gentle female students is a high calling, one that should only be undertaken by those who are of impeccable moral character. Miss King has been an excellent example to our delicate ladies for many years. Miss Curran, however, spends her time playing baseball with men. In public, where she's viewed by large numbers of spectators." Mr. Kendall paused, letting the words sink in as if they had the most devious implications.

Bea couldn't help herself. She surged from the hard seat and raised her voice so she could be heard by every ear in the room. "If I might defend myself, I don't play men's baseball. I am employed as an umpire for the Chicago City League, which is an upstanding semi-professional league that does not tolerate uncouth behavior any more than this fine institution would. I disclosed my status with the league before my employment as the women's baseball manager was approved, and it was not an issue for anyone at that time."

Several men at the table nodded as if her words put all concerns to rest.

But Mr. Kendall wasn't finished. "That may be true, but it

doesn't explain Miss Curran's penchant for spending time alone with single men. She's even gone so far as to seek out my company late in the evening in the empty dining hall. And she was recently seen sneaking out a side door at a fundraiser for the women's team with a man to whom she is not related."

The burning in her chest exploded. Bea gasped. "Mr. Kendall, you know none of that is true. I never sought you out. You planned that dinner."

For the first time, he turned to face her. "But didn't you disappear from the ball with Emmett Worland, a pitcher with a well-known reputation for abusing the affections of young ladies?"

Silence blanketed the room, heavier even than the stifling heat. Bea couldn't catch her breath. That moment outside the ball with Emmett had not only burst her unrealized dreams, but now it threatened to take away the opportunity she'd been chasing her entire career.

As she tried to find words to defend herself and Emmett, Mr. Willis took away the opportunity. He stood, that infernal chair grating out a creak that echoed off the high ceiling and started a headache pulsing in Bea's skull. "Mr. Kendall, I appreciate your desire to protect our female students. This board will consider Miss Curran's character at a later time. The women's baseball season is almost over, and her status as Miss King's successor isn't up for debate yet. Now, we'll take a ten-minute break and return to discuss the law department."

The men stood and began leaving the room.

Mr. Willis turned to Bea before he left. "Miss Curran, please be aware that Mr. Kendall is correct. We consider the well-being of our students above anything else. The staff who influence them must be upstanding and moral beyond a doubt. I'm not concerned about your job as an umpire, but as I warned you earlier this summer, we'll be keeping an eye on your... extracurricular activities."

With that caution hanging in the air, Mr. Willis joined his colleagues as they left the room. Bea swung around to confront Mr. Kendall, only to find the coward had disappeared while her attention was occupied.

With no other plans for the day and a huge weight on her shoulders, Bea retreated to the one place she was most comfortable—the baseball field. No teams were practicing right then, so she slid onto the bench in the home team's dugout and buried her face in her hands, too angry to cry.

The stillness of the campus on a hot afternoon was calming, along with the gentle lapping of Lake Michigan's waters against the shore not far from the field. The cries of seagulls split the air now and then, a sound she usually enjoyed after growing up in Iowa as far from a large body of water as possible.

But today, the beauty around her didn't soothe the ache in her heart. She was on the verge of losing everything she'd planned for since leaving home at sixteen to become an umpire.

Before she was ready to face anyone, feet shuffling in the dirt on the field alerted her to an approaching presence. Emmett came through the gate onto the field, the sight of him causing a tingle to race across her skin. He slid off his jacket and hung it over the fence, leaving him in a plaid vest and white shirt. Bea drank in the sight of him, so strong and sure of himself.

He hadn't noticed her, so she watched in silence as he walked to the pitcher's mound. He went through the familiar motions of his pitch, holding the ball in front of him, glancing around as if checking the field for players stealing bases, winding up, and taking a wide step forward as he released an imaginary ball toward home plate.

Despite the terrible day, Bea had to smile. He reminded her of the boys she often saw at the City League fields, playing pretend baseball by themselves or with friends as they watched their heroes in the real game.

Her heart warmed, but he'd been so angry the last time she'd seen him. Would he listen to her if she explained what had happened? And would he ever feel comfortable enough to trust her with the truth of what was going on in his life?

From the pitcher's mound, a movement in the home dugout caught Emmett's eye. He turned, startled to find Bea sitting in the shadows. He froze. Had she seen his childish antics?

The decision to visit Western College after the Lincoln Parks' practice hadn't been conscious. There had been enough time to go home for a while before he needed to be at the field. But he'd ended up on the campus baseball diamond as if drawn to the place he felt closest to Bea.

Now that he knew his grandmother hadn't revealed the truth, figuring out how to repair the damage he'd caused to his relationship with Bea had been weighing on his mind. He wasn't well-versed in the language of flowers, but he had a feeling there wasn't one that said "I'm sorry for jumping to conclusions and blaming you for something you didn't do."

Bea saw him staring at her and raised her hand in a hesitant wave. Awareness of the terrible way he'd acted the last time he'd seen her came crashing down on Emmett once again. With or without flowers, she deserved an apology.

So he jogged across the field to join her in the shade. Her smile was sweet, if a little sad. Far kinder than he deserved. "Hello, Emmett. What brings you to the field today?"

He wiped the sweat from his forehead as he dropped onto the bench next to her. "James is meeting me here in a while, and we're going to sweep out these dugouts. The storm the other day flooded them, and it doesn't appear the men's team is going to clean them up, since they don't have any home games for another week yet." She nodded, but her forehead wrinkled as her eyebrows drew together. "And what are you doing here?"

Bea hesitated. Emmett inspected her face, letting her deep-brown eyes and wide, soft lips fill his awareness. Even weeks later, he could bring to mind the feel of those lips under his in a heartbeat. Her voice was soft when she finally responded. "I've had a bad day. The baseball field feels more like home sometimes than my room at the boarding house, so I came here."

Now he was the one to nod. He understood that sentiment completely. "Want to tell me about it?"

She shook her head, and silence fell between them.

Emmett used the next few moments to gather his thoughts —and courage—to do what he knew was right. "Bea, I owe you an apology."

Her gaze shot up to meet his, cautious and hesitant. "For what?"

"For the way I behaved after the women's game last week. My grandmother explained that you two were talking about how to lighten my load, not what's wrong with me. I appreciate that you cared enough to ask, and I'm sorry for getting angry."

She leaned back against the bench, releasing a breath. Had she been worried about his reaction to seeing her? She'd had every reason to be after the way he behaved. "I accept your apology. I do hope that you'll consider sharing what's going on, though. You know I'm on your side. I'd like to think we've become friends."

After the way he'd kissed her at the ball, hearing her call him a friend felt a bit like a punch in the gut. But he shoved that aside. He had no right to demand any more than her friendship. If his feelings had taken a leap right past that into something much deeper, well, that was his problem to handle.

Swallowing a lump that had formed in his throat, Emmett

pushed himself to continue with the words he'd rehearsed, despite the way his stomach knotted. "I've been considering that. And you're right." Bea leaned forward, her eyes locked on him. Emmett had to look away. Otherwise, he would get lost in them and not say what he needed to. "Last year, a hit from an opponent's batter struck me right on the head. Knocked me out for a minute. But that's part of the game, so I didn't think much of it. I had a headache for a few days, then everything was fine."

Struggling to continue, Emmett stood and paced the length of the dugout as he spoke, giving his nervous energy an outlet. "In spring training, I started getting headaches again. Then came the dizzy spells. Those two things have been getting worse ever since. In the past few weeks, I started having trouble seeing clearly across the field. There have been a few days when I was so tired, I could hardly pull myself out of bed, without any reason to be."

He risked a glance at her, praying he wouldn't see revulsion or pity. Instead, those beautiful brown eyes reflected unshed tears. Tears, on his behalf. Not one hint that she thought less of him for his weakness. But would it come when she understood the gravity of his situation?

Turning to pace in the opposite direction, he finished the confession in a rush. "You remember the day I left the women's game without telling anyone? I went to the campus doctor because I had such a bad headache that I didn't think I'd be able to remain upright. He said I'm suffering delayed symptoms of a concussion from that hit. There's...there's no way to cure it. He thinks it will get bad enough that I'll have to quit baseball. Some men have lost their minds and been institutionalized. No matter what, my time in baseball is limited."

With the truth hanging between them, Emmett couldn't bring himself to look at her. After hearing it all, she had to be feeling horror, disgust, disappointment.

But a sniffle from her direction caused his gaze to swing to her unbidden. She watched him with lips parted, her entire face reflecting not disgust, but compassion. Concern. Possibly even something akin to love. Only love for a friend, of course.

A tear slid down her cheek, and all the emotions he'd kept locked up in his heart for the last few months broke free. Emmett lunged to her side and wrapped his arms around her. Bea returned the embrace without hesitation. She was strong from years of athletic pursuits, so her arms around his waist squeezed tight, almost enough to be uncomfortable, but he didn't care. Having her in his arms again was worth it.

They sat like that for longer than he could keep track of as she cried a little—he might have teared up a bit himself—and they both let the moment exist.

Eventually, Bea pulled back, raising one hand to press against his cheek. "Emmett, I'm so sorry you've been going through this on your own. I wish you would have told me from the start."

It did seem foolish now, seeing the understanding and concern in her every move. Why had he been so sure she would reject or pity him? "I'm glad you know now. But I have to ask you to keep it a secret. I want to play baseball as long as possible, and you know as well as I do that if there's any evidence that a player's health could cause issues on the field, managers don't hesitate to replace them."

"Of course. But you must promise me you'll take care of yourself. There must be ways to make it manageable, even if it can't be cured. You should see another doctor. Or two or three. I've heard there are doctors now who study athletes and treat health problems specific to sports. Perhaps you could see one of them."

Emmett's heart lifted, any remnants of worry over her reaction gone. Impulsively, he reached out and once again wrapped her in an embrace. But this time, she stiffened and didn't return it.

When he released her, Bea rose and walked to the fence, glancing around the campus as if concerned they might have been seen. Her suspicious reaction reminded him that he wasn't the only one who'd taken refuge at the field.

"Bea, what made your day so bad that you were out here hiding?"

She leaned both arms on the fence, her back still to him. "I attended the board of regents' budget meeting today. I was hoping to give them information on why we should expand beyond offering classes, to get them thinking about the possibility of starting a certificate program. I know I'm not in charge of the department, but I felt it wouldn't hurt to lay some groundwork. Even if I'm not hired, the program would still benefit the school and the students."

Her tone made the results of the meeting clear without him needing to ask. "I take it they didn't like that idea?"

She turned to face him, both hands thrown up in a gesture of surrender. "I didn't get an opportunity to bring it up. Aaron Kendall was there."

Emmett's stomach clenched. It didn't even matter what she said next. Mr. Kendall had ruined it for her, and it was because Emmett had confronted him at the ball. "What did he do?"

"He accused me of immoral behavior. Because we…disappeared during the ball. Now the board will be watching my every move, examining my conduct. I already felt the weight of being under their scrutiny as the women's manager, but it's so much worse now that they've been given reason to wonder about me."

Which meant Emmett would have to guard himself around her at all times. He'd already brought this on her by giving in to his anger toward Mr. Kendall at the ball and by taking her out of the reception room. He couldn't make it worse by doing anything else that would bring her character into question. "Then prove him wrong. You're an upstanding woman and a fine example to the ladies on your team. It won't be hard for you to show that."

The corners of her lips lifted, and Emmett's heart responded in kind. He did enjoy making her smile.

"Thank you for that encouragement. I needed it."

An idea sprang up, one that had been stirring in the back of his mind for some time, but now it might make her smile even more. "I've been thinking, perhaps we should reward the women for their hard work this season with a special outing. A celebration of all they've accomplished."

Sure enough, her lips tilted up farther, and a curious sparkle appeared in her eyes. "What kind of outing?"

"We could take them to a Chicago Cubs game. Most of them, as much as they love baseball, have probably never attended a major league game. I've only been to one myself."

A sparkle chased away the worry in her eyes, and her entire face brightened. "That's a wonderful idea. We have enough money left from the fundraiser to cover part of the cost if the girls can each help pay a bit. I know they'd love it."

A responding grin stretched across his face. "Or I could ask Grandmother to cover it as a gift to the team. She loves those ladies now, so I'm sure she'd be delighted. Maybe she'll even join us."

It was strange to hear those words coming from his own mouth. At the beginning of the season, Emmett never would have believed how much his life could shift in a few months. Yes, his health was a heavy weight dragging him down at times. But he'd also found a great deal of joy in helping the women's team, in using his limited talents for fundraising, in growing closer to Bea. His relationship with his grandmother had changed for the better.

Maybe the outlook for his future wasn't so grievous, after all.

CHAPTER 17

*B*ea marveled at the size of the West Side Grounds ballpark, the Chicago Cubs' home field. As the group from Western College made their way through the crowd to emerge in the stands, they all paused to look up at the upper deck, supported by wooden beams that soared above their heads. It was a cathedral honoring the game they loved. Bea never wanted to leave.

Behind her, Emmett placed one hand on Bea's shoulder as he leaned forward to speak in her ear, his head brushing her velvet-trimmed felt hat. "I heard more than twelve thousand people attend these games. Can you imagine being on the field with all those eyes on you? It's so many more than we get at our games."

A delicious tremor vibrated up and down her spine at his nearness. While most of the women started looking for seats in the lower bleachers, the three closest to Bea—Anna, Luella, and Ruby—exchanged knowing looks and giggled with their heads together. As soon as Emmett moved away from her, Bea turned to them, hands on her hips. "And what is so amusing?"

Ruby smirked. "Mr. Worland is awfully comfortable

touching you. We thought a wedding invitation might be in our future."

Bea had to fight to breathe through the visceral longing that hit her chest as hard as a solid hit to the outfield. Since she and Emmett had spoken at the college field several weeks ago, there had been a definite shift in their relationship. Reminding herself of the reasons why she needed to keep a wall between them was getting more difficult all the time, and reactions like she was experiencing now weren't helping. "Never mind that. We're friends and there's no wedding awaiting us. Now go find your seats."

They did as she asked, but the way Anna glanced back over her shoulder, examining Bea with thoughtful eyes from under the brim of her beribboned straw sailor hat, made Bea think they weren't ready to forget the matter.

That theory was confirmed when she reached the clump of seats the ladies had chosen. Mrs. Buchanan, who had decided to join them as Emmett had hoped, was seated at the end of one row. Much like Bea, the girls had taken a liking to Mrs. Buchanan, and several were bargaining with each other to decide who would get to sit nearest her. The glow that brought to the older woman's cheeks warmed Bea as much as the blazing August sun.

The problem was the rest of the women. In the short moment she spent standing on the steps observing them, Bea could tell they were finagling the seating order to get an empty spot opened up next to Emmett. He was unaware of their meddling, occupied with watching the Cubs and the New York Giants warming up on the field. As soon as everything was arranged how they wanted, Mary Beth waved to Bea, her voice syrupy sweet. "Oh, Miss Curran, your seat is right here."

Now it was mortification that warmed Bea, causing sweat to break out along her back and around the collar of her white linen shirtwaist. She paused, giving herself a moment to admire the way Emmett's suit outlined the muscles all his physical activity had built up. The idea of sitting so close to him for the duration of the game was both terribly appealing and distinctly a bad idea. But if she was going to avoid any more attention than Mary Beth was already bringing her, Bea would have to acquiesce.

After sliding past several seated girls to reach the empty spot, Bea pushed the wooden folding seat down so she could lower herself onto it. Emmett looked up from the field and greeted her with the warmest smile, his eyes glowing. Was it from the love of baseball…or her presence beside him?

Bea placed that thought into the back corner of her mind. It wasn't because of her, and it wouldn't matter if it was. They both had far too many reasons not to act on any bond they might feel toward each other.

Very important reasons.

If only she could remember what any of them were.

Bea shifted in the seat, trying not to lean against Emmett too much, which was quite difficult thanks to the narrow confines. "They try to fit too many people into these stands, don't they?"

Emmett shrugged. "Ticket sales pay the players and provide maintenance for the field and the stadium. The more tickets sold, the more baseball there is for fans like us. I'll take that trade."

A pang of irritability hit Bea, and she tugged at the sleeve cuffs that had grown uncomfortable. "I know how it works, Emmett. But it's too crowded in such heat."

And now she sounded like a petulant child. Bea clamped her lips shut as Emmett raised an eyebrow at her. But he didn't have time to further embarrass her before several of the girls decided to squeeze past them. Bea stopped them. "Where are you going?"

"To the concession stand. Please say it's all right."

"I hear they have Cracker Jack. I've always wanted to try it, Miss Curran."

Emmett nudged her side with his elbow. "I was going to visit the stand myself before the game starts, so I'll accompany them. Can I get you some?"

Bea hesitated. How would that appear, Emmett buying her treats at a ball game while they sat crushed together like a young couple?

Oh, but his piercing blue eyes were too convincing. She nodded, and the girls giggled in delight, rushing off arm in arm. Emmett stayed back a moment, gaze still locked on Bea. "Do you want anything else to go with it? A Coca-Cola, perhaps?"

She was as giddy as the girls at the prospect, but feeling off-balance because of him made her too defiant to show it. "A drink wouldn't hurt, I suppose."

He grinned as he walked away. But when a glance back over his shoulder allowed him to catch her watching his exit, Bea whipped around to face the field, unwanted flutters tickling her stomach.

Her emotions were getting entirely out of hand.

There must have been a line at the concession stand because Emmett and the girls didn't return until the first inning had already gotten underway. The three of them were laden with as much food as they could carry. It took a few minutes of standing in the aisle, reaching over people, and discussing who wanted what before they got everything passed out and Emmett rejoined Bea, handing her a wax box of Cracker Jack and a chilled glass bottle of Coca-Cola.

Once Bea had everything settled in her lap, she glanced at Emmett to thank him. But the words died on her lips as she noticed a thick sheen of perspiration on his face and deep creases on his forehead. "Emmett, is something wrong?" She lowered her voice, all too aware of how close others were to them. "Are you experiencing any symptoms?"

He offered one curt nod in response, pressing his fingers to his temple.

A headache, then. Bea tapped his hand, which clutched a glass bottle like hers. "Drink something. The heat might be making it worse."

She examined his movements as he tipped his head back and guzzled a long drink. He licked his lips and pressed his shoulder against hers. "That's a bit better. I can manage for a while. You're right—I'm probably a little overheated."

But his words didn't soothe the worry that rose like a snake to squeeze the air out of her chest. Now that she knew of his struggle, she was desperate to help him manage it as well as hide it from others. But she also found herself worrying about him all the time.

A roar went up from the crowd, and Bea turned her attention to the field in time to see Jimmy Sheckard sliding across home plate in a cloud of dust, giving the Cubs the first run of the game. He was soon followed by Frank Schulte, leaving the Cubs up by two for several innings.

As the game progressed, Bea watched Emmett almost as much as the action on the field, searching for signs that he needed help. But she also tried to keep an eye on the ladies. Most of them watched the game with interest, warming Bea's heart. Several were more concerned with the many young men shooting intrigued glances at their group—understandable since it was rare to see so many single young women present at a game. But even if romance was stronger in some minds than athletic pursuits, Bea knew women were often just as interested in and excited by sports as men. There was no reason they shouldn't be allowed to play those sports as well as watch them.

And that was Bea's goal, after all. Her purpose. Seeing these college girls enjoying the game increased her longing to be part of creating a generation of teachers who could go out and encourage both boys *and girls* to participate in sports. Having spent time at the Woman's Athletic Club with other females who practiced various sports with enthusiasm and passion, nothing could dissuade her from being part of continuing this trend.

Not even falling in love?

Beside her, Emmett shifted, and his arm was now nearly around her waist. She tried to scoot a bit, to put space between them, but there was nowhere to go. Emmett caught her eye, still trying to smile, though he looked strained.

Bea's heart ached for him, and worry crowded back in. "Are you worse? Do you want to leave? I can escort the girls and your grandmother back to the college."

Emmett shook his head. His hand searched for hers, enfolding her fingers in the strong grip of a pitcher once he found them, sending a rush of flutters through her. "No, I don't want to miss this time with you."

At least, that's what her heart heard, although she couldn't be certain she hadn't made it up. At the same moment, the crowd again exploded with excited cheers. Another run for the Cubs. But Bea couldn't pull her gaze away from Emmett's to see who had scored.

Her breath came in shorter bursts as Emmett's nearness filled her awareness. Her mind screamed reminders about the purpose she'd just been dreaming of, but her heart wasn't listening. Why did she have to make this choice between Emmett and her future? Why did her reputation even have to matter? Why did her caring for him have to be anyone's business?

Deep in the back of her mind, though, reality niggled at her. Emmett had made no promises. He wasn't the person the rumor mongers had fabricated, but there was Miss Ford to consider. Another woman who had fallen in love with Emmett and been hurt by believing he cared for her too. He'd already turned away from Bea once because he regretted his actions with her. If Bea was seen like this with him again and word got back to the board of regents, there was no reason to believe Emmett would commit to her to save her reputation. He hadn't with Miss Ford.

Bea needed to get her wayward emotions under control. But was she capable of such a feat when his mere presence stole the reasons why right out of her mind?

~

The thundering pain in Emmett's head intensified, threatening to rip his skull apart when the crowd howled around them. It was only Bea's warm hand in his and sinking into her brown eyes that kept him from bending over and moaning in agony.

Did she have any idea that her presence was sometimes the one thing that helped him swim through this nightmare?

It was still getting worse. Every time he thought it couldn't, the next day found some new way to torment him. That morning, he'd started seeing strange lights floating in his vision. He knew they weren't really there, because it didn't matter where he looked or where he went, they remained. But it made watching the game much more difficult and much less enjoyable.

He was beginning to understand how a concussion could lead to insanity.

Was it only a matter of time before he reached that point, as others had before him?

Emmett muddled through the rest of the game, but it sapped all his strength. As he watched the victorious Cubs players leave the field, a pang of regret hit him hard. He'd often dreamed of playing on that very grass and dirt. But if he couldn't take the noise of the crowd while sitting in a seat, how would he ever be able to handle the pressure of being on the field during a tense game? How would he make it through a raucous victory celebration?

It was becoming all too clear that the campus doctor had been correct. Emmett's future in baseball was bleak unless these symptoms cleared on their own.

But at least he had Bea. Emmett peered over at her, and his heart soared when she met his stare with a small smile. Since revealing the truth to her, he'd begun to rely on her presence more and more. She was the bright spot in his days. While every game he pitched made him wonder if it would be his last, spending time with Bea was something he'd started to crave.

As the spectators began filing out of the stands, the large group of women drew more attention than when the game had been going on. When Emmett glanced behind him and noticed two young men had stopped on the stairs too close to the women seated on the end of the row, a flame of protectiveness lit in his stomach. The ladies held themselves stiffly, shifting in an effort to create more space while the standing men loomed over them. Emmett couldn't let their discomfort go unchecked.

Turning in his seat, Emmett raised his voice to get the intruders' attention. "Gentlemen, the ladies are here to enjoy their day, not to be harassed by you. Please move on."

One of the men straightened and took a step backward. But the other didn't budge, lifting an eyebrow as he glared at Emmett. "And who are you to say they aren't enjoying our company?"

Emmett stood, refusing to let the throbbing pain make him sway. "I'm their chaperone. I wouldn't be so heavy-handed as to tell them what to enjoy, but it's very clear to everyone here that you are making them uncomfortable. I'll ask you again, please go."

The man stepped away from Miss Stevens and pulled up to his full height. But both he and Emmett immediately realized that Emmett towered over him. The man slunk backward a few paces, hands coming up in front of him. "Fine, we'll go."

Emmett didn't move, standing guard until the two men were well out of sight. Then he looked around to see the entire team, Bea, and his grandmother all staring at him. "I'm sorry, was that too much? The women looked uncomfortable."

With a soft grin lighting her face, Bea put her hand on his arm. "It was the perfect thing to do. Thank you for watching out for us."

The women started tittering amongst themselves, making the tips of Emmett's ears burn. Didn't other men stand up for ladies? He shifted his weight to the other foot. "That's what I'm here for, isn't it?"

Looking down into Bea's lovely features, Emmett's breath caught at the warm emotion lurking in her eyes. "You're here because we like your company and you're a part of our team. Having a strong male companion is nice, but we enjoy you."

On impulse, Emmett grabbed Bea's hand again, tucking it into the crook of his elbow as he led the way through the stands and out of the stadium. Walking with Bea on his arm felt as good as any victory he'd ever earned on the field.

Outside, the group headed together toward the carriages Grandmother had hired for the day. She, of course, had her own there as well. Climbing into hers while the women found their seats, Grandmother waved Emmett over.

He leaned through the open window, marveling at how he no longer dreaded being summoned by her. "Thank you for doing this for the ladies, Grandmother. It was a good experience for them."

She nodded but didn't seem as pleased as he expected. "Emmett, I won't beat around the bush. No one could miss the closeness that's developing between you and Miss Curran. You haven't forgotten the purpose of helping her with this team, have you? You spent most of that game in a crowded stadium holding hands and whispering with the woman. You might not be as well-known as the players on the field, but what if some reporter happened to see you and kept track of your activities? We can't have a repeat of the Charlotte Ford situation."

A chill chased away every tendril of satisfaction from the fine afternoon, allowing his headache to take over. Emmett straightened. "I thought you were ready to drop this nonsense. I'm not the rake I might have seemed in the past, and I've tried to prove that to you. Can't you trust me when I tell you who I am?"

"Emmett, it's not you that I don't trust. It's those dratted reporters, always digging for stories, not caring if they're accurate as long as they're sensational. They'll take any small mistake and turn it into a life-ruining headline, and everyone will believe it."

"Spending time with Bea is not a mistake."

Grandmother reached out to pat his hand, but Emmett stepped back. She sighed, eyes brimming with regret. "I don't think so either. But you need to be certain of what you're doing, that's all. It's not only your reputation at stake but also Miss Curran's. Don't ruin her chance at the career she wants so much unless you're willing to promise her something better."

Without waiting for him to respond, she leaned back away from the window, tapping on the roof to signal to the driver she was ready. The vehicle lurched into motion, but Emmett stood rooted to the spot for several more minutes.

What exactly could he offer Bea that was better than running the women's gymnasium and building up the physical education program as she'd dreamed of for so long? Continuing to grow closer to him without any commitment between them would be scandalous enough to take the opportunity from her. His actions had already hurt her, as proven by the budget meeting disaster she'd told him about. But how could he ask her to marry him knowing the future that awaited him if these symptoms didn't resolve?

It wasn't his grandmother's expectations or even the press. He was the problem.

Climbing into a waiting carriage, Emmett found the women on the team had once again contrived to push him and Bea together. Miss Tucker was in the process of scooting from the spot next to Bea to the only other seat available, which Miss Sims seemed to have held for her. Just like in the stands, they might have thought they were being clever, but several of them were nervous gigglers and gave the entire thing away.

Nonetheless, Emmett took the spot. As the carriages lurched into motion one at a time, he tried not to lean into Bea, wishing they had the vehicle to themselves so they could talk more openly. "Did you enjoy the game? From what I was able to watch, the Cubs put on a good show."

"They did. It was excellent. It's no wonder their record is so impressive this year."

He nodded, allowing his head to dip closer to her because he couldn't help himself. "It's a shame Three Finger Brown wasn't pitching this time. He's a sight to behold. You've never seen a ball fly like it does out of his hand."

"I was also hoping to watch Frank Chance play. I've heard the combination of him with Tinker and Evers makes for unstoppable double plays. But I suppose he can't play every game while managing the team."

Bea's eyes shone with her passion for the game. Was she sad to leave it behind, even though expanding the physical education program meant so much to her? He'd never thought to ask. But what right did he have to pry into that sort of personal business now, when he had nothing to offer her for a future except the possibility of a husband in an asylum?

He had to do something to stop that horror from becoming a likelihood. "Bea, didn't you tell me you know the name of a doctor who might have some expertise in the area of my...situation?"

She seemed surprised by the sudden turn in the conversation, but she nodded, letting out a slow breath before speaking. "Yes, I'll write it down for you when we get to the college."

The prospect of facing more bad news was terrifying. But if there was any chance he could stop what was happening to him so he could pursue a future with Bea, he had to take it.

CHAPTER 18

Three days later, watching the last game of the women's baseball season was like watching an entirely different team compared to their first game. These women operated with the assurance of knowing what they should do. Their passion and confidence had soared in the days since they'd attended the Cubs game, and they hadn't stopped talking about details they'd noticed in the professionals' actions that Bea had no idea they'd been aware of. Now, Anna showed all the marks of being a standout pitcher. The team's batting had improved so much between May and August that Bea could hardly remember how bad it was before Emmett.

Before Emmett. That was now a delineating point in her life. There was the time before Emmett and the time after.

If only the after didn't have to include ever being without him, then it wouldn't be so alarming.

But Bea had a career to focus on. It would take every bit of her attention and effort. Starting the new degree program was important enough to warrant that from her. Emmett, as much as she now had to admit she cared for him, had given no indication that he intended to be anything more than a helper for her baseball team. A friend.

Yes, he'd kissed her. But then he'd immediately recoiled in regret. Bea had to be strong enough to face the truth. If she was going to take over Marjorie's position and expand it, she would have to keep herself free from entanglements.

As if to solidify that reality in her heart, Chancellor Willis himself was in attendance at the game. When she caught his eye while taking her place near first base at the bottom of the fifth inning, Bea nodded a greeting. The women were leading by two runs and were playing like a coordinated team. It was a good time for him to decide to take in a game.

Across the field, Emmett sat in the dugout. He'd seemed more at ease that morning when he and James had worked on the field than he had in some time. Was it a good day for his symptoms? Or was his condition improving on its own? An urge to pray for a miracle that would turn his health around hit her. She tried to tell herself she'd desire that healing for any of her friends. But the strength of her longing for this prayer to be answered made it impossible to ignore that her heart was in too deep.

Bea pulled her mind back to the game in time to see Beth Marie Thorn take her batting stance, hovering over home plate. She swung the bat a few times to get the feel of it, then took a deep breath and settled into position as Emmett had taught the batters. The opposing pitcher released her throw, and the ball sailed toward Beth Marie.

The crack of the ball connecting with the wooden bat brought every eye to attention. The ball headed toward the outfield, straight over the shortstop's head. Bea watched it while keeping track of Beth Marie's pace as she ran toward first base. Seeing the outfielders scrambling, Bea urged Beth Marie to keep going toward second. And thank goodness, the younger woman tagged the base with her foot before the ball got back to the infield.

The game continued in the same way until the Western College women emerged victorious in the ninth inning. The large crowd of spectators erupted in cheers as the women congratulated each other with delight. Bea even caught sight of Mr. Willis grinning from ear to ear. Her heart lifted. It must be a good sign if he was enjoying himself at the game. Maybe now he would be on Bea's side as she fought for the chance to expand the physical education program.

Once the visiting team left the field and Bea's team had celebrated and begun packing up their things, Bea headed to the stands to greet the spectators that remained. Sitting next to Mrs. Buchanan and several other ladies from the Woman's Athletic Club, Marjorie gave a pointed look toward Mr. Willis, as if to silently ask Bea if she'd seen him. Bea answered with a nod as she made her way toward the distinguished guest.

"Mr. Willis, I'm so glad you could make it to one of our games. And it was a good one to watch."

Rocking back on his heels, Mr. Willis beamed. "That was quite exciting. I haven't had much interest in baseball, but I might have to change that now."

Bea responded with her perkiest smile. "That's very good to hear, sir."

"I believe you were going to say something at our budget meeting a few weeks ago before you were interrupted. Would you like to share your request now?"

Heart thumping, Bea nodded, trying to remember all the things she'd intended to say. "Thank you for asking. As you're aware, I intend to apply to replace Miss King. If hired, I would love to discuss expanding the physical education department. I was hoping to give the board some information now to think about so we could be ready to implement changes for next school year."

"And why would we need to do that? The physical training program seems to serve the needs of the students fine now. We have the gymnasium with athletic offices and plenty of courses aimed at keeping the students active. What more could they need?"

Bea settled into her topic, feeling confident thanks to the genuine curiosity in his voice. "Yes, the program has been very beneficial for the Western students. And I think students at all levels should have the same access. Primary schools across the country are beginning to add physical education to their formal curriculum, along with recess and games at lunch. That means teachers need to be educated on how to use the most current, accurate, age-appropriate information and practices. I'm proposing we develop a degree program that would certify students who want to bring physical education to all schools."

Mr. Willis looked thoughtful as he stared across the baseball field. Bea followed his gaze to see Emmett and James hard at work cleaning up the dugouts and packing equipment. The chancellor turned back to her before she could pull her eyes away from Emmett. "That's an interesting proposal, Miss Curran, one I'd like to hear more about once you're installed in the department. But Mr. Kendall, despite his unsuitable approach, did have a legitimate concern. Our staff members— females especially—*must* maintain spotless reputations, or parents won't be comfortable sending their young ladies to be educated here. If you can stay far clear of any compromising situations, I'd like to see where you'll take the department."

With that, Mr. Willis tipped his hat to Marjorie and Mrs. Buchanan—sitting near enough that they heard everything— then nodded to Bea before he turned and left the field. Bea released a deep breath, letting her shoulders drop.

Marjorie rushed down from the top bench to grab Bea's hands. "That's an endorsement if I've ever heard one. It's such a relief that he won't hold Mr. Kendall's accusations against you."

Following more slowly, Mrs. Buchanan reached them in time to amend Marjorie's claim. "Ah, but he didn't make any promises. You know he'll still be watching for the slightest mistake."

Bea's cheeks heated as both women's gazes turned toward Emmett. "There will be no mistakes. I've managed to maintain the spotless reputation he mentioned for years while umpiring baseball games. I can continue to do so."

Majorie nodded, confidence radiating from her. But Mrs. Buchanan raised a skeptical eyebrow. Bea tried not to bristle at the unspoken insinuation. She could keep herself away from Emmett. It wouldn't be that difficult. After all, she'd spent the last few years fending off much more ardent suitors than he was. Emmett Worland showed no intention of pursuing her.

So there shouldn't be any problem with her avoiding entanglements.

Theoretically.

~

A week after the women's last game, Emmett walked through the hallway that ran along one side of the college gymnasium building at a brisk pace that matched his excitement for the news he had to share with Bea. He found her in Miss King's office, where one of the women from the team had told him to check when he'd arrived at the campus.

Standing in the frame of the open door, he paused to watch Bea, who hadn't noticed his approach. She sat at a desk that took up most of the floor space, with her head bent over what looked like a journal, the scholarly type that he had quite frankly never had a reason to pick up. Every so often, she reached out without even looking up to scribble on a notepad next to the journal. The soft pile of her dark hair was disheveled, as if she'd spent the morning digging through and engrossed in the rows of books that lined Miss King's shelves.

Emmett's heart hammered in his chest as he admired her delicate nose and the way her lips pressed together in a tight line of concentration. A soft white shirtwaist covered her shoulders, tempting his fingers to reach out and stroke the fabric, feeling the warmth of her skin through it.

With a shake of his head, Emmett pulled himself immediately from that line of thought. He rapped his knuckles on the doorframe he was leaning against. Bea's head shot up, eyes wide with alarm. He grinned as a pink flush tinged her cheeks. "I didn't mean to startle you. Miss Tucker told me you might be here."

Bea put down the pencil on top of the journal and rose from the wooden desk chair, arching her back to stretch it. "It's all right. I was so focused on this article that I didn't hear you. I'm gathering information to give the board if they're open to hearing about my hopes for the department. Please, come in."

The office wasn't very large, so it only took Emmett two steps to reach the desk. "I've come on an errand for my grandmother."

A teasing light appeared in Bea's eyes, her beauty when she was cheerful making Emmett's breath catch in his throat. "You run errands now? I'll have to remember that in the future."

Grinning, he held out the envelope Grandmother had entrusted to him that morning. "I do for you."

She came around the desk to take the envelope from his hand, holding his gaze for a long moment as if trying to figure out any double meaning underneath the words. His tone had turned far more serious than her teasing warranted, but he couldn't help it. He wouldn't deny the deeper implication that he would do anything for her. It was entirely true.

Sliding the paper from the envelope, Bea perched on the edge of the desk as she read. Emmett tried not to drum his fingers on the smooth wood while he waited. Grandmother had told him what the letter contained when she asked him to visit Bea in her place since she was feeling unwell. They were both sure the contents would make Bea happy.

And making her happy was becoming ever more important to him.

He knew the moment the words on the page sank in. Bea looked up at him as if for confirmation, her lips parted. "Does this mean...?"

"Yes. Not only is your membership now official, but the Chicago Woman's Athletic Club is offering regular donations to women's teams in all sports at Western College. They'll be your patronesses. Once you're the department head, you can ask them for anything you need, and they'll help you find the funds."

Bea's eyes returned to the paper, but it hung limp in her fingertips as she appeared to consider the impact of it. Finally, she turned to him with the widest grin he'd ever seen from her. "Thank you, Emmett. You've been more than just helpful to the baseball team. You've made it possible for us to grow the women's athletic program here in ways I never would have hoped for."

Her tone was so soft and awe-filled that his heart wrenched in his chest. Before he could think better of it, Emmett reached out to pull her into his arms. "I connected you to my grandmother. Everything else you earned with your brilliance."

Emmett soaked in the feeling of Bea in his arms, her cheek resting against his chest. Every thought faded from his mind except the memory of her kisses that night at the ball. The way she'd so sweetly responded to him, the complete trust in her eyes when he'd pulled back. Before he'd let her believe he regretted it.

Because no part of him could ever regret kissing Bea Curran.

In fact, he'd like very much to do it again.

Using his fingertips to grasp her chin and tilt her face toward him, he started to lean in to do just that. But Bea pushed against his chest before their lips met.

He released her immediately, as much as he didn't want to. Bea spun away from him and somehow managed to find enough space in the cramped office to pace. "We can't do this again, Emmett."

He'd made such a mess of it at the ball. But now everything had been put into perspective. He needed to make her see what he'd come to understand. "I know, Bea. I never meant to let you think I regretted kissing you. I most certainly didn't. I was afraid I couldn't offer you anything, that you would be horrified if you knew the truth. The headaches were getting worse, other symptoms were appearing all the time, and I was terrified to let you in. But now things are different. That's all under control."

Finally meeting his eyes again, she stopped mid-step. "Did the doctor I recommended help you?"

Nodding, Emmett gave in to the urge to be closer to her and followed her path to the window. "He gave me a different medicine for the symptoms. So far, everything is much more manageable. The dizziness and spots in my vision have completely disappeared."

Her lips lifted, taking his heart along with them. "That's so good to hear. Does he have a positive prognosis for your future?"

Emmett nodded again, reveling in the hope that had returned in recent days. "He does. He thinks we can get all the symptoms under control enough that I can continue to play. Provided I don't take any more hits to the head."

Her eyes lit up with humor at his jest. With his heart hammering in his chest, Emmett licked his dry lips. He couldn't let the moment slip away without trying to tell her how he felt. If his symptoms weren't going to keep him from playing baseball, it might be possible for them to have a future together. But could he convince her of that before they had no reason to see each other anymore?

Continuing with the playful tone he'd established, Emmett shot Bea a grin while he leaned against the window frame and reached for her hand. "Then perhaps you'd give this newly optimistic baseball player a chance to spend a little time with you. We don't have the excuse of the women's team anymore, but that doesn't mean—"

Before he could get to the part about his feelings, she shook her head and took a half step back, twisting her fingers together instead of letting him grasp them. "I'm happy about your health, Emmett. I am. But the chancellor was very clear the last time we spoke. I can't allow any scandal to damage my reputation. I can't have my name splashed across the papers like Miss Ford."

He suddenly couldn't draw enough air into his lungs. The hopefulness faded. She didn't take him any more seriously than any of the other baseball players she'd rebuffed over the years.

That truth settled over Emmett in the form of an ache that felt strong enough to bruise his chest. He'd been living in an imaginary world where Bea returned the feelings he could no longer deny. But in reality, she still saw him as the rake people had decided he was, not as a man who wanted to spend his life with her. Good enough to be her friend and helper, but not for her to love.

Stepping back, Emmett drew himself up straight, determined to walk out of the office with his dignity intact. "You're right, of course. We both have images to uphold. I've completed my errand, so I'll leave you to your work."

She called his name as Emmett strode from the room, but he didn't pause or turn back, pretending he didn't hear her. Outside the building, he finally stopped to collect himself, dropping back against the wall in a sheltered corner where he wouldn't be noticed. He pulled in several deep breaths, the stifling air doing nothing to help relax him.

Bea's rejection brought a pain to Emmett's heart that he'd never experienced before. The women who had tried to catch his attention in the past had never meant anything to him. They'd all been like Charlotte, pursuing a relationship they thought he wanted, not accepting that he didn't return that interest.

But Bea...her opinion of him was all that mattered. Everything—including his desire to play baseball—paled in comparison to the longing to have her in his life. He was now faced with wondering why God would allow him to grow so close to her when He didn't intend for them to be together.

His newly refreshed faith struggled under the weight of the doubts that sprang up, but one thing became perfectly clear in that shady corner of the campus.

Without meaning to, Emmett had lost his heart to Beatrice Curran.

CHAPTER 19

$\mathcal{B}$ea walked into the stadium with mixed emotions warring in her chest. It had been over a week since she'd had to reject Emmett's advances, and since the women's team was done playing, she hadn't seen him since he'd walked out of Marjorie's office. Part of her was excited to see him again at this game, had been looking forward to it since the moment he disappeared from her view.

But a larger part was terrified to look in his eyes and see whatever might lurk there. Would he be aloof? Angry? Hurt? He hadn't given her time to gauge his response before rushing from the office.

Her own reaction had been much easier to ascertain. All the days since had been terrible. She hated thinking about him but couldn't seem to stop. She longed to go back in time and let him hold her. What would have happened if she'd encouraged him to kiss her again, as she'd been dreaming of since the first time?

In that moment in the office, he'd been a temptation. The smooth, convincing tone of his voice and that playful, crooked grin had brought to mind all the headlines she'd read, all the things she'd heard about his way with women. It had reminded her that if Charlotte Ford could misunderstand his intentions, Bea might be unwittingly following the same path.

Surely, she'd made the right choice. Marjorie had sent in her resignation and submitted a recommendation for Bea to be her replacement. After speaking with Chancellor Willis at the women's last game, there was every reason to believe that she'd be hired.

As long as she could keep her emotions from clouding her judgment in the presence of Emmett Worland.

Bea dressed in her navy skirt and white shirtwaist in the small umpire's locker room. On her way down the hallway situated behind the stands like at most stadiums, she forced her thoughts toward the game ahead. There were only a few weeks left in the season and then she would be finished umpiring and would move on to the next chapter in her life. She wanted to end this career with the solid reputation she'd built intact. That meant clear thinking and flawless attention to the game.

And absolutely not allowing herself to be distracted by a certain charming, handsome pitcher.

Finding a spot to wait near the home dugout, Bea observed the players as they warmed up. The Lincoln Parks were playing the Blues, a team that trailed them in the standings by only two games. Without meaning for it to, her gaze slid across the field until she spotted Emmett's tall, athletic frame dressed in a pristine white-and-black pinstriped uniform. She made her best effort not to stare while he finished a few stretches and started warming up by tossing a ball back and forth with a teammate, but he was so nice to watch. Her traitorous heart thumped harder than it needed to, as if she'd taken a run around the bases instead of standing by the fence.

Keeping her mind clear was going to be more difficult than she'd imagined.

Before she could get herself under control, Emmett turned

and looked right at her. The timing was so perfect, she could imagine he'd felt her eyes locked on him. Even from across the field, she could feel the pain emanating from his expression. Then, without any acknowledgment of her presence, he turned away and continued warming up.

Hurt it was, then.

She was a little relieved that he cared enough to be wounded. But the agony of knowing she'd caused him pain outweighed it by far.

Was there any way she could make it up to him without compromising her future?

The team managers gathered their players into the dugouts for final encouragement and reminders. Bea took her preferred spot behind the pitcher's mound, waiting with a ridiculous amount of anticipation for the moment when Emmett would come out and stand less than ten feet from her.

As the visitors, the Lincoln Parks would bat first, meaning Emmett wouldn't be near her unless he got a hit and reached second base. Since he wasn't early in the batting order, it would likely be a while before Bea could try to get his attention.

Not that she'd planned on doing so, of course.

After an uneventful start, Emmett finally emerged from the dugout in the second half of the inning. Bea had to fight to take a full breath as he stalked across the field toward her. He refused to even glance her way, though, instead rotating his arm a few times while the first opposing batter took his practice swings. Bea tried to drown out the noise from the crowd, which was large that day as the end of the season approached. She had a job to do, and she would do it well, no matter what was going wrong in her life off the field.

Emmett struck out the first two batters, playing very much the same as the first time she'd seen him pitch, before the concussion symptoms affected him. The third batter got a solid hit and made it to first base. Bea called him safe, thankful for the chance to settle into the game and put her irrational emotions out of her mind for a while.

The game progressed without incident. There was a run by the Blues in the third inning. Then Hank Foreman from the Lincoln Parks scored in the fifth to tie the game. Bea loved games where the calls were non-controversial, and this one was that sort. Not one fan or player even grumbled about the outcome of a single play or call she made.

If only she could find a way to apologize to Emmett, it would be the perfect day.

But he never once looked her way. Finally, in the ninth inning, she decided she had to get his attention before the game was over. Otherwise, he'd escape the field in the usual mad crush afterward. And who knew when she'd run into him next? She couldn't visit him without raising questions about their relationship, and she couldn't leave their next meeting to chance. She would have to try now.

So when Emmett jogged across the field to the mound, she made an effort to get his attention before losing her nerve. "Emmett, I know you can hear me. Please listen for a moment."

He didn't look back, but she had to try again. "I'm sorry about what happened in Marjorie's office. I never thought it would hurt you. I thought..." She hesitated, not used to revealing her true emotions. "Well, I thought you only saw me as another dalliance."

Finally, he spun around, raising his arms as if calling for a time-out, which drew so much more attention than she'd wanted. With his eyes locked on her, he waved off his team-mates who were starting to run in from the outfield. He stopped at a respectable distance from her, but it was near enough for Bea's breathing to turn shallow. The entire time, his gaze never left hers. "You thought that of me? After all the time we spent together, all the things we shared, you believed I could be so deceitful?"

"No, not deceitful. Unsure, maybe? I don't know why I thought it, Emmett. I only know you've never spoken of a future for us or a willingness to commit to any woman, much less me. And I couldn't—can't—take the chance with my career at stake."

Emmett took one step closer to her, and Bea was aware of every eye in the stadium, all the attention that was on them. She straightened under the weight of not only that but the anger and pain in his expression, emotions that made his voice rough. "And you're willing to choose your career over the chance that I might have serious intentions this time? That I might care? Do I mean so little to you?"

The conversation wasn't going at all how she'd imagined. "That's not how it is, Emmett. I'm not choosing my career over you. I've worked for so long, and I'm close now, finally. I can't take a chance on a future that's not certain. Unless you want to tell me anything that would take away that hesitation...?"

Bea's cheeks burned. She hadn't intended to essentially ask him if he cared for her, but there was no way to take the words back now. Emmett stared at her, his gaze intense in a way she'd never experienced from him. He was upset, and she wasn't explaining her reasoning as well as she wanted to.

To make matters worse, the Lincoln Parks' manager chose that moment to run out onto the field and find out what was happening.

Emmett stepped back onto the mound, his gaze still never breaking from hers even while he assured Mr. Anders that everything was fine and they were returning to the game. Once the manager had returned to his spot by the dugout, Emmett finally turned back to face home plate without another word to Bea.

Her heart sank into the dirt at her feet. Now he was angry *and* hurt. She'd wanted to smooth over the situation and had somehow made it worse. How was she going to repair their relationship now?

And why was it so imperative that she did?

As the batter prepared his stance and Emmett lined himself up to pitch, Bea tried to return her focus to the work ahead. But now her confidence was shaken, and that didn't bode well for her ability to referee the game.

Emmett released the ball in a perfect throw that earned him the first strike of the inning. He followed it with several more until the batter was out. The second batter hit the ball and made it to first. The third got another hit, but it flew straight to the first baseman, his catch causing an immediate out. Bea spun around in time to call the runner from first safe at second.

Another hit followed, putting players on first base and third base with two outs. A strapping rookie stepped up to bat. Emmett took the signal from his catcher and released a beautiful fastball that might have thrown off many players, but not this young man. He swung the bat at the perfect moment to connect with the ball, sending it straight between the shortstop and second base and on out to center field.

The runner on third made his way to home plate, then whipped around to see the situation at second base. Unfortunately, a combination of excited Blues fans and grumbling Lincoln Parks spectators who all clearly thought the game was over after the run were flowing onto the field, making it impossible to continue.

Bea stood frozen in place as the runner who had been heading toward second base noticed the crowds on the field, and rather than completing the play by reaching second, started making his way back to the dugout without ever setting foot on the base. Bea attempted to get his attention, but the young player was cheering, following the crowd in thinking the Blues had won. That might be a career-ending mistake. If the ball somehow made it to second, he would be out, and the score would remain tied while his team left the field, thus forfeiting the game.

$$\sim$$

Despite his best efforts to focus, Bea's presence plagued Emmett the entire game. He couldn't help watching her when he was in the dugout. He felt her behind him at the pitcher's mound. So he was fully aware when she came to a standstill while the field gushed with spectators and the players began heading toward their dugouts. It only took a moment for him to grasp what had happened. The ball was still in play.

Frantic, he yelled to any of his teammates remaining on the field to get the ball to second. The ones closest to him caught on right away. Fred Reneau, who was still in his position at shortstop, ran a few steps and scooped up the ball, throwing it in one smooth motion as he came upright. Big Ben Barnes caught it at second base with his foot squarely, undeniably on the bag.

"He's out! The game is still a tie!" Bea's voice was a whisper compared to the din of the crowd, but enough people heard her to bring the immediate area to a standstill. As the word spread, a hush fell over the crowd. Emmett was close enough to see Bea swallow hard before repeating herself in a clear, authoritative voice. "The runner is out at second. No run is counted. The game remains a tie."

Pandemonium broke out, shouted repetitions of her words and anxious discussion swelling across the field as everyone tried to understand what was happening. Emmett glanced at Big Ben and gestured for him to stay where he was, one foot on base with the ball in his glove. No Lincoln Parks players moved while more spectators surged onto the field, many arguing with each other as the atmosphere grew heated.

The managers from both teams approached Bea, Jet giving Emmett a nod of approval as he passed. Emmett kept a close eye on the trio standing a few feet from him, trying to hear them but unable to. He gave up and moved closer in time to hear Bea explain the situation. "The runner left the field without ever touching second base. The ball was caught and the base tagged, so he's out."

The Blues' manager—a burly man who could intimidate even Emmett in the right situation—scowled at her. "Young lady, my runner made it home. He scored. The game was over right then."

Bea shook her head. "The run doesn't count if a third out occurs during the play, no matter if it's before or after a runner reaches home. That's the league rule, not my opinion."

The manager threw up his hands, raising his voice so everyone nearby could hear. "I think you're trying to make sure the Lincoln Parks win. Everyone saw that little discussion between you and the pitcher earlier. You can't tell me it's a fair game happening when the umpire is sweet on one of the players."

Every muscle in Emmett's body stopped working at once. He might have been hurt by Bea's dismissal of him in Miss King's office, but he would not allow her to be accused of playing favorites on the field. He'd seen firsthand how hard she worked to avoid even the hint of that being true. She'd never given the Lincoln Parks a call they didn't earn.

But the fans around them all had their own opinions when they heard the manager's allegation. There were more shouts as word of what was happening now was repeated far and wide. What had been murmurs of confusion turned into frustrated yells. The situation was going to get out of hand fast.

Emmett whipped around, motioning for the bat boy who'd

accompanied Jet to the mound. "Kid, you know who the league president is, right? Mr. Rosen?" Kid nodded with wide eyes and Emmett patted his shoulder, hoping to reassure him. "I saw him here earlier. Go see if you can find him. I know there are a lot of people, but we need him. Check the offices, the press box, outside the stadium. Hurry."

Kid ran off, darting between the clumps of people clogging the field. Emmett turned back to see that Jet had interrupted the other manager's accusations with a calm tone. "Now, Miss Curran has always been a fair ump, and you know it. Yes, my pitcher has helped a college team she manages, so they do know each other off the field. But that doesn't mean there's anything untoward going on. And accusing a lady of such a thing isn't what this league is about."

The buzz of voices murmuring about him working with Bea all summer became a thundering crash in Emmett's skull as a headache began pounding. The Blues' manager grew redder in the face by the minute, if that was possible. He took an intimidating step toward Jet, his voice an angry bark. "You saw what we saw, Anders. There's more than baseball between those two. And now you expect me to believe she's got this silly rule that takes the win away from us? No, we won this game."

The Blues fans shouted their agreement, which made the Lincoln Parks fans start yelling back. The air in the stadium was charged with frustration and confusion, making it a volatile situation. Where was Kid with Mr. Rosen?

Bea stepped right up to the Blues' manager, her chin held high and shoulders straight. "Sir, I assure you, I would never allow any personal relationship to interfere with doing my job well. The rule exists and must be enforced. Your team has not won yet. If we can get everyone off the field and the players back in place, we'll continue. You'll have a fair chance to earn a win."

The ever-growing crowd roared. It wasn't going to be

possible to contain them, much less get them back in their seats and continue the game. Emmett started to make his way toward Bea to convince her of that when uniformed policemen began gathering around the edges of the field, attempting to corral the spectators. Behind them, Kid finally appeared with Mr. Rosen on his heels.

As people pushed in until he was separated from Bea and the managers, Emmett shouted, thankful he was tall enough to see over most of them. "Jet! The league president is here. He'll clear it up."

Jet turned toward him but didn't seem to be able to hear what Emmett was trying to say. All around the field, upset spectators tossed angry comments back and forth. Outlandish ideas, everything from claiming Fred had tossed Big Ben a ball he'd had in his pocket to Jet paying Bea beforehand to favor the Lincoln Parks. Angry Blues fans were everywhere, filling the infield.

From what he could see, the managers were in a heated discussion now, with Bea standing between them looking worried. As Emmett gave up being polite and tried to force his way toward them, several spectators began shoving one another. One even bumped into Bea, causing her to stumble into a man nearby. That man turned, eyes blazing, and began shouting accusations at her.

That was it. With growing urgency, Emmett pushed several people out of his way, not caring about the angry shouts following him through the rushing crowd. He would not allow anyone to put a hand on Bea.

God, help me reach her. Please protect her.

But getting across those ten feet of dirt between the mound and Bea was becoming more difficult all the time. The league president was having the same difficulty but was making some headway. Despite the headache that now threatened to bring him to his knees—the first he'd had in several weeks—Emmett pressed forward again. A few people gave way for him to pass, and those who didn't he simply elbowed and pushed past until there was a path.

Finally, he reached the trio at about the same time Mr. Rosen finished listening to Bea's explanation of what had happened. Bea glanced up at Emmett, her expression fierce until she realized it was him. Then her entire body sagged. While Mr. Rosen turned to the two managers, she took a step closer to Emmett, as if seeking shelter in his nearness.

No matter what she'd said or done to hurt him before, in that moment, nothing could have kept him from being at her side. He didn't even care if their actions confirmed the Blues' manager's accusations. Emmett still moved toward her until his arm brushed hers. He slid one hand around her to rest on her waist. The way she looked up at him with thankfulness radiating from her eyes made Emmett's heart swell.

Mr. Rosen was in deep conversation with the two managers. Jet visibly attempted to remain calm, while the other manager continued to escalate until he was screaming in Mr. Rosen's face. The league president finally raised both hands and shouted to silence those around them. A little at a time, the volume level across the field decreased until the man could be heard—at least, by those closest to him. "While I didn't see the final play, I've listened to all sides of the story. According to the rulebook, Miss Curran's understanding of the matter is correct, and her call stands. The game is a tie."

Before he even finished the sentence, all the energy and emotion that had been building in the crowd burst forth. Shouts echoed around the field. More intense shoving ensued. Several punches were even thrown. People pressed in from every side.

On instinct, Emmett turned his body toward Bea and wrapped his other arm around her, forming a protective circle. He tried to push them toward the edge of the field, but there was too much chaos. The noise pounded in his head, and a wave of dizziness threatened to overtake him. The bright spots were back, dancing in the corners of his vision. But he forced it all back and focused on protecting Bea.

Several men noticed the two of them and started shouting at others nearby. "There's the crooked umpire. Let's show her what happens to cheaters."

An uproar arose, and Emmett tightened his arms around Bea, giving up trying to leave and instead using as much of his body as possible to shelter her. She curled in toward his chest while a few punches landed on his back and shoulders. The shouts of his teammates trying to come to their rescue swam in his awareness as the dizziness took over.

The last thing he was aware of was several of his teammates and a few policemen reaching him and Bea and circling around them.

Then blackness.

CHAPTER 20

$\mathcal{B}$ea felt the loss of Emmett's body protecting hers the second before he fell to the ground. Thankfully, his teammates and police officers had made it to the epicenter of the riot and gained enough control that at least Bea and the men around her were no longer being hit and spat at.

But Emmett could still be trampled. She wasn't strong enough to lift him, so she dropped into the dirt next to his prone body, pulling as much of him into her lap as possible and leaning over to shield him the way he'd protected her moments before.

Eventually, the shouts died down and space opened around her and Emmett. The dust that had been stirred up by so many shuffling feet settled, and she could draw a breath of fresh air. Policemen and league officials were all around, enforcing calm and explaining what would happen next.

But the outcome of the game didn't matter one bit. When the Lincoln Parks' manager glanced her way, she called, "Mr. Anders, it's Emmett. Please help."

The man blinked a moment as he took in the scene, then jumped into action, calling several of his players over as he raced toward Bea. The men converged while Bea backed away, giving them room to kneel so they could lift Emmett from the dirt. She followed them into the locker room, not caring if there were any men in a state of undress there.

All that mattered was getting a doctor to see Emmett.

Emmett's teammates pushed together two benches so the others could lay him down. Bea took a folded towel from a stack and gently slid it under his head. He was so pale and motionless, with only the shallow rise and fall of his chest to keep Bea's heart from shattering into a thousand pieces. Desperate prayers flew through her mind, jumbled pleas for him to wake up, to recover, that he wouldn't be taken from her.

Thankfully, one of the men had the presence of mind to call for a doctor, and it wasn't long before a short, stout man burst through the doors with a fine leather case in his hand.

Bea started talking before he even reached Emmett. "He collapsed during that mess on the field. He had a concussion last year and has been battling headaches, dizziness, blurry vision, and other symptoms since spring. He's been undergoing treatments that he said were helping, but this must be related."

Murmurs reached her ears from every corner of the room, reminding Bea that no one else present had been aware of Emmett's condition. Her heart plummeted. She'd revealed his secret to the entire team.

And, as she looked around, she realized she'd also told his manager and Charles Rosen, who had both halted inside the door while she'd been speaking.

Trying to swallow away the lump in her throat, Bea stepped back to let the doctor do his work. But she refused not to hover nearby, no matter what looks she got from the men in the room. The doctor examined Emmett, checking his head, feeling around his neck, tugging aside his shirt to look over his torso. He listened to Emmett's heartbeat, took his pulse, and looked in his ears and mouth.

Finally, he turned to address both Bea and Mr. Anders, who stood side by side. "Physically, he's fine. No damage from the fall or the crowd. I commend you both for protecting him from that madness."

Mr. Anders glanced down at Emmett, looking as concerned as Bea felt. "But why isn't he awake?"

The doctor dropped his instruments into his bag before turning his attention to the question. "There's not much we understand about concussions, Mr. Anders. The symptoms are varied and unpredictable. Especially so long after the original injury occurred, it's difficult to know how things will progress. Men have recovered. But most get worse until life in an institution becomes necessary, both for their safety and that of others.

"No." Bea's resolve was anchored in that simple word. She would not accept that an asylum was Emmett's only possible future, and she wouldn't allow anyone to claim it was. "I don't believe that's going to happen to Emmett. Since he's been seeing a specialist, the symptoms have improved considerably. What happened out there was the result of too much happening at once."

The doctor nodded but still appeared solemn. "Quite possibly. But think about all the situations when there might be chaos, loud noise, or large crowds pressing in. Think about the physical and mental strain of playing baseball. How long can he continue to hold up under such pressure? At any moment, he could lose control of himself. It's happened before, and it's not a risk I would advise taking."

Mr. Anders shook the doctor's hand, thanking him for his visit and his opinion while walking him to the locker room door. Then the manager turned back to Bea and the room full of men who stood waiting behind her. "The doctor had an ambulance summoned to take Emmett to the hospital for observation until he awakes. I also sent word to his grandmother. So you fellows can all pack up your things and get home. Miss Curran, I'm certain you have some work to do after this mess. Perhaps you should go on and get to it, as well."

The last thing she wanted to do was leave Emmett's side. But Mr. Anders's words reminded Bea that the entire reason chaos had ensued in the first place was because of accusations about her relationship with Emmett. Staying with him much longer would only bring her reputation further into question.

So, while it tore her heart in two, Bea nodded, gave Emmett's limp hand one last squeeze on the way past, and left the locker room. All she wanted as that door shut behind her was to find a corner away from prying eyes and let the tears welling in her eyes fall until there were no more.

But she didn't make it as far as the umpire's locker room. Charles Rosen stood in the hallway, his eyebrows drawn together in a pensive expression. As if he'd been waiting for her, he straightened when he saw Bea approaching. "How is Mr. Worland?"

Bea rubbed her palm over her forehead, not caring if dirt was now smeared across her face and wishing she didn't have to relay the truth. "He's unconscious. Mr. Anders is getting him to the hospital, but the doctor who came said there are no visible injuries."

"Then what happened out there?"

Bea sighed. What reason was there to try to keep Emmett's secret now? "He's been struggling with lingering effects from a concussion last year. His condition had been improving, but I suppose what happened today was intense enough to make even a person in good health succumb."

"About the situation on the field, Bea—"

A group of Blues players entered the hall from the far end, their conversation stalling when they saw her and Charles. Tension emanated from them. Bea met Charles's gaze, resigned to the reality that the consequences of her recent decisions were about to catch up with her and there was no avoiding it. "Shall we talk in the stadium manager's office?"

They escaped into the nearby door before the men could decide to confront them. Bea dropped into a wooden chair while Charles paced the spacious, sparsely decorated office.

"Bea, the Blues' manager has leveled quite a few accusations at you. I hate to take any of it seriously because I know you're trustworthy, but I must ask. What is the nature of your relationship with Mr. Worland?"

Bea's heart stuttered in her chest, leaving her breathless. How was she to answer that when she didn't even know herself? "Whatever it is, I assure you it hasn't affected my work. For my entire career, I've been very careful not to allow personal feelings to impact my calls. That hasn't changed and it won't."

"You and I may know that, but this will keep occurring as long as other teams believe it to be true. I'm not certain finishing the season is in your best interests anymore. You have a new position at the college lined up, don't you?"

Not entirely, but she wasn't prepared to explain it at that moment. "I understand the position you're in. But I know I can handle whatever comes in the remainder of the season. I'm only scheduled to work five more games. If you fire me now, you're essentially saying the Blues' manager is right and that I'm biased. That's not how I want to end my career, Charles."

She could read the hesitation on his face, but she found hope in the fact that he'd always gone to great lengths to build up those around him. After a moment, he seemed to make up his mind with a brisk nod. "Five more games, then. I'll be present at each one, and we'll issue a statement to all the teams that your decisions are not to be debated. You've done too much for our league for me to let one bad situation be the way you go out."

Relief spread through Bea's chest, but it didn't make the

slightest dent in the worry for Emmett that permeated every inch of her. "I appreciate your belief in me all these years, Charles. More than you know."

Coming around the desk, he rested a hand on her shoulder. "It's been a pleasure to work with you, Bea. I can't wait to see what you accomplish at the college."

Swallowing hard, Bea tried to smile as she shook his offered hand and left the office. She managed to hold herself together until she had marched through the front entrance of the stadium. But the moment she was out of sight of the gate, the events of the day crashed down on her.

Bea stumbled toward the small park tucked behind the stadium and sank onto a bench nestled in the shade of several trees. She sniffled for a few minutes, trying to hold the tears back. But it finally all became too much. Burying her face in her hands, she let silent sobs wrack her body.

News of what had happened today was going to reach the board of regents. The incident was big enough to be splashed across the front page of every newspaper in Chicago. There was no possibility that they wouldn't learn about the questions surrounding her and Emmett, the near riot at the stadium, and the way she'd helped him cover up his health issues. Any one of those things might be enough to keep them from hiring her permanently, but all together?

Her hopes for running the physical education department were nothing but a ruined dream now.

She'd been so close to accomplishing what she'd set out to do, what she thought God was leading her toward. Why would He let her get so close only to tear the dream away from her? The Bible promised that God would bless those who were faithful to Him, but this felt nothing like a blessing.

And through it all, Bea's thoughts kept returning to Emmett, repeating the moment when he collapsed over and over. Every time, she felt anew the way her entire world had shattered with fear as he hit the ground.

Did her career even matter if Emmett didn't wake up?

~

mmett's first impression was the smell. Antiseptic mixed with a warm breeze that carried hints of the lake he'd known all his life. It wasn't the most pleasant combination.

The next thing he became aware of was the voices. Quiet tones—almost whispers but not quite—coming from somewhere to his right. He couldn't make out what they were saying, and that made him want to sit up and demand an explanation.

But he couldn't. The moment he tried to lift his head, pain ripped through his skull, radiating through the rest of his body in a flash. He dropped back against a soft pillow and turned his attention to trying to open his eyes.

He could only keep them cracked for a moment at a time, barely long enough to take in the high ceiling with a single electric light hanging from it. On the next effort, he noticed austere white walls, with an open window set into the far one, a simple white curtain fluttering with the breeze. On his third try, he was able to keep his eyes open for a bit longer, revealing that the hushed voices belonged to Jet, Boot, and Fred, who sat in wooden chairs by the window, paying no attention to him.

Emmett let his eyes remain shut as he tried to make sense of what was going on. He remembered wrapping his arms around Bea to protect her from the surging crowd at the ball field. Then there was an overwhelming dizziness. He must have lost consciousness. Was this a hospital? Had he been injured? Where was Bea?

The men's voices stilled as footsteps entered the room. Emmett managed to peek through one eye again to see it was a doctor, the specialist he'd been seeing for the last few weeks about his symptoms. Before he could try to get the man's attention, the doctor noticed Emmett's gaze and headed toward the bed. "Mr. Worland, it's good to see that you've woken up. Are you able to speak?"

With an effort that felt greater than any training he'd ever done for baseball, Emmett forced a nod and croaked out a hoarse, slightly slurred, "Yes."

The doctor nodded while Emmett's visitors gathered on the other side of the bed. "Very good. Welcome back."

Emmett managed to lick his dry lips and, after several tries, pushed out one of the questions clamoring through his mind. "How long have I been here?"

The doctor leaned over Emmett to listen to his heart with a stethoscope. "Overnight. We were concerned when you didn't wake right away, but you appear to have come through without complications."

"I wasn't...injured?"

Straightening, the doctor offered him a slight smile. "No, you were very lucky. Another hit to the head might have been catastrophic. And I hear a lady was your protector against being trampled by the crowd."

Bea. His hopes crashed to the ground. Of course, he was relieved she must not have been hurt in the riot. But he should have protected her, not the other way around.

He couldn't bring himself to speak again, so he let the doctor finish his examination. The man promised to return in a few hours and let Emmett know how long it might be before he could return home. Then he left Emmett in the care of Jet, Boot, and Fred.

As the door closed behind the doctor, Jet stepped closer to the bed. "You gave us quite a scare there, Worland."

Emmett tried to muster a smile, some kind of lightheartedness to put the obviously uncomfortable men at ease. "Someone has to keep things interesting."

Boot leaned around Jet and explained to Emmett that the game had been declared a tie, but the chaos was too much for it to be continued, so they would reschedule the rest for another day. Emmett tried to listen, but his head was pounding. And he had bigger concerns at that moment than the results of a game.

Like the question of whether or not he still had a job.

When Emmett scrubbed both hands over his face, Jet shooed Boot and Fred out of the room. As soon as they were gone, Emmett asked one of the many questions on his mind. "Has anyone else been by to see me?"

Jet nodded. "At least one man from the team has been here most of the time. You just happened to see Boot and Fred. Your grandmother sent word that she'll visit as soon as she's feeling well enough to get out of bed unless you're released before that. I can tell she's quite worried and wants to be here. She's sent me...many messages demanding to hear about your condition." The grimace that accompanied Jet's words was almost enough to make Emmett smile.

It was good that Grandmother had remained in bed, lest her lingering pneumonia grow worse again when she'd been so close to recovering. It did make him want to smile to imagine the kind of messages Jet must have been receiving from her.

But Jet hadn't mentioned the one person Emmett had been most hopeful to hear had visited. Bea.

Before he could get any more answers, the door opened again, and a nurse in a crisp gray dress covered by a spotless white apron blocked the doorway while asking, "Are you up to another visitor, Mr. Worland?"

Emmett wanted to say no, but the familiar form of Mr. Rosen, the Chicago League president, hovered behind the nurse. If only he wasn't prone in bed and dressed in loose white cotton pajamas and his Lincoln Parks sweater, he might have felt more confident about facing this moment.

But the news wouldn't change whether he was in Mr. Rosen's office or his current embarrassing position. So Emmett nodded, and the nurse stepped back, pushing the door wide and allowing Mr. Rosen to step inside. On the way out, she issued a final instruction for Jet and the newcomer. "You both have ten minutes to visit with him, then you'll have to leave. Mr. Worland needs rest."

Mr. Rosen claimed one of the chairs Emmett's teammates had abandoned and dragged it closer to the bed. "Mr. Worland, how are you feeling?"

Swallowing back the lump that blocked his throat, Emmett managed to croak out an answer. "I've been worse, but not by much." Both men smiled slightly, but the serious atmosphere in the room remained. Emmett drew a breath and cleared his throat before pushing through. "I need to know where I stand with my position on the team."

Mr. Rosen straightened his jacket sleeves and collar as that small hint of amusement faded from his expression. "I'd planned to meet with you once you've recovered. Why don't we address the matter then? That's not what this visit is about."

Emmett tried to push himself up on his elbows, but it was too much, and the room tilted around him. He let his head fall back. He couldn't wait any longer to know his fate, though, weak or not. "Please, I need an answer now. Worrying about it until I'm released won't help me recover any faster than if I know."

With his lips in a tight line, Mr. Rosen nodded once. "Then we'll discuss it now. We learned from Miss Curran that you've been hiding your worsening health for some time now. That deception is unacceptable to the league."

A powerful wave of regret would have knocked Emmett back if he'd been upright. He'd involved Bea, made her part of his deceit, though he'd never intended it that way. Did she hate him now for putting her in that position?

Mr. Rosen was still speaking, so Emmett shoved that thought aside to worry over later. "Your team is also concerned about your ability to play. You could collapse again at any time. It's difficult to imagine because I know you're a decent man, but there's the possibility you could become violent. For the sake of your health and because of your actions, we have no choice but to expel you from the league."

Deep down, he'd known it was coming since he realized the headaches were recurring. But the reality of hearing the words out loud was too final, too cold. Emmett's chest constricted, and the room started closing in. His first try at responding turned into a choked gargle that sent a flush of heat up his neck. He couldn't even accept being dismissed with dignity.

Finally, he cleared his throat enough to speak. "I understand. But please know that I never meant to deceive anyone. I just wanted to play baseball as long as I was able."

With his expression softening, Mr. Rosen rested a hand on Emmett's shoulder. "I'm sorry it had to be this way. But I want to see you get your health in order, and I'm sure Jet feels the same. That won't happen while you're pushing yourself to play baseball most days for months at a time, not to mention spring training and keeping yourself in shape over the winter. This might even turn out to be a blessing for you."

Emmett wanted to scoff. He'd prayed for months for God to take away the symptoms. The new treatment had seemed like a divine answer. Now he had to face a future without any of the things he'd begged God for.

But he restrained himself, determined not to look any more foolish than he already did. When the nurse once again appeared at the door, the men bid him goodbye and both exited, leaving Emmett alone with his thoughts in a too-silent room.

Despite the devastation that accompanied losing his dream, Emmett wished more than anything that Bea was there. Her presence would have lessened the hurt. She might have smiled that gentle way she often did, and his heart would have lifted enough to make the loss tolerable. Maybe she could help him unravel why God would deny him the one thing he loved.

No, two things he loved. Because Bea wasn't there. And he couldn't help wondering why.

Was she embarrassed by his weakness? Upset that he hadn't been able to protect her? Had she known that he would be let go and decided she wasn't going to waste time on such a failure of a man? Or perhaps she still believed he didn't have serious intentions toward her.

As much as Emmett longed for her company, once reality hit, he was rather glad he didn't have to face her yet. Whatever the reason, Bea's absence was a sign that she wanted nothing more to do with him.

And Emmett wasn't going to force her to care for a man who wasn't worth her time.

CHAPTER 21

$\mathcal{B}$ea sat in one of the salons at the athletic club, putting all her attention into surreptitiously tugging a loose thread on the trim of her black-and-gray-striped gown while Marjorie and Mrs. Buchanan prattled on to several other club members about Bea's hopes for the college physical education department. The women seemed delighted with the idea of a program to train teachers who would pass on a love of athletics to the next generation.

But as much as Bea had dreamed of a time when others might support her vision, the victory felt hollow without Emmett there to share it.

He was home from the hospital, according to Mrs. Buchanan. His grandmother had seen him that morning before heading to the club and, when asked by one of the ladies, had told the group that he looked well physically, although his spirits were low. The specialist he'd been seeing wasn't concerned about any lingering problems from his collapse, and they planned to continue treating the symptoms as best they could. But Mrs. Buchanan had arched a meaningful eyebrow in

Bea's direction when she admitted he was no longer playing for the Lincoln Parks.

Bea couldn't forgive herself for letting his secret slip, thus causing him to lose his job. If she'd kept that information to herself or told the doctor at the stadium quietly rather than announcing it to the entire room, he might still be able to return to playing once he recovered.

Instead, he was discouraged and very likely blamed her. As he had every right to.

To make matters worse, Bea couldn't stop remembering the sight of Emmett's pale, dirt-streaked face as she blocked him from the angry crowd. She would never get that image out of her mind as long as she lived. It haunted her dreams. It was there when she blinked her eyes. It danced in the back of her mind at the most inopportune times.

Like now, when she should be reveling in the excitement these women had for the dream Bea held most dear.

Mrs. Buchanan's voice finally cut through her morose thoughts. "Ladies, I'm so glad you see the value in Miss Curran's plans for the program. We'll have a bit of an uphill battle to get her hired on, I imagine. My grandson's choice to hide his health situation has put scrutiny on everyone around him, and the board of regents was already hesitant about Miss Curran, though we all know that to be nonsense."

One of the ladies, Mrs. Petersheim, wife of steel magnate Reginald Petersheim, flicked her fan in indignation. "As if we would allow a woman of questionable morals into the Athletic Club. Humph."

The other five women, including Marjorie, nodded vehemently. It warmed Bea's heart to know they would stand beside her in the face of whatever was to come. Feeling that they deserved to know how much that support meant, she spoke aloud what was brimming in her heart. "I hope the board will listen to the letters of recommendation you all sent, and that they'll believe in me with as much confidence as you do. It's wonderful to know I have friends here."

Marjorie reached over to pat Bea's hand. "The board is a reasonable bunch, although quite cautious by nature. I'm certain they'll see the truth once it's all explained. The riot at the game was not your fault. To the contrary, you were attempting to uphold the rules, which should be commended. We'll make them understand."

The gathered ladies all agreed, and the conversation moved on to the club's upcoming fall golf tournament. But Bea's thoughts couldn't be as easily redirected and returned to worrying about Emmett almost immediately.

Hoping to hide her distraction, Bea rose from the plush sofa and stepped over to a sideboard set with refreshments. Although she had no desire to eat, standing at the table for a few moments as if deliberating over the sweets would buy her time to breathe through the ache tearing at her heart.

Emmett could have died on that field. He could have been trampled. He could have hit his head again and never woken. And in the long minutes Bea had spent holding and protecting him, all she'd been able to think about was how empty her life would be if he wasn't in it.

The ache had started with that realization, and it had stubbornly refused to go away in the days since. If Emmett had died, would any of her previous concerns matter? How much could baseball, or the physical education department, or her reputation matter if his light was gone from the world?

As she'd begun doing the night after he collapsed, Bea let her mind fill with prayers to drown out the fear of losing the man she'd never even wanted in her life. *Lord, please heal Emmett. Please give me a chance to repair the damage I've done to our relationship. Let him see that I believe in him.*

There was a niggle of doubt in her mind, though, a question of whether the prayer was even worth praying. Why had

God allowed all this to happen? What would it have hurt for her to get the job at the college easily? For Emmett's symptoms to go away so he could do what he loved?

Those unknowns were still flooding her mind when she felt a presence close by her side. She found Mrs. Buchanan standing there with raised eyebrows and amusement lifting her thin lips. "Is the choice of desserts so difficult you must stand here and ponder it that long?"

Bea tried to smile in return, but tears had inexplicably welled in her eyes.

Mrs. Buchanan set her plate on the table, glanced over her shoulder at the other ladies, who were occupied with their conversation, and took Bea's arm to steer her from the salon into the deserted hall. Only then did she speak again. "My dear, whatever is wrong? Are you worried about the board? Marjorie is right, women are more powerful than men want to give us credit for. We'll show them you're the only choice for the department."

Bea shook her head, any responses she could think of dying before reaching her tongue.

Mrs. Buchanan's eyes softened. "Are you worried about Emmett? I understand you haven't seen him since that game."

The tears began to fall at once, spurred by the immense kindness in Mrs. Buchanan's voice. All Bea could do was nod once, then cover her face with her hands.

Mrs. Buchanan pulled Bea close, letting her cry without making any attempt to talk her out of it. When the tears finally slowed, the older woman pulled a lilac-scented linen handkerchief from her reticule and handed it to Bea, giving her time to get herself in order.

Still sniffling, Bea finally found her voice again. "I'm sorry for taking you away from the others. But thank you for indulging me in a weak moment. I feel much better."

And she did. For the moment. Until the worries about Emmett inevitably returned later.

As if seeing her thoughts, Mrs. Buchanan speared Bea with a direct gaze. "Now, I will not accept any argument. Once we're finished here, you'll accompany me home to visit Emmett. I intended to spend some time with him this afternoon, anyway. I miss his presence these days more than I used to when he was away traveling for games."

Bea tried to protest. "I don't know if that's wise. Going to visit Emmett won't help my cause with the board."

Mrs. Buchanan waved off her arguments as she turned back toward the parlor. "Never mind that. It's my home, and I won't leave your side, so there's not a thing improper about it. The position at the college will work out—you needn't worry."

There was no way Mrs. Buchanan knew that for sure, but her fortitude was contagious. And Bea was desperate to see Emmett for herself, even if she could never admit such a thing to anyone else.

An hour later, she was settled into a carriage with Mrs. Buchanan, staring out the window as they traversed the wide, quiet streets that led to the most elegant neighborhood in all of Chicago. Bea chewed her lower lip, taking a bit of comfort from the habit. What would Emmett say when they were together again? Would he still be angry about her behavior in Marjorie's office that day? Would he be upset that she'd revealed his condition?

Twisting her fingers together until they ached, Bea couldn't stand it any longer. She had to address Mrs. Buchanan. "This is a terrible idea. You can drop me off at the next corner, and I'll go home. I can see him in a few weeks when all the conjecture has calmed down and he's more up to receiving visitors."

To Bea's surprise, the older woman chuckled. "Oh, no. You're going to face him right now. You're both moping about like lovesick fools, and I'm rather tired of it. If he doesn't have baseball anymore, he's going to need someone to support and encourage him while he decides what to do with himself. And there's no one better suited for that than a woman who's in love with him."

"In love?" Bea's words came out in a squeak that would normally mortify her. "Why would you think I'm in love with him?"

But the truth sank deep into Bea's mind. It explained the ache in her heart, the worry, the way she missed him so much.

She had to admit she cared about him. Fanciful daydreams about what it would be like to marry him had even popped up on occasion. She'd spent far too much time wishing for the chance to kiss him again. But love?

Was she in love with Emmett Worland?

In love with a baseball player, the one thing she said she'd never do?

Mrs. Buchanan sat in self-satisfied silence, letting Bea work it out for herself. But before Bea could attempt to convince either of them that it wasn't true, the carriage stopped and the driver pulled the door open, allowing a swirl of one of fall's first cool breezes to fill the inside. Mrs. Buchanan exited the vehicle, tapping a foot on the brick drive as she waited for Bea.

There was no avoiding it. Bea was going to have to face Emmett. And now she had to do it with the awareness that she, least likely of all women to let herself get entangled with a baseball player, was in love.

~

*E*mmett was not prepared to enter Grandmother's parlor and find himself staring into the beautiful chocolate eyes he'd been dreaming of all week.

He'd dreamed of them since the first time he'd met her, if he was honest.

But the last thing he'd expected when a footman informed Emmett he had a visitor was to see Bea Curran perched on a damask-covered sofa looking for all the world as though she wanted to run straight out the front door.

Gathering his wits, Emmett dropped a kiss on Grandmother's forehead—a new custom he'd taken up since they'd started growing closer—and nodded to Bea, giving himself a moment to drink in the sight of her while he addressed his grandmother. "I wasn't expecting you back so soon, Grandmother. You said you would likely be at the club until supper."

Grandmother dismissed his comment with a wave. "Oh, don't be daft. I returned early so Miss Curran could see for herself how you're doing. She was hesitant to visit a single man on her own, which is quite reasonable. But she has been concerned. Haven't you, Miss Curran?"

A noticeable nudge from his grandmother's elbow to Bea's ribs made her jump. Bea's eyes were wider than he'd ever seen them, she kept fidgeting with the black velvet that lined the front of her gown, and her lips were parted as she shook her head in denial. "A normal amount of concern, of course. As any friend would be."

If he didn't know better, he'd think she was nervous about being there.

But that was ridiculous. She was uncomfortable because she had reasons for not visiting sooner that had nothing to do with propriety and everything to do with her feelings toward him. Or lack thereof.

Emmett dropped into the nearest chair and faced the ladies with no idea what to say. How did one start a conversation when the guest didn't want to be there, and the host could think of nothing more than kissing her?

Thankfully, his grandmother always knew the proper way to converse in any situation, no matter how unusual. "Emmett, do update Miss Curran on the state of your health. And from what I heard, she deserves thanks for keeping you safe during that vulgar display by the spectators at the game."

Emmett cleared his throat. If only it were the two of them alone, he might be able to say the words burning inside him, to ask Bea why she'd stayed away. But with his grandmother there, he could hardly bring up something so intimate. "Well, the specialist I've been seeing believes the collapse was due to the overwhelming strain of that particular situation. He doesn't think it means I'm worsening or that it will happen in normal situations."

"That's very good to hear." Bea's voice was soft and kind, but there was a hesitancy in it that he wasn't used to hearing from her.

"And Grandmother is correct. I owe you my gratitude for protecting me from being trampled or injured. You're..." His voice cracked, forcing him to stop and clear his throat again. The way she searched his face so earnestly, her eyes wide with emotion, made it an enormous feat for him to continue. He pushed the rest of the words out in a rush. "You're one of the bravest women I've ever met to stay in the midst of that chaos and make sure I was taken care of. I only wish you hadn't had to."

"I wish the same thing."

Emmett nearly reeled back in his chair. After his heartfelt admission, her words cut deep. He hated that his weakness meant he hadn't been the one doing the protecting out there. But to hear that she agreed and that she would rather not have had to risk herself that way...the knowledge created a shroud of regret so heavy, he wasn't sure how he'd manage to hold it.

Jumping to his feet, Emmett wiped his damp palms on his trousers. "I'm sorry to cut our visit short, but I still feel out of sorts. I'm going to get some rest. Grandmother, I'll see you in the morning. I'll take supper in my room."

To his shame, Emmett bolted from the parlor without

waiting for a response, passing an eavesdropping maid without acknowledgment and taking the stairs two at a time to his room.

It was a long night spent reliving and regretting nearly every part of that summer and fall rather than sleeping. The only thing he couldn't bring himself to wish hadn't happened was meeting Bea. Falling in love with her had been foolish on his part. But meeting her had changed him so much for the better.

Once the sun began peeking over the horizon, shining a much cooler light on the world now that fall weather had arrived, Emmett dressed in loose trousers and his Lincoln Parks sweater and escaped to the one place that had always distracted him from the harsher realities of life.

Walking onto the empty Lincoln Park ball field after convincing the young groundskeeper at the gate that he was still allowed to be there, Emmett let the familiar smell of damp grass and dirt soothe his spirit. He shuffled his feet on the way to the mound, the baseballs he'd grabbed from a basket in the dugout a comforting weight in his hands.

On the mound, he stood in pitching position with his eyes closed, letting the sounds of the city waking up outside the stadium wash over him, twirling a ball around in his fingers. Prayers rolled through his mind. They were somewhat unintelligible, but the minister at Grandmother's church had once preached that the Holy Spirit could understand even wordless groans, so he continued, anyway. He didn't know if they did any good, but he felt less untethered when he released his fears to the Lord.

Without opening his eyes, Emmett secured the ball in his fingers and pulled his arm back, lifting his front knee for momentum. He took a wide step forward as his arm came around, releasing the ball on instinct without needing to see where he was aiming.

When he finally opened his eyes, it was just in time to see the ball fly in a perfect line over home plate, hitting the backstop with enough force to shake the entire fence.

Slow clapping broke the silence on the field.

Emmett whirled around to see Jet walking toward him, a lazy half smile on his face. "You're still the best pitcher I've had the privilege to work with."

With his quiet morning now interrupted, Emmett couldn't keep the bitterness from his voice. "Then hire me back."

Jet sighed as he handed Emmett another ball. "You know that's not up to me. I'm the manager of this team, but I answer to the owner and the league. I fought for you, Emmett. I really tried. If you'd only been honest with us, I might have succeeded. It was the deception that was too much for them."

That wasn't anything Emmett hadn't already known, but it would never get easier to hear the harsh truth. He rubbed his palm over his face, tempering his tone. "I know. And I'm trying not to be angry. I regret so much about how I handled this and...everything."

"Meaning Miss Curran?" Jet shot him a knowing expression.

Emmett was tired of trying to deny the truth, so he nodded. "Her most of all."

Jet chuckled, bringing Emmett's gaze up to see what was funny about the situation. "Sorry to laugh, but I'm plenty familiar with troublesome ladies."

"Unfortunately, I'm the troublesome one here. Every bit of trouble she's had is because of me."

Slinging his arm over Emmett's shoulders, Jet pulled him toward the dugout. "Come sit with me a bit before the team starts arriving for practice."

They settled on the long bench, which was damp and cold from a heavy dew overnight. But Emmett didn't care. He had far worse problems than wet trousers.

Jet leaned back, spreading his arms across the back of the bench and looking relaxed enough to irritate Emmett all over again. "Why do you think everything that's happened is your fault?"

Emmett sighed, the weight of his terrible choices making it difficult to breathe. "I'm the one who decided not to tell the truth about my health, and then I shared it with Bea but asked her to keep my secret too. I let myself get too involved in her life despite knowing she thinks I'm a hopeless womanizer. And even with my best efforts, I haven't been able to convince anyone that my reputation isn't who I truly am."

Jet rubbed his jaw, looking thoughtfully across the field. "You could look at it that way. Or you could realize that what other people do isn't your responsibility. Yes, it was your choice to keep your health problems from us. But you didn't force Miss Curran to do the same, even if you asked her to. She made that choice. And I don't care what your grandmother said—you didn't need to prove yourself to anyone. Those who take the time to get to know you realize immediately that all the sensational headlines in the papers were hogwash."

How could he be so positive and encouraging in light of all Emmett had done—and failed to do? "But it was my responsibility to be respectful and decorous enough to change people's minds. I couldn't even change Bea's, and I've spent countless hours with her."

Jet barked out a loud laugh that echoed across the empty stadium. "If people don't want to change their minds, nothing you do will make them. And most don't. As for Miss Curran, I don't know why you believe otherwise, but that woman admires you. I'd even dare to claim she returns the feelings you're trying to hide."

A tendril of hope rooted in Emmett's heart, but letting it grow was a terrifying prospect. Was it possible Jet could be right? Emmett had already been in such agony these days without Bea, certain she was better off without him in her life, even if by some chance she wanted him there. But everyone around him believed she cared more for Emmett than he'd told himself she could. Were they right? Or was Emmett condemning himself to face another heartbreak if he followed through with his growing desire to pursue her?

CHAPTER 22

The acknowledgment of feelings for Emmett that Bea hadn't recognized before made her experience everything in a different way. When she umpired the next game on her schedule, all she could see were players who weren't Emmett. When she visited the Athletic Club with Mrs. Buchanan, all she could think of was that she'd rather be playing golf with Emmett. And when she walked across the college campus to meet with the board of regents about her possible appointment as Marjorie's replacement, all she wanted was for Emmett to be at her side.

But he wasn't. And it seemed he might never be.

It had only been a few days since Mrs. Buchanan had insisted on visiting Emmett, and although Bea knew he'd been out and about, he'd made no effort to see her. Two weeks ago, that reality might not have bothered her in the least. But now that she'd realized the depth of her feelings for him, a future without Emmett Worland in it seemed untenable.

Try as she might, Bea struggled to keep her mind focused on the meeting ahead and what it meant for her dreams. After tugging on her sensible brown jacket and making sure the buttons down the front of the matching skirt were straight, Bea entered the administrative building and headed to the conference room where she'd been asked to join the board. *To discuss the recommendation of hiring you for a position with the college in light of the recent situation* was the exact wording of the letter. Or perhaps more accurately, the summons. Because it felt as if she was on her way to be tried for her actions, not offered a job.

To Bea's relief, Marjorie was already waiting for her in the conference room. Several other familiar faces occupied chairs ringing the outside wall of the room, including the gymnasium director and three girls from her team, who grinned and waved when she entered as if this wasn't likely the end of Bea's dreams. Surprisingly, Mr. Kendall was nowhere to be seen. She had no doubt, however, that he had been the one to make sure that the board members heard about the chaotic game and Bea's part in hiding Emmett's health concerns from the league.

Taking a seat beside Marjorie, Bea reached for her friend's hand.

Marjorie smiled, confident and cheerful as always. "I can see the worry written all over your face. Take a breath, and let the Lord go before you. The board is sure to see your true character shining through, no matter what they've heard."

If only she was right. "Marjorie, I helped Emmett hide the truth from his team and the league. I don't know how to explain that to the board in a way that won't make them believe I'm deceptive by nature."

Before they could say anything more, the door opened and most of the board members filed in, speaking together in low tones as they found their seats at the large table in the middle of the room. Several of the men glanced her way, but Bea couldn't tell if they were friendly toward her or ready to declare judgment.

Mr. Willis stood to address the room while the others

settled in. "We'll wait a few minutes for any more attendees, but I plan to begin promptly at four o'clock. There will be time for everyone to speak, provided they have something of value to add to the matter. I'll have no besmirching of character without proof."

The pointed reference to Mr. Kendall's accusations at the last meeting sparked a flame of hope in Bea's heart. Perhaps her fate wasn't already sealed.

Over the next ten minutes, the door opened several times with three more board members arriving. Bea focused on looking out the windows instead of staring them down as they gathered around the center table, so she didn't see the last person to walk in until Marjorie sucked in a breath and nudged Bea's side. Bea glanced up to find herself looking right into Emmett's ice-blue eyes.

Suddenly unsure how to manage herself, Bea could only swallow hard and bask in his presence as he occupied the empty chair next to her. He was mere inches away, close enough for his shoulder to brush hers every time he moved. Bea searched his face for some idea of what had brought him there. It had to be more than her wishful thinking.

Emmett shifted to meet her gaze, and he mirrored her examination with the hint of a smile lifting the corners of his lips. Warmth spiraled through her, and she glanced away before he could see what must be showing in her eyes. If only her heart would control itself until this meeting was over. She'd longed for him to come, but now that he had, what a distraction his presence would be!

After a few more minutes with the occasional shuffle of feet or rustle of clothing making the only sounds in the otherwise silent room, Mr. Willis cleared his throat. "It's now four o'clock, so we'll start. We've called this meeting today to determine the suitability of Miss Beatrice Curran for the position of head of the women's physical training department upon the retirement of Miss Marjorie King." He nodded in their direction. "Both women are present today, I see. This isn't the way we usually handle employment decisions. But given the circumstances and the fact that fall classes begin on Monday, we need to reach a satisfactory consensus as soon as possible."

On one side of Bea, Marjorie squeezed her hand. On the other side, Emmett shifted, his arm pressing against hers from shoulder to elbow. She didn't know if it was purposeful or not, but the contact bolstered her courage. She raised her chin and met all the curious eyes that turned her way when her presence was announced.

Mr. Willis continued by laying out Bea's qualifications as she'd listed them in her application for the position. Then he read aloud Marjorie's letter of recommendation, which warmed Bea's heart with kind sentiments about her suitability and passion. Finally, he glanced around the room. "Now we'll give a few moments to anyone who wishes to speak on the matter of Miss Curran's potential employment. As I stated, only relevant *facts* will be allowed."

One of the board members rose with a letter in his hand. "I feel the information we received last week about Miss Curran is relevant and needs to be discussed before we can make an informed decision." The man began reading from the page, giving a detailed account of the Lincoln Parks game and Bea's part in it, along with a mention of Emmett losing his spot on the team because he'd deceived the league and the revelation that Bea had known about his health for some time before divulging it to those in charge.

How Mr. Kendall, who she presumed sent the letter, had learned so much about the incident only crossed her mind for a moment. What lingered was the way her heart ached to hear it all laid out in such a matter-of-fact manner. She'd only wanted to support Emmett. But how could she convince the board that her intentions had never been deceptive?

Before she could figure out a way to defend herself, Emmett stood. The room went still as he spoke in a humble tone. "I'm Emmett Worland, the pitcher mentioned in that letter you just read. And while those facts may be true, there's much more to it than that."

Taking a small step forward, Emmett glanced at each man around the table before speaking again. "Miss Curran and I met on the baseball field. She's the most sought-after umpire in the semi-professional Chicago City League and one of the most qualified umpires I've ever had the privilege of working with. On the field, she's fair, firm, and quick-thinking. She upholds rules while maintaining compassion for those around her."

One of the board members sighed. "Is this indulgent speech going to go on much longer? Miss Curran's qualifications as an umpire have nothing to do with her appointment here at the college."

Emmett hardly reacted, maintaining a calm demeanor. "I mention this to show that Miss Curran's natural personality shines through in everything she does. The way she acts on the field is the way she acts in all facets of her life. Fair, compassionate, invested. Not only can you count on her behaving the same way if she's employed here, but I think she'll be those things to a greater degree because this position is her dream. She's worked hard to become qualified to lead others in sharing the merits of physical education, and I know she'll be a benefit to the college overall."

Bea's heart melted with every word Emmett spoke. He'd come not only to support her but to defend her. He was her champion. But would it be enough?

Several of the board members muttered to each other, and at least half of them looked doubtful. The one who'd sighed spoke up again. "Still, that doesn't address the grievous mistakes she made in her relationship with you, Mr. Worland. Those are the matters we're concerned with today."

The room seemed to grow smaller and tighter around Bea. It didn't matter that Emmett had come. These men were only going to see her mistakes.

But when he spoke again, Emmett sounded undeterred. "Miss Curran made the best possible choices in response to actions beyond her control. She kept my health a secret because I begged her to. It was my responsibility to disclose it. I admit my failure there. But she exhibited the compassion I mentioned by giving me time to be the man I should have been and face my future rather than ignoring it."

To Bea's surprise, Emmett's heartfelt confession appeared to be softening the men around the table. Heads nodded as if they understood the predicament Emmett had been in.

At that moment, Emmett glanced over his shoulder at Bea. She hoped he could see in her eyes how much his words and effort to take responsibility for the situation meant to her. A long gaze passed between them before he turned back to the board. "As for the chaos at the game, Miss Curran was upholding the rules of baseball. The fault for that event lies with the players who chose to argue with her call and the spectators who shouldn't have been on that field in the first place because the game wasn't over. She could hardly be held responsible for the madness that overtook the crowd when she was doing what was right."

Emmett stepped back toward his seat. "I'll conclude by saying that not hiring Miss Curran would be a loss for this institution. She's already been a driving force for positive change, given the energy, effort, and care she's put into this place and the students she works with. Thank you for listening."

Then he dropped into the chair as his words hung in the silence that fell over the room. After letting Emmett's words sink in, Mr. Willis opened the floor for other comments. The girls from her team rose together and spoke about Bea's dedication to them when they'd been the worst team on campus. Then Marjorie reiterated what she'd said in her letter, telling the board she still stood by her recommendation. But Bea hardly heard any of it. Emmett's praise was thrumming through her veins, warming her spirit in a way that wouldn't be dimmed even if the board rejected her application.

When no one else had anything to say, the board members began discussing the matter amongst themselves. Bea leaned close to Emmett—who looked a little overwhelmed at his own actions—and spoke in a near whisper. "Thank you. I can't believe you came to defend me."

Emmett reached over and took her hand in his, the calluses on his fingers from pitching thousands of baseballs over the years sending shivers along her skin. "I'll always be there to defend you, Bea. Any time you need it. I hate that I didn't make that clear to you a long time ago."

The tenderness in his expression made her heartbeat quicken. Without meaning to, she licked her lips and watched his eyes dip down to follow the movement. When the memory of his kiss at the ball months ago came rushing back, heat worked up her cheeks. She remembered every sensation as if it happened yesterday.

But another memory pushed aside thoughts of kissing. She could see anew the way his face crumbled when she expressed her doubts about his intentions at the game, right before the world went to pieces. Was this statement a confirmation of what she'd longed to hear him say then? Did he mean that he wanted to be with her no matter what happened in this meeting or with his baseball career?

She thought back on his actions throughout the summer. While she'd interpreted every move he made through her initial assumptions about who he was, his behavior continued to prove her wrong. He'd been more concerned about others than himself. He'd worked hard to be her assistant without letting his pride undermine her. He'd shown endless confidence in her and support for her dreams. He was always respectful, kind, and patient.

And she'd nearly forced him away by believing lies.

What did it matter if he was a baseball player? God had placed him in her life, the man she never expected but now couldn't imagine being without.

Bea's breath caught, her chest tightening. How could she convince him she regretted her assumptions and the way she'd treated him? How could she ever live up to the way this man cared for her?

Those weren't questions that could be answered at that moment, sitting in the conference room. But Bea was determined to find a way.

~

*E*mmett was far too busy trying to communicate his feelings wordlessly to Bea to see the chancellor stand and push back his chair, but the screech of its wooden feet on the floor broke the moment, much to Emmett's regret. If it wouldn't have further damaged Bea's reputation and chance to get the job she wanted, he would have kissed her right there in that conference room. After seeing the warm wonder in her eyes and feeling her squeeze his hand as if it was her lifeline, claiming her lips was all he could think about.

Ever since talking with Jet at the ball field earlier in the week, Emmett had become more and more convinced of what he needed to do. He'd hatched this plan to try to repair his mess, but he still wasn't convinced he had any right to ask for a place in her life. A man should be able to offer something of value to the woman he loved. And Emmett did love Bea. Undeniably, unexpectedly, unconditionally.

It wasn't what he'd ever imagined would happen, but that

was the truth. He loved her patient, hardworking, self-controlled nature and her ability to care for others while helping them rise to the standards she believed in. He loved her laugh, her eyes, the lips he couldn't help glancing at again when he should have been listening to Mr. Willis.

Right. The meeting. Emmett dragged his gaze away from the beautiful woman at his side and contented himself with cradling her soft hand in his as they listened to the result of the meeting.

At the head of the table, Mr. Willis had finished reiterating the responsibilities of the position they were trying to fill. Then he looked at Bea and nodded. "I believe Miss Curran would not only be capable of filling this role but that she'll bring more to it than we could hope. My vote is yes. Gentlemen, please go around and give us a yay or nay."

Emmett rubbed his thumb over the back of Bea's hand as the men voted, thrilled when they concluded with only two dissenters. Mr. Willis nodded in approval, gesturing toward Bea. "The recommendation to hire Miss Curran is accepted. Let's welcome the newest member of the Western College administration."

Emmett released her hand when they stood up, then lingered nearby and let Bea enjoy the congratulations from the board members and the others in the room. He couldn't have been prouder of her as she accepted their handshakes and words of welcome.

Bea and Mr. Willis began discussing when she would start and other details while Miss King sidled up next to Emmett, eyeing him with an almost smug expression. "Coming here to stand up for Bea was quite a wonderful thing to do. Your grandmother would be proud. Although something tells me you didn't let her know you intended to do this."

Emmett stuffed his hands in his pockets, feeling rather like a schoolboy caught doing something sentimental for a girl he was sweet on. Really, that wasn't so far from the truth. "No, I didn't see any reason to tell Grandmother where I was going today."

Miss King's eyebrows arched. "Has she changed her mind about making you repair your reputation, then? Because this is the kind of thing that would prove to anyone that you're not the kind of man to leave a woman with your mess to clean up."

It was the truth. His grandmother would love to know that he'd been there to support Bea. But Emmett had already wrestled through that line of thought. "The last thing I want to do is use this attempt to fix the problem I created and embroiled Bea in to make myself look better. Coming here wasn't about me. It was about Bea getting what she's worked so hard for, what my mistakes almost cost her. That's what matters."

An approving smile spread across Miss King's face. "That's exactly what I hoped to hear from you, Emmett. Bea is a special woman. I'm so pleased she's met a man who can see that and live up to it."

Beads of sweat broke out across Emmett's forehead. "No, that's not me. I'm nowhere near good enough for Bea. I've failed too many times for her to look past what everyone sees."

Surprise brought Miss King around to face him with her back to the room. "Now, that's the silliest thing I ever heard. Being good enough for her has nothing to do with your ability to play baseball or to have a career at all. Even what others think of you doesn't make a bit of difference to a good woman. It's about the way you care for her and support her. This is a modern time. Your life doesn't have to look like your parents' or grandparents' lives. You can figure out together what matters to the two of you."

That sounded too good to be true. "I can't expect a woman to earn a living for me while I do nothing, Miss King. Bea won't respect a man who's too damaged to work and needs his grandmother's money to live."

Miss King's snort of laughter brought several glances their way. Emmett turned her away toward a more private corner of the room, where she put a hand on her hip and speared him with a no-nonsense glare. "Most people in this world dream of having the kind of freedom your grandmother's money can bring. And don't get me started on why you're not damaged or a failure. What nonsense. Why don't you let Bea decide how she feels about these things instead of assuming her response?"

Before he could respond, Bea called Miss King. The older woman gave him one more pointed look before turning to join the others. As soon as he was alone, Emmett slipped from the conference room while everyone was distracted. The last thing he wanted was to overshadow Bea's joyous day with the presence of his troubles. Because whether he was ready to face it or not, he was now jobless and without any future prospects.

But was Miss King right? She assumed a future where he and Bea spent the rest of their days together doing whatever they wanted. He couldn't deny that at some point during the summer, he'd started dreaming of that very thing. But could he let go of baseball and embrace what his grandmother had always held over his head? Everything was so different now than it had been at the beginning of the summer. He could hardly even remember why he'd been so sure Bea would reject him for his weaknesses.

Similar thoughts swirled through his mind for the next week, with no resolution in sight. On Wednesday, Emmett joined his grandmother for lunch. With the women's team finished for the season and his career at a standstill, he didn't have anything else to do. Plus, he'd hardly seen her in the time since his collapse, since she'd been busy catching up on the many social obligations she had to set aside while she'd been ill.

And, surprisingly enough, he missed her company.

It was strange to realize that after so many years of trying to avoid her, his relationship with his grandmother was as different as it could be compared to six months ago.

So he anticipated an enjoyable meal as he settled in at the small table she had once again set up in the drawing room, rather than the larger dining room. "Good afternoon, Grandmother. You look wonderful today. I'm glad to see you've recovered fully."

His grandmother brushed a loose strand of hair back up into her coiffure, preening under his compliment. "That illness was a terrible trial. I'm happy it finally passed."

They took a moment to fill their plates in silence, and then Emmett prayed for the meal. As his grandmother cut a piece of ham into bites, she began to speak again. "The time I spent confined to my bed worrying about you and wishing I could be at your side in the hospital did give me cause to think, though."

Emmett had just taken a large bite of bread, so all he could do was mumble, "Oh?"

Grandmother shook her head at his muffled response, a long-suffering twinkle lighting her eyes. "I came to a conclusion that might surprise you. I was wrong."

Now he had to speak. That wasn't a statement he could allow to pass with no response. He swallowed hard to clear his throat and offered a teasing smile with his words. "That is shocking. How on earth so?"

Grandmother paused before responding, turning more serious. "I should never have believed the press over my family, and I shouldn't have tried to coerce you into behaving the way I wanted. You're a grown man, and one I'm very proud to call my grandson, no matter what anyone else believes about you."

Emmett froze mid-bite. Those were the kind of words he'd always longed to hear from her, and the blessing of being able to experience this moment was not lost on him.

Reaching across the table, he took Grandmother's wrinkled

hand in his. "Thank you. It means a great deal to me to hear you say that."

"That's not the only realization I had." Grandmother reached into a hidden pocket in her skirt and slid out a folded piece of paper. Handing it to him, she leaned back in her seat. "Holding on to my money seems trivial when it would be much more useful to the person I love the most. You'll find that's a letter handing over the management of my estate to you. As long as you agree to take care of me in my later years, the family fortune is all yours. I know you'll make me even prouder with it."

As Miss King had said, Emmett now had a fortune at his disposal and would no longer need to pursue any career if he didn't want to.

But it felt far emptier than he'd expected the moment to be.

Grandmother must have noticed his reticence. Her brow furrowed and one grey eyebrow arched. "You don't seem pleased."

The last thing he wanted was to offend her. "I'm honored that you trust me with this. And I'm thankful our relationship has come so far. It's only..." How could he explain his dissatisfaction? He had no claim to Bea's heart, so it seemed presumptuous to admit that he wished she could be part of this moment.

But his grandmother proved to be as perceptive as ever. "It's our dear Miss Curran, isn't it? Young man, why don't you go get her? Your feelings are clear to the rest of us. Go tell her so you two can get on with it. Hesitating is a waste of the time God has blessed you with. If you're waiting for the perfect situation to pursue her, I can assure you, things will never seem right enough. Don't miss your chance because of fear."

When he heard it that way, it all seemed so clear to Emmett. God had brought Bea into his life. Why couldn't he accept that there was a good reason for it? Why was he so convinced he had to have everything in his life figured out for Bea to care about him?

Suddenly, the wait until he'd planned to see her again at the Lincoln Parks' game the next day was far too long. He was ready to step forward with confidence and prove to Bea that she could trust him and the sincerity of his feelings.

Bea stepped into Marjorie's office, now bare except for the empty desk, wooden rolling chair, and a bookcase by the window. The large window bathed the room in cool fall sunlight. Where only a few weeks ago it had been a mess of papers, research books, and ephemera from Marjorie's time there, now it was a blank space that should have represented the reality of Bea's dreams.

After the day Emmett had visited Bea there, however, the room never ceased to remind her of his presence, of his nearness when he'd almost kissed her, of the way she'd hurt him when she pulled away.

Now the office was hers and he wasn't there. Would she have to get used to that? Or would there be a day when he joined her here again?

Drawing a deep breath and straightening her shoulders, Bea marched the few steps from the door to the desk and dropped the crate of her personal items on top of it. This place would become a sanctuary for her in time. Even if Emmett wasn't part of her life going forward, the memory of him here would fade with time.

At least, she had to believe it would.

The staccato beat of footsteps on the plank floors brought her around to find Marjorie entering the room with a wide smile on her face. "Welcome to your new office, Miss Curran."

Bea managed a small smile. She *was* happy to be there. If only other aspects of the summer had gone differently, there would be no reason for her to have mixed feelings.

So she tried to match her friend's lighthearted, teasing tone. "Thank you, Miss King. I'm quite pleased with the condition the previous occupant left it in. I hear she was a bit of a pack rat."

Marjorie swatted her arm, and they both laughed—a good excuse to release the tension that had been building in Bea's chest ever since Emmett had disappeared from the conference room the week before.

As if she sensed the way Bea's heart was torn between joy and misery, Marjorie perched on the edge of the desk and tilted her head, examining Bea's face. "What's bothering you? This is what you worked so hard for, and you earned it with overwhelming support from the board. But there's a distinct sadness lurking in your eyes."

Bea joined her friend, letting the heavy wooden desk support her while voicing the words she was finally unafraid to admit. "I miss Emmett. After the meeting, I thought he'd find a reason to see me—if nothing else, to congratulate me on the position he helped me get. But I haven't heard a word from him."

Marjorie slid an arm around Bea's shoulders, and Bea leaned into the gesture, letting herself be mothered a bit. The comforting touch made her remember how long it had been since she'd visited her family in Iowa. She would be more thankful than ever for a hug from her mother when she made the trip back at Christmas.

"You love him, don't you?" Marjorie's tone was soft and

filled with such understanding that Bea could only nod as tears she didn't want to shed welled in her eyes. "And as a proper lady, you have very few ways to approach him yourself."

For a few minutes, silence filled the office, punctuated by sniffles Bea couldn't contain. Without warning, Marjorie jumped up, nearly sending Bea to the floor. The older woman snapped her fingers, eyes alight. "I've got it. Since you're taking on much more as the new women's physical training director and with expanding the program and all, the women's baseball team needs a new manager for next season. Someone with plenty of experience and knowledge to continue guiding them. Who better than an experienced pitcher who not only had a semi-pro career but also worked with the team before?"

Bea could only blink at Marjorie while her mind raced to catch up to what the other woman was proposing. "You think I should extend an offer for Emmett to manage the women's team? Do I even have the authority to do that? And why on earth would he agree to it?"

Marjorie moved to stand in front of Bea and put her hands on Bea's shoulders, claiming her full attention. "You have the authority to ask the board to approve it before you approach him. And as for Emmett...he'll agree because he loves you and he'll want to be near you. Plus, he loves baseball. He might not be able to play, but managing isn't out of the question, even with his health concerns. You and I both know the league expelling him was more about what they considered to be a deception on his part than about his health. But we also know that's ridiculous. He's completely trustworthy and would be the perfect manager."

The idea swirled around in Bea's mind, lifting her heart even before she decided if it was a good plan or not.

Marjorie took her hesitation as acceptance and smiled in satisfaction. "Now you have an excuse to seek him out."

Bea wanted to shake her head, to describe all the reasons

why that was a bad idea. But deep down, she was growing more excited about it by the minute.

Still, though, there were so many unknowns. Bea released all the questions she'd been stewing over for weeks out in a wild rush of words. "You think he loves me, but if that's true, why did he come in and save the day, then disappear without a word? What if I can't convince him that I know the kind of man he is now, and I don't doubt him any longer? What if you're wrong, but he agrees to manage the team, and I'm stuck daily facing the reality that I'm in love and he's not?"

Marjorie had the gall to let out a lilting laugh in the face of Bea's agony. "Oh, my dear. If only you could see what the rest of us see."

Bea was afraid to ask but couldn't help herself all the same. "And what's that?"

"A couple in love. And both deny it for reasons none of us understand. Bea, don't battle against your feelings for him. Fight for them. Find a way to show him what's in your heart, and give him the courage to do the same. Don't miss the good that God placed in your life. You will regret it if you do."

Marjorie's tone had turned serious, even wistful, reminding Bea that while her friend seemed happy enough with the work she'd dedicated her life to, there had always been hints of sadness, of choices she might have made differently in hindsight. Was Bea willing to risk having those same regrets when she reached the end of her career?

The answer to that question drove Bea forward the next day as she walked into the Lincoln Parks stadium for her last game as an umpire. The team's regular season was over, but the Chicago Cubs had scheduled games with some of the semi-professional teams in the break before the World Series. It was a huge opportunity for the Lincoln Parks to play against a major league championship contender which also happened to be the previous year's World Series champions. The idea was so exciting for baseball fans that the stadium was already filled near to capacity by the time Bea made her way to the field.

As she waited by the home dugout, she chatted with the second umpire Charles had hired for such a big game. It was a good thing she wouldn't have to watch every bit of action on the field by herself. But the entire time, Bea's heart ached over Emmett's absence. The same as in the office, memories of him filled every corner of the stadium. How she was going to stand behind the pitcher's mound with another man in Emmett's spot and get through the game, she didn't know.

Whispering a prayer for strength while pulling her jacket closer around herself, Bea went over the plan she'd hatched with Marjorie yesterday as a distraction. Emmett might not be at the game, but that didn't mean he would never be in her life again. God had put them together—Bea was certain of it now. His plan for her might not look like she'd imagined, but He knew better than she did. When the time was right, she would fight for the good gift He'd given her, as Marjorie had advised.

Cheers rose from the stands as players began making their way into the dugouts, finally pulling Bea's thoughts from Emmett and to the game ahead. Most of the spectators were celebrating the Cubs, but the committed Lincoln Parks fans tried their hardest to match the intensity of the opponent's praise.

Many of the Lincoln Parks' players stopped to greet Bea, although she tried to maintain proper restraint so there would be no question of bias on her part this time. That wasn't the way she wanted her last game as an umpire to go. But she couldn't resist smiling and greeting the men who had supported Emmett so well.

As the players congregated in their respective dugouts, encouraging each other to have a good game and getting their equipment in place, the managers emerged onto the field. Bea and the other umpire had met with Mr. Anders and the Cubs' manager, Frank Chance, while the players warmed up, but now a third man was with them.

It only took a moment before Bea recognized the height, the broad shoulders, the gait of his walk. *Emmett.*

Unable to help herself and definitely against her better judgment, Bea rushed toward him, her breath coming in short spurts. But uncertainty took over when she got within a few feet, and she halted mid-step. Tipping his hat to her with a knowing wink, Mr. Anders continued walking with Mr. Chance, leaving Bea and Emmett alone. As alone as they could be in front of five thousand fans, anyway, not even counting the ones standing wherever possible around the edges of the stadium.

Bea had no idea what to say as Emmett looked down at her, his expression filled with emotions that reflected her internal turmoil. Hope, worry, tenderness, and so many more. She wanted to wrap her arms around him and bury her face in his chest, but she found enough self-control to resist the urge. When she managed to tear her gaze from his face, she noticed his freshly pressed uniform, covered with one of the knit sweaters the players wore while warming up on chilly days. He looked dashing enough to take her already short breath completely away.

Thankfully, Emmett wasn't as tongue-tied as she was. "Maybe I should have had Jet tell you I'd be here. I didn't mean to upset you, Bea."

His voice was rough, but it still acted as a balm to her battered heart. When his words pierced the fog clouding her thoughts, Bea took stock of her expression. Did she look upset? She shook her head. "You didn't upset me. I...I've missed seeing you on campus and at games."

"I've missed you too." His soft, warm eyes roamed her face as if memorizing it, melting Bea to her core.

Before she could figure out the next proper thing to say, Mr.

Anders called Emmett's name, waving him over. Emmett nodded, then turned back to Bea. "The team somehow convinced the league to let them send me off as if I'm retiring, rather than being fired. So they invited me today to sit with them for one last game. I'm looking forward to watching you work since you're usually behind me for half the game. But I'll find you afterward. I need to speak with you."

Emmett started to jog toward the home plate but turned to send Bea a wink and a crooked smile over his shoulder on the way. Her legs went weak. Thank goodness she had a few minutes to lean against the fence and compose herself before the game started.

～

It had been a strange experience to rejoin Jet and the Lincoln Parks players in the locker room before the game, trying to join in their banter while also feeling not quite a part of it all. It was surprising how quickly he was able to let his baseball dreams go when he had something better to look forward to.

Now on the field, all it took was a glance at Bea, irresistibly wonderful as she leaned against the fence with her eyes glued to him, to remind Emmett just how much better his new dream was.

As the players from both teams lined up down the first and third baselines, Emmett joined his former manager at home plate. Jet spoke in a near shout to reach those on the field and as many spectators as could hear him. "Today we're honoring our former starting pitcher, Emmett Worland. Emmett only played with us this season, but he is one of the best pitchers I've had the privilege to work with and an important part of our team. While the circumstances aren't what any of us would prefer, we're better men for having spent this season with Emmett."

The Lincoln Parks all cheered, along with more people in the stands than Emmett expected. He gave a brief wave, wishing there was a way he could express his gratitude for all those who supported the team and cheered for him now, after everything that had happened.

Jet held up a celluloid button printed with the outline of a baseball and the year, attached to a metal Chicago City League pin by a bright blue ribbon. "Emmett, this medal is a reminder of your time here and a way for us to express how much we've appreciated your playing ability and your leadership on the team. We hope you'll come back and join us to watch games often."

Pausing to pin the medal onto Emmett's sweater, Jet patted Emmett on the back. Mr. Rosen stepped forward to shake his hand, and then the ceremony was over. Emmett and Jet returned to the dugout while the crowd applauded and the players got into their positions on the field.

Once they reached the team's bench, Jet turned to Emmett. "I meant every word, you know. You've been more than just a good pitcher. You lifted this team to be better than they ever were before, on and off the field. We'll miss you."

They shook hands, Emmett's heart aching for what he was being forced to give up. But a glance at the field where Bea was taking her place behind the pitcher's mound lifted his heart immediately. His future wasn't as bleak as he'd imagined it would be without baseball. As the Bible said, God had taken the hardest moment in Emmett's life and used it for good. And that meant Emmett's job was to take that blessing and glorify God with it.

As the game progressed, Emmett got almost as much enjoyment from watching Bea in her element on the field as he used to get from being out there himself. There was a slight pang in his heart when his replacement, a young rookie named Harvey Johnson, took the pitcher's mound. But it passed quicker than Emmett would have guessed.

Then, for the first time in several years, Emmett sat and enjoyed watching a game of baseball. No headaches, no dizziness, no analyzing the players or imagining what he would do in their place. Just a man enjoying America's national pastime.

The Lincoln Parks played well that day. In the first inning, they stopped every play the Cubs tried to make, refusing to let a single runner make it on base. In the second inning, they allowed a run but also got one of their own. Emmett found himself leaning forward on the dugout fence, thrilled to watch his former teammates make such a good game of it against a successful, seasoned team.

But with each inning, he grew more and more distracted by Bea and the conversation he needed to have with her after the game. The Lincoln Parks scored again in the fourth inning, but Emmett was too busy watching Bea's beautiful eyes follow the action of the game, and he missed it.

In the fifth inning, Joe Tinker, the Cubs' shortstop, slid into home plate to score a very close run right in front of the dugout, but Emmett was focused on the graceful way Bea moved as she spread her hands wide to call him safe.

By the ninth inning, when the Lincoln Parks were up five runs to two, he'd given up watching the game. It was exciting that the semi-pro players were about to beat a team that might win a second World Series in just another week. But Emmett had found something that mattered more to him than baseball. Only a few months ago, he would have thought that impossible, but now Bea constituted his dreams for the future. God might have taken baseball from him, but what He'd given in return made that struggle worthwhile.

Being apart from Bea so much in the last few weeks had been difficult, to say the least. But the time had allowed

Emmett to gain some perspective. No matter what he'd assumed, Bea's actions showed that she cared for him and respected him. After looking back at the way she'd reacted when he revealed his condition, how could he have thought she would despise or pity him? She'd proven herself time and again. He had just been too afraid to see it.

The game ended with the Lincoln Parks celebrating their unexpected victory. The Cubs players left the field, and the stadium emptied. Near the dugout, Bea talked to his former team, laughing at their joyous antics and congratulating them on such a momentous win. She met for a few moments with the league president and managers to confirm the scores. Then she turned with a graceful swirl of her navy-blue skirt to walk across the field.

Emmett hurried to intercept her before she disappeared inside and he missed his opportunity.

When she caught sight of him in her path, Bea paused. She held his gaze, and the whirlwind of emotions in her expression —the same now as it had been before the game—increased his hope and his worry at the same time.

Swallowing hard, Emmett took a step closer to her. "Bea—"

He hardly got her name out before she flew forward and launched herself into his arms. Emmett caught her, grateful for the quick reflexes his baseball training had fostered. Holding her tight, he savored the feel of her body pressed against his for as long as he dared.

Finally, he pulled back so he could look into her face. "What brought that on?"

A pink flush rose in her cheeks. She was rarely embarrassed. It was charming. "I'm sorry. I've missed you, and I was worried about you."

Emmett's heart soared, all the fear over how she would respond drifting away. "A man likes to hear that."

She met his gaze again, this time with a warm smile lighting her face. "Emmett, I have a proposal for you."

A wave of shock hit him in full force. A proposal? As in the life-altering question he'd been hoping to ask her once they worked through all that had stood in their way?

Tongue-tied, Emmett nodded cautiously, waiting for her to continue. Bea stepped out of his arms and paced a few feet along the fence behind home plate before turning back to him again. "You were wonderful with the women's team this summer. They learned so much from you and improved under your instruction. Since I'm taking over the women's physical education department now, I won't have time to dedicate to the team next season. So would you like to be their manager?"

That was not what he'd expected her to say, but the relief that she hadn't taken on the task of proposing marriage over-shadowed the surprise for a moment. Feeling ridiculous that he'd assumed she was as consumed with thoughts of matrimony as he was, Emmett lifted his cap and ran a hand through his hair. "Are you sure you trust me to do that? What if we're traveling and I collapse again? What if my condition gets worse?"

They both paused as the victorious Lincoln Parks players passed, many winking at Emmett or clapping him on the shoulder as they left the field.

Once he and Bea were alone, Emmett leaned against the wall that separated the stands from the dirt. Bea stepped close and rested her hand on his arm as she picked the conversation up where they'd left off. "If your health worsens, we'll figure out what to do. There's a myriad of reasons that any of us could have our health fail unexpectedly. Unless that becomes a reality, we should continue making the most of every day of good health you have."

As if that issue had been the last string of fear holding his heart back, a lightness filled his chest. Emmett slid one arm around Bea's waist, pulling her close. Her eyes softened and her lips parted, starting a fire inside him. "There's more we need to discuss."

"Oh?" She responded absently as she raised a hand to rest her fingers on his chest.

"Yes. We should talk about *how* we're going to make the most of those days, as you said."

Her attention seemed focused on running her hand over his shoulder and down his arm.

Emmett controlled a shiver. "Bea."

"Hm?"

To get her attention, Emmett slid the fingers of his free hand over her cheek to tip up her chin. She stared at him with another resolve-melting smile, and it was impossible not to grin in response. "If we're going to make the most of our days, maybe we ought to start by deciding how many of them we're going to spend together."

Bea bit her bottom lip but didn't answer his half-teasing comment, leaving Emmett waiting for her next move with a pounding heart.

CHAPTER 24

$\mathcal{B}$ea hesitated to say the first thought that popped into her mind, but she and Emmett had spent months not saying what they wanted to. At that moment, wrapped in his wonderful embrace, she didn't want to do so any longer. "Oh, I have that figured out. All of them."

"Bea, did you say you want to spend the rest of your days with me?"

"Yes. I don't want to be apart from you another minute that I don't have to."

Emmett leaned back to look her in the eyes. "You mean that?"

Hoping he could see that she'd never meant anything more, Bea smiled up at him. "With all my heart. I was so frightened to think of letting a baseball player into my life that I almost missed the wonderful gift God had planned for me. Emmett, I made you feel like less than the strong, honorable, incredible man that you are. I'm not ever going to make that mistake again."

Hesitation from Emmett made Bea's confidence falter. He searched her eyes as if looking for signs that she meant it. After all the hurt between them, was it too late to prove to him what she really thought, how she felt? She swallowed hard, tempted to pull away from his side as the silence stretched out too long but not ready to accept anything other than what her heart now longed for.

When Emmett leaned down and pressed his lips to hers, warmth spiraled through her. A weight lifted off her heart. He wouldn't kiss her like this if he held reservations about the truth of her words.

Bea savored the sensation of being surrounded by his strength, of feeling dainty and delicate and feminine in comparison. His lips moved over hers, and she stashed away the memory of every shallow breath, every delicate sensation. When they finally parted, he took her hands in his.

But as he opened his mouth to speak, the Lincoln Parks' bat boy ran full speed onto the field, shouting, "Mr. Worland! I have a message you're s'pose to see right away!"

Emmett's grimace when he had to release her hands to take the note the boy held out warmed Bea, even as she wondered what was so urgent. He reached out to ruffle the boy's hair with obvious affection. "Thanks, Kid."

The boy ran back inside while Emmett unfolded the paper and skimmed it. By the time he was finished, the color had drained from his face. "It's from our housekeeper. Grandmother slipped and fell, and the doctor has been called for some sort of injury. I need to go to her, Bea. But I have so much more I want to say to you. Will you let me call on you?"

Bea's throat tightened. She'd come to love Mrs. Buchanan, despite the woman's often intimidating manner. As much as she hated to leave things unspoken between herself and Emmett, part of what she loved about him was the way he cared for those around him. She nodded. "Yes, of course. Any time."

He took a step toward the stadium entrance, then turned

back and grabbed her hand, tugging her into his arms again for an all-too-brief embrace. "You're certain a visit from me won't damage your reputation? You still have an example to uphold as a staff member of the college."

He looked so forlorn at the thought of hurting her career. Bea's heart swelled. If only there was time to reassure him properly. But he needed to see that his grandmother was all right, so she'd have to say what she could and trust God to help Emmett believe it. "No matter what I might have thought before, Emmett Worland, you are the most respectable, upstanding, thoughtful man alive. Spending time with you could only ever be worthwhile and good. Now go see your grandmother, and tell her I'm praying for her."

While there was still worry in his eyes, Emmett's face cleared. After one last long, lingering look, he strode out of the stadium, taking Bea's heart with him.

While she changed and returned to her boarding house, she prayed for Mrs. Buchanan. During the hours she couldn't sleep that night, she prayed for Emmett. And on her way to campus the next day to meet with the board of regents about the new physical education certificate they were going to offer the next year, she prayed for herself, that she would never again take Emmett for granted or make him feel as though he was less than the best thing God had ever given her.

After the meeting, which went as well as she ever could have hoped, Bea stopped by the gymnasium to watch the educational gymnastics class in session. The instructor, Miss Bessie Clark, led the female students through several stretches and exercises, stopping to adjust their postures and correct their movements. The women paired off and practiced showing each other how to do the same positions as if they were showing students of their own.

Bea's heart welled with gratitude that she got to be part of a program that would expand access to physical education, just as she'd dreamed.

When the class was over and the last women were leaving the gymnasium, distinctive giggles came from the stragglers, the kind that could only mean a good-looking man was present. When the girls walked out, there, framed in the open doorway, stood Emmett.

For a long moment, they stared at each other across the cavernous room. Then he started forward, moving with determined steps straight to Bea. He stopped in front of her, but neither said a word at first.

Finally, Bea swallowed hard before breaking the silence. "How is your grandmother? I prayed for her all night. And for you."

From the corner of her eye, Bea saw his fingers twitch as if they wanted to reach out but he wasn't sure he should. "She slipped off the last step of the staircase and thankfully only twisted her ankle. You may not know this, but she can be a tad dramatic when it suits her. The housekeeper thought she was gravely injured and insisted on a visit from the doctor, and that's what caused all the panic. But she'll be fine as soon as the swelling goes down."

Relief warred with humor at the vision of stately Mrs. Buchanan on the floor, moaning and clutching an ankle that was barely sprained. Emmett's lips lifted at the corners, revealing that she wasn't the only one amused. She'd missed being lighthearted with him. "I'm very glad it's not serious."

Emmett gave in and reached for her hands, his thumbs rubbing circles on the backs of them as he spoke in a low voice. "I'm sorry we were interrupted at such an inopportune moment yesterday. I believe you'd mentioned something about never leaving my side."

There was still a hint of humor in his eyes that made Bea's

responding grin inevitable. "You might be right. But you didn't say whether you would welcome that."

Emmett framed her face with both his hands, drawing her forward. "I won't make you wait any longer to know the truth. I love you, Bea. You're everything I could have hoped for in a woman and more. I didn't give you the chance to make this choice before. I let my fear push you away but won't make that mistake again. We may not face the easiest future together, though. Are you sure you want that?"

A pang of regret tempered the warmth that spread from his touch. Bea reached up to rest her hand against his cheek as well. "Without a doubt. I'm sorry that you have to ask, that I didn't make it clear weeks ago. I love you, and I could never leave you to face the uncertainty of your future alone. I meant what I said yesterday. I want to enjoy every moment God allows me to be with you, no matter what comes."

Pushing up on her toes, Bea claimed Emmett's lips this time, every nerve tingling when he wrapped his arms tight around her. It was quickly becoming her favorite place to be.

They separated after too short a time, and Emmett rested his forehead against hers while they caught their breath.

Bea pulled back so she could look up into his face. "Don't forget, Emmett, you didn't answer me about managing the women's team. What do you think?"

A slow smile belied his excitement. "I'd be honored to do it. I guess something good could come out of my short baseball career, after all."

She shook her head. How could he be so blind to the positive impact he had on people? "That was never in question, but I think this is the perfect way for you to remain involved in the sport you love. I'll tell the ladies this afternoon that we have a new manager. They'll be so thrilled."

As she and Emmett headed toward the gymnasium door, joy

overflowed Bea's heart. She would miss her career as an umpire, of course. But she had so much more hope for her future now than she would have guessed when she decided to give it up.

Not only had she found new strength in the Lord and been hired to run the physical education department as she'd wanted, but God had surprised her with Emmett, the most unexpected blessing of all.

Outside in the fresh, cool air, Bea slid her arm through Emmett's, her heart swelling with contentment. Their future had unknowns in it, but now Bea could rest in the certainty that God would lead them through.

~

Three weeks later, Emmett once again stood at the entrance to the Western College gymnasium, this time watching Bea as she mingled with the women from the baseball team and the alumni who had supported them over the summer. Their banquet for the team had been a well-deserved celebration of all that the women—and Bea—had accomplished.

Emmett's heart warmed to see Bea and his grandmother sitting together, both chatting in unbridled delight with the Western College ladies. There was a new lightness in his chest when he considered how close the two women in his life had become. And that was only intensified by how happily the ladies on the baseball team accepted his announcement that the Board of Regents had hired him to be their manager in the spring.

But this afternoon was about more than baseball for Emmett. It was time to move forward in the life he hoped to share with Bea. He could only pray she still meant it when she'd said she intended to remain at his side for the rest of their days. Otherwise, he was about to make an embarrassing spectacle of himself.

The team members, alumni, and faculty who had attended the banquet were beginning to leave, many of them stopping Bea to congratulate her on the improvements of the season or her new position. Emmett tried to be patient, but the knowing eyebrow Grandmother raised when she approached him revealed that he was not succeeding. "Emmett, dear, stop tapping your foot. I told Bea we'd wait for her outside. She'll be done soon enough."

"Last week wouldn't be soon enough."

Grandmother laughed and slid her arm around Emmett's waist. "You've waited this long to propose to her. A few more minutes won't hurt you. Let her enjoy her victory."

Emmett grinned, giving her a pointed look. "And you should, as well. I can hardly believe my grandmother was chosen to replace Mr. Kendall as president of the alumni association."

With pink creeping up her cheeks, her lips twitched upward. "It's high time they gave a woman the job, don't you agree?"

Emmett squeezed her shoulder in response, and Grandmother reached up to pat his hand. "Let's go outside and check on your plan."

Outside the gymnasium, Emmett smiled when he noticed his former teammates congregating near the building. They'd been surrounding him when he met Bea, so he'd asked them to be there when he surprised her today. He greeted several of the men, half listening to their excited chatter while his attention remained inside, where Bea was.

After waiting far too long, Boot nudged Emmett and tipped his head toward the building. "Here she comes."

Emmett spun around, longing for a glimpse of her. Next to him, Jet chuckled. But the moment Emmett moved to go to her side, Jet stopped him with a restraining arm. Emmett pulled his attention from the woman he loved to glare at his former manager. "Jet, what are you doing?"

The only response was a mischievous grin.

Looking back toward Bea, Emmett watched Fred Reneau walk up to her. She paused in her conversation with Emmett's grandmother, who had met her by the door, to stare with wide eyes as Fred lowered himself to one knee. "Miss Curran, will you marry me?"

Fred must have winked during his proposal because Bea smiled, swatted his arm, and shook her head. "Certainly not. But whatever are you doing here?"

Rising, Fred only grinned at Bea as he went to stand with the others again.

Emmett glanced at Jet, who still held him in place. "What's going on? Why did Fred do that?"

Jet shook his head with an indulgent shrug. "I know you just asked us to be here for support, but they had an idea. Go with it."

Emmett watched the Lincoln Parks' new pitcher as he walked up to Bea and repeated Fred's actions, dropping to his knee. "Miss Curran, I've never seen a lovelier umpire. Will you marry me?"

Now her eyes narrowed as she caught on that this was something more than a joke from one player. Her voice was still firm, though. "I'm sorry, but no."

The scene was repeated with Hank and Boot each approaching Bea in turn and proposing, then joining the others once they'd been rejected.

Emmett glared at Jet, a bit bothered that the men seemed to be testing the woman he loved. "When I asked you to let them know I wanted to propose to Bea today, I didn't expect any of you to participate."

Jet winked, finally dropping his arm. "We couldn't help

ourselves. Once she accepts you, no other players will get the chance to propose to the lovely lady umpire. We couldn't stand to let the opportunity pass."

It must have been Jet's turn, as he left Emmett's side and headed toward Bea.

Emmett followed until he was close enough to catch the amused twinkle in Bea's eyes. A bit of the tension drained from his shoulders. If his friends were going to commandeer his proposal, at least Bea was enjoying herself. Still standing next to her, his grandmother watched Bea with a fond gleam in her eyes.

Jet took Bea's hand and knelt in front of her. "Please marry me, Miss Curran?"

"No, thank you, Mr. Anders." Her voice was sweet and dripping with humor. Was she hoping Emmett would approach next? Did she have any idea that a genuine proposal would follow these false ones?

Emmett stepped forward as Jet walked away. Bea's gaze flew up to meet his, and her smile widened. All the air left his lungs in a rush at the joyful anticipation in her expression. He longed to pull her into his arms and kiss her soundly, but he had an important task to do first.

When he stood close enough, Emmett took both of her hands in his and lowered himself to one knee, raising his face so he never lost contact with her eyes. "Bea, you've changed my life. In everything we've gone through since meeting, you've been unwaveringly compassionate, caring, and supportive. I know you've rejected quite a few proposals from baseball players, including some today. But perhaps you'll allow a failed former player his chance."

Emmett drew a deep breath, encouraged by the way her lips parted in expectation. "Bea, I love you. I thought baseball would be my life, but it turns out that your love has shown me meaning beyond what I ever imagined. Will you marry me?"

At first, she only nodded. Then laughter bubbled from her lips, and she pulled his hands to get him to stand with her. Emmett wrapped his arms around her, relieved to hold her once again. Against his chest, she finally responded with the words he'd been desperate to hear since the first time he saw her on the baseball field. "Yes, Emmett. I love you and I'll marry you."

The men cheered and rushed to surround them, offering their congratulations while slapping Emmett on the back and shaking Bea's hand. His grandmother had uncharacteristic tears in her eyes when she grasped his face with both hands and nodded her approval. Emmett's heart welled to overflowing. After a lifetime spent longing to experience love, he'd not only found a way to repair his relationship with his grandmother and with God, but he'd also found Bea, the catch he'd never expected.

The End

Did you enjoy this book? We hope so!
**Would you take a quick minute to leave a review where you
purchased the book?**
It doesn't have to be long. Just a sentence or two telling what
you liked about the story!

Receive a FREE ebook and get updates when new Wild Heart
books release: https://wildheartbooks.org/newsletter

Thank you for joining me on this second journey in the Adventurous Hearts series. I looked forward to writing this story for several years before I finally got the chance. My family loves baseball, so it was incredibly fun that we could all participate in the writing of this book together.

Bea is my second heroine to be inspired by a real historical figure, a delightful woman named Amanda Clement. In 1904, Amanda became the first woman on record who was paid to umpire a baseball game—at just sixteen years old! She went on to umpire for six years in amateur leagues.

You might notice throughout the book that Bea umpires from behind the pitcher, while we're used to seeing an umpire behind the catcher. Historically, umpires started out behind the pitcher's mound. By the last few years of the 1800s, the trend had changed, and they most often stood behind the catcher. But there are references to Amanda Clement umpiring from the earlier position, behind the pitcher, and I couldn't resist that opportunity for Bea and Emmett to interact on the field.

Emmett is one of my favorite heroes. The real history that

inspired his struggle with what we now call post-concussion syndrome broke my heart. There are many records of athletes in the early days experiencing memory loss, mood swings, changes in personality, and other symptoms that were often attributed to insanity at that time. These are possible side effects of undiagnosed post-concussion syndrome, so it's not hard to imagine that could have caused the issues some of those players dealt with. Instead of receiving treatment, these men were often arrested, ostracized, or sent to mental institutions.

I did take one large liberty with the history, and that related to the timeline. The Chicago City League was active in 1887, from 1890-1894, and then again in 1909-1910. You'll notice 1907 was not one of those years. But I loved the idea of a minor league that would play predominantly in Chicago, rather than traveling like most teams would. So I adjusted the timeline a little to use the league.

Baseball in the early 1900s was wild. The player nicknames, the team names, the in-game antics. It was such a delightful time. The chaotic game at the end of this story is, to the best of my ability, accurate to a well-known game that was dubbed "Merkle's Boner." Rookie Fred Merkle of the New York Giants made a disastrous mistake that allowed the Cubs to win in a make-up game...and it probably cost his team the National League championship. It was fun to learn the ins and outs of that game (as well as the controversies that still surround it) so I could retell the details in the story.

If you would, please take a moment to leave a review for *An Unexpected Catch* online. Reviews are vital to help readers connect with stories they would enjoy. And they're a free way for you to support authors!

You can find me on Facebook (AbbeyDowneyAuthor), Instagram (abbeydowney), and Pinterest (abbeydowneyauthor).

I love to put together book club kits and flash fiction stories that relate to my published books, and all these bonus materials are free for my newsletter subscribers! You can sign up at www.abbeydowney.com.

ABOUT THE AUTHOR

Abbey Downey started writing inspirational romance stories during naptime when her kids were babies and found she couldn't stop. She previously published two books with Love Inspired Historical under the pen name Mollie Campbell. She also works with Spark Flash Fiction producing a quarterly digital magazine that contains love stories under 1000 words.

A life-long Midwestern girl, Abbey lives in central Indiana with her husband, two kids, and one rather enthusiastic beagle. She loves watching her kids play sports and fixing up a 1900 farmhouse with her husband. Connect with Abbey at www.abbeydowney.com.

f X ⓟ

If you love historical romance, check out the other Wild Heart books!

Byway to Danger by Sandra Merville Hart

Everyone in Richmond has secrets. Especially the spies.

Meg Brooks, widow, didn't stop spying for the Union when her job at the Pinkerton National Detective Agency ended, especially now that she lives in the Confederate capital. Her job at the Yancey bakery provides many opportunities to discover vital information about the Confederacy to pass on to her Union contact. She prefers to work alone, yet the strong, silent baker earns her respect and tugs at her heart.

Cade Yancey knows the beautiful widow is a spy when he hires her only because his fellow Unionist spies know of her activities. Meg sure didn't tell him. He's glad she knows how to keep her mouth shut, for he has hidden his dangerous activities from even his closest friends. The more his feelings for the courageous woman grow, the greater his determination to protect her by guarding his secrets. Her own investigations place her in enough peril.

As danger escalates, Meg realizes her choice to work alone isn't a wise one. Can she trust Cade with details from her past not even her family knows?

~

A Summer at Sagamore by Lisa M. Prysock

Can summer love survive amid mystery and mayhem?

When Abigail Greenwood and her cousins settle in for their annual summer retreat at the stunning and impressive Sagamore Resort in the Adirondacks, all she wants is to spend as much time as possible plunking out stories on her typewriter. But when her cousins insist she join them in the tradition of choosing a beau to adore from a distance during their stay, she reluctantly plays along, setting her sights on a mysteriously quiet and aloof guest. What started as harmless fun soon changes as Abby finds herself captivated by debonair—and handsome—Jackson Gable. Who is he, and why does his arrogant amused smile exasperate her so much?

When a series of events causing mayhem and mischief begin to occur at Sagamore, journalist Jackson Gable is determined to get to the bottom of it, since his father is an investor of the resort. Jack has a nose for mysteries, but he may have to use his recently earned law degree and some of his posh family connections to sleuth out the culprit. Are the events connected? Why are they happening? And why can't he get the beautiful Abby off his mind?

A Not So Peaceful Journey by Sandra Merville Hart

Dreams of adventure send him across the country. She prefers to keep her feet firmly planted in Ohio.

Rennie Hill has no illusions about the hardships in life, which is why it's so important her beau, John Welch, keeps his secure job with the newspaper. Though he hopes to write fiction, the unsteady pay would mean an end to their plans, wouldn't it?

John Welch dreams of adventure worthy of storybooks, like Mark Twain, and when two of his short stories are published, he sees it as a sign of future success. But while he's dreaming big with his head in the clouds, his girl has her feet firmly planted, and he can't help wondering if she really believes in him.

When Rennie must escort a little girl to her parents' home in San Francisco, John is forced to alter his plans to travel across the country with them. But the journey proves far more adventurous than either of them expect.